NICK POINTED TO THE RARE AND BEAUTIFUL CACTUS

"Kelley," he whispered. "Over there."

In an instant Kelley was on her knees before the Queen of the Night, drinking in the scent of its gorgeous white flowers. Her beauty, her womanly innocence, magnetized Nick. He watched her smile like a mother cradling a child.

"She's so exquisite, Nico," Kelley breathed. "There's nothing quite like her, is there?"

Quietly he knelt down beside her, slipping his arms around her waist. "No, there isn't," he concurred. "She is without question the most beautiful sight I've ever seen...."

Slowly Kelley turned to meet his gaze, and Nick realized that nothing else mattered now. He'd wanted this woman north of the border, no less than he wanted her south. He wanted her more than anything in the world....

To hell with Liliana, his eyes promised her. *Tonight there's only you and me.*

ABOUT THE AUTHOR

Suzanne Ellison lives in a small rural Californian town that's largely Mexican-American. Fluent in Spanish, she taught grade school before turning to writing full-time. Working on *For All the Right Reasons* gave her the opportunity to revisit Arizona and Mexico. Additional research on cacti and herbal medicine proved fascinating. In fact, Suzanne discovered a practicing *curandero* not far from her house!

Books by Suzanne Ellison

HARLEQUIN SUPERROMANCE
165–WINGS OF GOLD
258–PINECONES AND ORCHIDS

HARLEQUIN INTRIGUE
46–NOWHERE TO RUN

Suzanne Ellison

FOR ALL THE RIGHT REASONS

Harlequin Books

TORONTO • NEW YORK • LONDON
AMSTERDAM • PARIS • SYDNEY • HAMBURG
STOCKHOLM • ATHENS • TOKYO • MILAN

Published November 1987

First printing September 1987

ISBN 0-373-70283-3

For my father
Reverend J. Wesley Pierson
with love.

CHAPTER ONE

IF THE SIGN that read Nick's Auto Repair hadn't been painted in bright red block letters, Kelley McKinney never would have spotted the shop in the heavy rain. It was already nine o'clock in the morning and she should have been at work, but Kelley considered her recruitment of Nick Morales vital enough to the Institute of Southwestern Studies to justify a short detour through East Los Angeles on her way downtown.

Slipping into her light gray raincoat, Kelley scrambled out of her old Datsun and hurried into the warm, dry shop. It appeared to be a small operation, but the place was clean and orderly and had several cars waiting for attention. Just inside the door a pair of long, overall-clad legs protruded from beneath the front of a spanking-new Chevy sedan, and near the back wall a wiry blond mechanic wrestled with the engine of a Jeep. Above him hung a crisp new American flag and a bright blue Dodger pennant.

Miss Martinez had described Nick Morales as "memorable," adding with a twinkle in her eye that he had a smile that could have warmed the state of Texas. She'd also raved about his muscular build and thick black hair, so Kelley was certain that the blond in the back couldn't be her quarry. Unfortunately the waffle-soled work boots that poked out from under the Chevrolet didn't offer many clues about their owner.

As she debated her next move, it occurred to Kelley that she hadn't really approached this interview very professionally. She should have called the man and set up an appointment instead of letting her eagerness get the better of her. But when Kelley had dropped off her nephew at school this morning, she'd barely outlined her botanical expedition to Bobby's teacher before Miss Martinez had urged her to drop by the auto shop at once. The charming young woman had given Nick Morales such a glowing recommendation that Kelley had been absolutely certain that she'd found the perfect guide to the high desert country of Sonora. Now she regretted her impulsiveness.

Before she could decide if it was considered good form to roust a mechanic from under an engine, a deep male voice drifted toward her from the ground. "Do you need some help or are you just looking for a warm place to dry off?" His friendly tone held a note of laughter and the charming lilt of a faint Spanish accent. "Either way, there's hot coffee in the office."

Taken aback by the warmth of his greeting—not to mention the jovial rumble of his masculine voice—Kelley answered in the same spirit. "Thanks for the offer, but I'm not lost. I'm looking for a fellow named Nick Morales."

A metal part hit the floor with a clunk and a rattle as he replied, "Well, you've found him . . . and just in the nick of time."

"I beg your pardon?"

He chuckled as he slid farther toward the front of the car, revealing most of a solid torso and the open V of his mechanic's coveralls. A silver religious medal nestled in the thick dark hair of his chest. Bracing one brown elbow against a muscular thigh, he scrunched up closer to some hidden piece of the sedan. "You've got a sticking piston. It's not likely to leave you stranded anywhere, but it wreaks havoc with your mileage and ages your engine mighty fast." The grinding sound of a wrench and bolt doing battle punctuated his off-the-cuff diagnosis of her ailing car. "And since your engine is already eight or nine years old, there's no point in hustling it to an early grave."

Surprised by his acute hearing and ability to interpret the harsh rattling that had beset her old Datsun for the past few days, Kelley asked, "I suppose you know what make and model it is, too?"

He laughed. It was a rich, happy sound that made Kelley feel good all over. She almost forgot that it was a rainy day and she was late for work. "It's a foreign car—economy model. V-6. Honda, Datsun, Toyota...something on that order. None of them are particularly prone to sticking pistons, though, so beyond that I'd just be taking a shot in the dark."

With that comment he slid out from under the car, revealing the sunny smile that Bobby's teacher had so accurately described. His white, straight teeth accentuated the handsome darkness of his face; long, thick lashes framed his friendly eyes. As he stood up, Kelley was surprised to discover that he was only a few inches taller than she was. His powerful biceps, clearly visible in the rolled-up broadcloth sleeves, were so solid that they lent an impression of great height.

At five feet seven Kelley didn't often feel dwarfed by a man, nor was she in the habit of feeling tongue-tied when she first met a stranger. But for some reason, Nick Morales had been easier to talk to when most of his masculine attributes had been hidden from view. Now that he stood just a foot or two away—muscles rippling, brown eyes smiling—she was having trouble thinking of him as a possible employee for a rather unusual sort of guided tour of the Mexican desert. He was just a single man in his mid-thirties—handsome, virile and undeniably appealing.

She couldn't tell if he viewed her in a similar way. While his features showed a polite interest in his unexpected female visitor, any flicker of awareness of Kelley as a woman was carefully concealed. Of course, he probably thought she was a customer...a misconception she'd do well to correct.

"Uh, actually, I didn't come here to ask about the 'car," she began, surprised by how quickly she'd forgotten her carefully planned sales pitch. Suddenly she didn't want to ask him if he'd take her plant-hunting in Sonora; she had a crazy urge to ask if he was free for dinner tonight. It was a notion she smothered at once.

"Considering the fact that I don't usually work on imports, that's probably a good thing," he answered cheerfully. "However, it does make me wonder just why you've chosen to grace my humble shop with your presence. You don't look like an insurance agent or a cop, I don't see a subpoena in your hand and—"

"Oh, it's nothing like that!" Kelley assured him with a smile. "Miss Martinez sent me."

If Kelley expected this revelation to clarify her position, she was mistaken. Bobby's teacher had implied that she and Nick were very close...or at least had been at one time. Yet now he stared at Kelley uncertainly while he asked, "I don't suppose you've got a first name to go with 'Martinez'? I probably know a dozen people by that name on this side of the border alone."

Suddenly Kelley felt ridiculous. She'd left the school full of hope that this man might be the solution to her problem, but if he didn't even know Miss Martinez well enough to remember her name, it was likely that the rest of the teacher's information was less than accurate. However, her description of Nick's appearance had been flawless....

"I'm sorry, Mr. Morales, but I don't know her first name. She's my nephew's first-grade teacher at Ralston Elementary School in—"

"Juanita!" he supplied instantaneously, pronouncing the other woman's name with such great warmth that Kelley wasn't sure whether she felt relieved or just a tiny bit jealous. "If Juanita sent you, you've definitely come to the right place. Whatever you need, just name it." He gave her an expansive gesture that included the confines of his orderly shop. "*Mi casa es su casa*, as we like to say."

"You're very kind," she assured him, then tacked on belatedly, "I'm sorry, I forgot to introduce myself. I'm Kelley McKinney."

He gave her another irresistible grin as he plopped down the wrench in his hand on the Chevy's bumper. "With that curly red hair and green eyes, I can't say I'm surprised. You look like you stepped right out of an Irish picture book."

If her freckle-faced looks appealed to Nick, he gave no sign. Kelley knew from long experience that it was a distinctive appearance that most men either really liked or really didn't—even on days when the rain hadn't turned her tight natural curls into a red ball of frizz. Allan had often called her "cute" or "peppy," but never "pretty," let alone "beautiful." Not that beauty in itself was so important to Kelley, but since she knew that she'd never quite made the grade with Allan, the memory still rankled.

"Third generation, actually. My grandfather came over just before the Depression when he was only twenty-two." *And made a real success of himself in spite of it,* she wanted to add with pride. Instead she said, "Miss Martinez...Juanita...indicated you came to this country yourself as a teenager, too. If I'm not mistaken, you were born in a village in the Sonoran desert, right?"

"Wrong," he answered quickly. Despite the sunny smile that remained on his face, a shadow crossed Nick's eyes and his chin lifted a proud inch or two as he quietly declared, "I was born in Tucson, Kelley."

"Oh, really?" she asked, surprised that she'd managed to confuse one of the few facts about his background that Juanita had disclosed... and more than a little regretful that she'd already managed to offend this incredibly appealing man. "I used to live there when I was a kid."

He nodded, the brief tension disappearing from his handsome face as he summoned up another smile. "Small world, neighbor. I'd shake your hand like a hospitable soul but I'm too greasy." Before she could reply he gestured toward his office. "May I get you some coffee? I always keep a pot going inside. Might have a doughnut or two leftover from breakfast... maybe even some *pan dulce.*"

As chilly as she was, Kelley decided that some hot coffee and a Mexican sweet roll certainly sounded appealing. Besides, it might be easier to talk to Nick if they both sat down in an office. She felt like a fish out of water in the male bastion of the repair shop. Her stylish black pumps, heather-green sweater and matching skirt just didn't blend in with the decor.

Nick's office was as clean and well-organized as the rest of the shop, though it, too, smelled of metal and oil. The shelves were lined with small boxes of parts and repair manuals for several makes of cars; fan belts of various dimensions hung on the walls in the order of their size. Nick offered Kelley the padded swivel chair by his desk, then perched on the countertop a scant foot away. The office didn't really seem big enough for the two of them, let alone for the wiry blond mechanic who joined them moments later.

"You're going to have to help me on this engine, Nick," he pleaded. "I've been fussing with it for an hour now, and I can't find a thing wrong with—" He stopped abruptly when he spotted Kelley at the desk. It was obvious from the startled look on the young man's face that he was not accustomed to having his boss entertain female strangers in his office.

Nick, however, showed no trace of discomfort as he introduced Kelley to his employee. "Jeff, this is Kelley McKinney, a friend of Juanita's." To Kelley he said, "I've been training Jeff for two years, and he's a lot better mechanic than he thinks he is. I only hire the best."

Jeff flushed under the praise, then asked Kelley, "How's Juanita doing? I haven't seen her since—" he glanced at Nick for confirmation "—last February or March."

"March," Nick clarified, then asked his guest, "How *is* she doing? Still teaching at Ralston, you said?"

Kelley nodded, embarrassed by the focus on Bobby's teacher. She hardly wanted to admit that she'd only met the woman that morning and they'd talked for all of five minutes, but she didn't want to lie, either.

"I just met Juanita, actually, but I've heard so many wonderful things about her from my sister-in-law that I feel like we've been friends a long time," she managed to say. That much was certainly true. She looked at Nick. "Juanita certainly seems to think a lot of you."

His expression didn't change but he seemed to avoid Kelley's eyes when he answered, "It's quite mutual." Grabbing a jacket hanging from a hook on the wall behind him, he tossed it across the desk to the other man. "Why don't you take the Jeep out for a spin, Jeff. Make sure you get her hot; Mr. Wilson says she dies at every light. If she doesn't start sputtering when you brake, I'll take a look when you get back."

Jeff protested mildly, "Are you sure it wouldn't be easier for you to fix it and let me work on Don's Chevy?"

"Of course it'd be easier," Nick agreed with a grin. "But then you might go through a whole day without learning something new. Besides, I promised Don I'd have his car ready by noon, and you know I never like to disappoint a customer."

The young man slipped on the jacket and gave Nick a quick salute. "Spare me the lecture, sergeant. I know you'll make something of me no matter what I do." The two mechanics shared a chuckle, as though they'd been over the same ground many times before. Then Jeff excused himself and trotted back to the floor.

A moment later Kelley heard him rev up the Jeep and drive out of the shop. Nick listened intently to the sound of the engine, but Kelley found herself studying his profile as he faced the office door. His features were smooth and even; only his prominent cheekbones hinted of some Indian blood in his past. His lips were soft and full, and though he looked fresh-shaven, it was obvious that he kept a running battle with his dark beard to avoid a five o'clock shadow.

When the sound of the Jeep faded away, Kelley suddenly realized that she and Nick were alone in the shop. Only the pelting rain on the roof and the uneven lurch of her heartbeat seemed to fill the tiny office, and she desperately hoped that Nick could hear only the rain.

Ignoring the awkward silence, Nick stood up and crossed the room to pick up a coffeepot near a small sink in the corner. He reached for a Styrofoam cup, then changed his mind and pulled a mug off the rack on the wall. "Hal's out sick today, so I don't think he'll mind if you use this," he declared, filling the mug before he carried it back to Kelley. "I wash the mugs every night, so I'm sure it's clean."

Kelley thanked him for the coffee and accepted some cream and sugar before he handed her a box of baked goods. "That's called a *semita*," he informed her as she chose a flat, round roll with a diameter of five or six inches. "You can get them in the Mexican section of the grocery store if you find you really like the taste."

"I already know I like the taste," Kelley assured him, glad to have something safe to say. "My grandmother used to bake these for me. They were always so warm and fluffy right out of the oven!" She smiled at the memory. "To this day, every time I eat one I think of Mama Chayo and feel...well, like somebody's just given me a special hug."

Busy pouring some coffee for himself, Nick didn't answer right away, but he looked slightly puzzled as he hopped back up on the counter near his desk. "Forgive me for sounding doubtful, but I'm having trouble picturing you with a grandma named 'Mama Chayo.'"

Kelley chuckled. "Well, it's a long story, actually. But, in a nutshell, my dad hired Mama Chayo to take care of the house when I was three and we lived in Arizona. My mother was pregnant with my brother, Jimmy. She was very sick and already had five of us—big Catholic family, you know—and the doctor ordered her to bed. At first we all hated the idea of having a stranger in our house, but by the time we moved to Kansas several years later we all cried so hard at the thought of leaving Mama Chayo behind that Dad asked her to come with us as part of the family."

"And she came?" he asked, as though Kelley's answer really mattered to him.

"Oh, yes! She lived with us—well, with my parents—for twenty-four years."

Nick sipped his coffee gravely, swinging one long leg between the counter and the desk. Up close, Kelley noticed that his thighs were as well-muscled as his arms.

"And then?" he queried softly. "When she got too old to work?"

Despite the lazy warmth that his nearness engendered in her, Kelley couldn't help but stiffen at his unspoken implication. "When she got too old to work, we took care of her the way we take care of my eighty-year-old Irish grandpa." She tried not to sound emotional, but it was a losing effort. "Mama Chayo died last summer. My mother hasn't gotten over it yet."

Neither have I, Kelley could have added, but she knew she'd already said too much. But how else could she explain to this intriguing stranger why her trip to Sonora was so important to her? Oh, it was part of her job, and she was fascinated by medicinal plants as well as enthralled by the harsh, dry beauty of the desert. But there was a debt to be paid, a promise to be kept, that forced her to complete this trip before the chance slipped through her fingers.

For the first time since she'd arrived at the shop, all trace of humor died in Nick's eyes. "I'm sorry, Kelley," he said quietly. "I'm sorry I misjudged you and I'm sorry for your loss."

It was a surprisingly humble statement for such a virile specimen of a culture known for its adherence to arrogant *machismo*. But Kelley had loved Mama Chayo too many years to believe that race or culture could wholly determine the essence of any human being, and it was already obvious to her that underneath those long lashes and laughing eyes there lived a very complex man of warmth and depth. A man whose help she really needed . . . and a man whom she was already itching to get to know better.

"Nick—" it seemed right to call him that now "—Mama Chayo was an Opata Indian from the Sonoran desert. Her father was a *curandero* who cured everybody in the village using ancient herbal remedies—"

"And witchcraft." There was a strong note of disapproval in his tone—an attitude Kelley often encountered when discussing her project with middle-class Mexican-Americans. "I suppose you know that half of the people who live in those desert villages still don't get any decent medical care. There's nothing the doctors can do for you in L.A. that they can't do for you in Guadalajara or Mexico City, but once you get out in the mountains or the jungle or cactus country, it's like going through a time machine to the turn of the century.''

Kelley swallowed uncertainly. Nick had already disavowed his desert birthplace, and now he was speaking adamantly against the very field of botany she'd chosen to research. Juanita's heart might have been in the right place when she'd urged Kelley to come see him, but Kelley had an uneasy feeling that the other woman had badly misjudged Nick's response to her proposal.

"Time is running out for the Opatas, Nick," she pointed out, unwilling to give up so soon. "There are only a few thousand of them left. They're largely assimilated now, but—"

Nick shook his head. "The Indians will never be assimilated in Mexico. It's not a matter of time, Kelley, it's a matter of money and education. It doesn't make much difference whether the poor folks are Indians or not—they live pretty much the same way." Suddenly his tone sobered, as though he were speaking of something too personal to be analyzed from a scholarly perspective. "Where I come from, Kelley, they live in hand-pressed adobe huts with roofs made of palm leaves. They survive on prickly pear and jackrabbits . . . and desert quail if they're lucky."

Glad that he'd at least admitted he had roots in Sonora, Kelley decided to tell him a little more about her own background. "Mama Chayo used to feed us the leaves and fruit of the prickly pear, Nick, and she also used cactus poultices whenever we got scraped up falling off our bikes. All her life she conjured up herbal remedies of one kind or another. She gave my mother some kind of tea for morning sickness, Jimmy something else for colic, and zapped my sinus headaches with this foul-tasting drink that worked better than codeine. It was incredible.''

"It was dangerous," Nick said softly, his tone surprisingly serious. ''You're lucky you're still alive.''

Not quite sure if he was kidding, Kelley protested, ''She wasn't trying anything experimental, Nick. Some of her cures had been handed down by five or six generations of Opata medicine men. Now Opata herbal healing is a specialized knowledge that's dying out, and—''

''Why do you think that is?'' Nick's demeanor was just as courteous as ever, but there was a hint of challenge in his words.

''Well, there aren't too many Opata folk healers left, even though a lot of their remedies have been adopted by other Mexican *curanderos*. You know, the Aztecs had a terrific store of knowledge in this area, which was virtually lost after the conquest. I'd hate to see the same thing happen to the Opatas' herbal medicine as well.''

''Would that really be so bad?'' He crossed his arms and studied her intently. ''I mean, was it such a tragic loss to future generations when they stopped burning witches in Salem, Massachusetts?''

For a moment Kelley was too stunned to answer, then she declared, ''Nick, there's a difference between witchcraft and *curanderismo*.''

''That may be so, but I don't think it matters much when you're dead, Kelley. I don't know anything about Opata herbal medicine in particular, but I know that most Mexican *curanderos* still aren't much past the 'eye of newt' stage. In spite of that, the villagers trust them so completely that they refuse to see a real doctor even when money's not a problem. They also believe that their witches can make them sicken or die from a curse. Believe it or not, I've seen people get terribly ill just because they honestly believed that they were under an evil spell.'' Kelley could see that he was struggling to stay calm, but he couldn't conceal the depth of his feelings. "Frankly, Kelley, I can't imagine how any educated person could waste a minute on that sort of quackery.''

"I'm not condoning witchcraft or quackery,'' she insisted, appalled at the abrupt downward turn of the conversation. "I'm simply a botanist trying to learn what *plants* have been traditionally used for healing. Some of those plants may be useful to modern science; some may parallel drugs already in use. Some may be ineffective, or even harmful, but we can't determine that without scientific data.''

"Maybe you can't, but I—'' Nick stopped abruptly and took a deep breath. Then he shook his head and lifted both hands in surrender. "Forgive me, Kelley. I know you mean well, and I've got no call to give you a hard time about your research. I'm not in the habit of arguing with people I don't even know. It's just that you . . . well, you managed to bring up a subject that's a very sore point with me. I can't talk about folk medicine as though it's the subject of an article in *Newsweek*. For me, it's—'' he sighed and took another deep breath to steady himself "—it's just very personal.''

Kelley wasn't sure what to say. It was a safe guess that somebody Nick loved had died or suffered greatly at the hands of some inept folk healer, but she would never be insensitive enough to ask. In fact, Kelley wondered why Juanita Martinez had been insensitive enough to send her here. The teacher had seemed like a very astute person who obviously adored Nick and probably knew him well enough to have predicted his response to Kelley's project.

"Forgive me for intruding on your busy morning," Kelley apologized, knowing that there was no way she could present her plan to him now. Rising quickly she said, "Thanks for the coffee and the—"

"Whoa, girl." Nick stopped her with another one of his heart-melting smiles. She wasn't sure if this one was genuine, but it would be a nice memory nonetheless. "Sit back down and tell me how I can help you. I said I was sorry; let's forget this herbal-cure stuff and get on with what you came to say. It wouldn't do for me to send away a friend of Juanita's without lending a helping hand."

Kelley sat back down, helplessly shaking her head. "Nick, I'm working on a project that Juanita thought you might be able to help me with. But now that I've met you, I really don't think you'd be interested."

Chagrin flashed across his smooth, square features. "Was I really that obnoxious?"

"Oh, Nick!" Kelley burst out in frustration, wishing she could start this conversation over. "Of course not. It's just—"

"Juanita knows me pretty well, Kelley. If she recommended me for something, I'd lay odds I'm the best man for the job." His tone was apologetic rather than proud. "Besides, you've already found my Achilles' heel, so you can't rile me again. I'm not touchy about anything else except the Dodgers, maybe, when they're having a bad season." This time his grin was so disarming that she knew he'd all but forgotten their brief disagreement. "I couldn't care less about politics."

Kelley studied him silently, trying to decide what to tell him about her research. There was no way she could get out of it now. He'd be insulted if she didn't ask him to help her—and offended when he found out what she had in mind.

"Well?" he prodded, leaning toward her expectantly. "How can I help you?"

Kelley sighed in defeat. "I need a guide to take me to Sonora, Nick. I'm an ethnobotanist at the Institute of Southwestern Studies, and I'm studying the use of medicinal herbs by the Opata. It's partly a professional interest and partly... well, a promise I made to Mama Chayo before she died. I've done all the book research I can possibly do. Now I need to spend some time with the people and talk to their *curanderos*. I need to collect samples of the plants they use. I went to Juanita because my sister-in-law thought she might know somebody who's from that neck of the woods and would appreciate a healthy salary to lead me back there. She suggested you." She met his eyes and added softly, "I'm sorry."

Not a flicker of emotion crossed Nick's handsome face as he slowly crossed the room to rinse out his mug and hang it back up on the wall. A full minute passed before he slipped both hands in his coverall pockets and turned to face Kelley again. Despite the undeniable virility of his rock-hard biceps, now rigid with tension, the stray lock of black hair that spilled forward gave Nick a surprisingly vulnerable look. The tarnished silver medal—an image of a madonna with gentle eyes and outstretched hands—gleamed in the overhead light. Kelley belatedly recognized the figure of the Virgin of Guadalupe, patron saint of Mexico.

"Go on," he prodded softly, sorrow rather than anger lacing his tone. "I'm still listening."

She didn't want to continue; she didn't want to add to this kind man's obvious distress. But she knew that his innate courtesy would keep him attentive until he thought she'd finished, so she decided to rush through the rest of her rehearsed presentation.

"Juanita said you use to live east of Hermosillo, Nick, which is where most of the Opatas still live. Granted, they're scattered here and there in tiny settlements with lots of mixed-blood Mexicans, but she thought you might have enough contacts in the area to help me get a foot in the door. I need somebody who knows somebody who knows somebody...that sort of thing. I know it doesn't sound like a very sophisticated way to find a *curandero*, but the Opatas aren't very sophisticated people, and the normal rules of twentieth-century research simply don't apply." Kelley took a deep breath and finished quickly. "I've already tried all my official contacts in Mexico to no avail, and I don't think I'll ever get an Opata *curandero* to reveal his secrets unless I've got the green light from some local soul he trusts."

There was a lot more that she could have said, but it was suddenly obvious that Nick could no longer hear her. Although his eyes were still courteously trained on Kelley, his smile had vanished. He didn't look angry so much as ineffably sad.

For a long moment after Kelley finished, he studied her worried expression. Then, without speaking, he took a step toward his desk and slowly began to rifle through a small box of safety pins, paper clips and photos near her right hand. When he came to a battered black-and-white snapshot, he plucked it out and studied it briefly, then tossed the photo down on the blotter in front of Kelley.

The whole picture looked as though the photographer had been unfamiliar with the rudiments of taking photos and had merely pushed a button when instructed by somebody else—but it had obviously been taken in the desert. A "fence" made of prickly pear framed the crude shack made of hand-shaped adobe bricks and the palm-leaf roof Nick had described. A handful of people were gathered near the front door...or rather the serape-covered hole that served as such.

One elderly lady with bowed legs and braided snow-white hair leaned on a young man, who looked like a teenage version of Nick Morales. The boy had flashing white teeth and a jubilant smile. Clad in blue jeans and a T-shirt that said "Go Dodger Blue" on the front, he wore a religious medal around his neck that could have passed for the one he wore now. Beside him stood a young girl with waist-length black hair and a small but nicely curved figure. Like the older woman, she wore a shapeless dress that hung below her knees. Her only jewelry was a silver chain with a tiny medal the size of Nick's, but the rapt adoration that shone from her eyes as she gazed at him enhanced her somewhat pedestrian beauty.

"This is all I have left of Cielo Solo," Nick confessed, his deep voice echoing throughout the empty shop. "And it's all I *want* of Cielo Solo. Juanita knows that, but she's always had this idea that I needed to go back there to settle some unfinished business, to lay some old ghosts to rest. To this day she probably thinks that if I'd gone back for one single summer vacation, I would have come home ready to marry her."

It was the first time that Nick had specifically described his relationship with Juanita. While Kelley was not surprised that they had once been lovers, she found herself feeling an unaccountable twinge of jealousy.

"The simple truth is that I left Sonora because I didn't want to live there, Kelley. Cielo Solo means 'nothing but sky,' and never was any lonely hole in the ground better named. I hate the poverty, I hate the clannishness, I hate the ignorance and backward ways of the people and I hate the hellish desert." His tone was even, controlled, but he couldn't conceal the fact that his words barely scratched the surface of what he was feeling. "But I do... like *you*, Kelley McKinney, and I wish I could help you with your problem. I think your interest in the Opata Indians is sincere, if a bit misguided and naive, but I wish you good luck."

Nick took a step toward the door, signaling an end to the conversation. His eyes were sober now, unhappy, even regretful as he gazed upon her. His tone was surprisingly nostalgic as he asked, "Did your grandfather ever go back to Ireland? Even for a visit?"

Slowly Kelley shook her head. She hated to think she'd caused this appealing man pain, hated to think she'd failed utterly to achieve her purpose in coming to meet him. She would have no reason whatsoever to see him again. "No," she answered gently, "but he... he always says he still wants to go just once before he dies."

Nick picked up the faded photograph and ran one callused thumb over the ancient black-clad lady in the center, then focused intently on the face of the young girl. "I know just how he feels, Kelley." He dropped the picture back in the box, then lightly touched the medal at his neck before he turned and headed back toward the dismantled Chevy. "I know just how he feels."

CHAPTER TWO

NICK RARELY QUIT WORK before five o'clock in the afternoon, but it wasn't even four-thirty yet when he reached Ralston Elementary School. He'd felt like a bear with a sore paw ever since that lovely Irish girl had left his shop this morning, and he blamed Juanita for the conflicting feelings at war within him. He hadn't even taken the time to shower and change before he'd tracked down his former lover.

She was writing at the blackboard when he sauntered into her classroom; his easy gait belied the haste with which he'd come. Almost a year had passed since he'd last seen Juanita, but she looked the same as ever—petite, sleek and happy. With her big brown eyes and smooth black hair, she couldn't have looked less like Kelley McKinney, but it occurred to Nick that the two women had a lot in common. They were both intelligent, forthright and sensitive and seemed to appreciate his sense of humor. Nick simply couldn't abide a woman who didn't know how to laugh.

"The teachers weren't so pretty when I was in school," Nick said by way of greeting. Then he tacked on with an impish grin, "Of course, I didn't start school till I was eight. They always said I'd missed something important in first grade."

At the sound of his voice, Juanita quickly turned around. "Nico! How good to see you!" She swept across the room and slipped easily into his arms for a quick kiss.

Nick gave her a hug and a peck on the cheek, then let her go. "I'm mad at you, Juanita," he chided his friend, though no trace of anger colored his good-natured tone. "Didn't we break up because you were always trying to send me back to Sonora?"

Taking a step back, Juanita shook her head. It was obvious that she knew why he had come. Despite his joking greeting, her reply was very serious. "No, Nick. We broke up because I always wanted more of you than you were able to give me. More than you'll ever be able to give any woman as long as half your heart still belongs to Liliana."

He couldn't help but stiffen at the name, and a vision of long black hair, and adoring eyes appeared before his mind's eye. He didn't think he was still in love with Liliana—he was sure he'd gotten over her years and years ago. But he couldn't deny that the mere thought of her could still dampen the most joyous of occasions. He'd never called Juanita by the other girl's name—a mistake he'd made with a couple of earlier girlfriends—but more than once he'd had a vision of another face at a rather awkward moment.

Of all the women he'd ever dated since he left Cielo Solo—Mexican or Anglo—Juanita had been the most special, the most likely candidate for Señora de Nicolás Esteban Santiago Morales Ríos. And she had wanted to marry him. Desperately.

But even though he had great respect and affection for Juanita, Nick had always felt that he could get along just as well with or without her. He was waiting for a woman whose essence was so compelling that he couldn't imagine shutting her out of his life. So far, the only one he'd never been able to forget was Liliana . . . who had become a widow just a few short months ago.

"Juanita, if you wanted to see me, why didn't you just give me a call instead of dragging Kelley McKinney into it?" he asked directly. "We didn't part so badly, did we? I thought we were still friends."

She smiled. "Of course we're still friends. I was planning to invite you to my wedding."

"Wedding?"

Glowing, she nodded. "He's a new teacher here this year. John Sherwood. We're getting married as soon as school's out in June."

Glad for her and more than a little relieved, Nick asked, "You're sure? I mean, he's really what you want?"

"Oh, Nick!" Her joy was undeniable. "He's as fine a man as you are, and he's got the only quality you lack."

"Just one?" he inquired skeptically.

Juanita laughed, then answered half seriously, "He adores me. He can't live without me. He says he's never felt that way about anybody before."

Nick couldn't meet her eyes while she said those heartfelt words. Not because he still wanted Juanita—he didn't—but because he hadn't felt that way about anybody since he was seventeen, and he didn't expect to feel that way ever again. The first woman who'd even aroused his interest in months was that spunky, redheaded beauty who'd come to his shop today, and he wasn't likely to see her again, considering the absurd proposal Juanita had encouraged her to make. Nonetheless, he liked Kelley's quick mind, her jaunty smile and her casual beauty. He liked her fondness for *semitas* and her love for her Mama Chayo... and the fact that she felt the need to honor a promise to a Mexican "grandma" long since dead. And above all, he liked the way she looked at him—as though she'd never tire of the sight.

"I'm happy for you, Juanita," he assured his old flame. "Really I am. But I came by to tell you not to do me any more favors. I'm not in need of a travel agent or a blind date."

"Oh, Nico, come on!" she implored him. "I didn't set you up on purpose. Kelley is my room mother's sister-in-law. Bonnie's a super lady who's done volunteer work in class every week all year, corrected papers for me, arranged wonderful parties for the kids... oh, all kinds of things! When she sent Kelley to see if I could help her find somebody to take her to the back country of Sonora, of course I thought of you."

"I'm the only person you know with ties to Sonora?"

She winked as she assured him, "You are my *favorite* person from Sonora. If I had to go down there, I wouldn't want to trust my safety to anybody else."

"Juanita, what on earth made you think I'd take on a job like that?" he demanded. "You know I don't need the money and I certainly can't spare the time. Besides, I haven't been over the border in nineteen years! I've got no use for the desert, and the only way to reach Cielo Solo is to hike the last twenty miles through cactus country overrun by rattlers, drug smugglers and villagers who are positively allergic to strangers."

"Kelley knows that! That's why she wants somebody who knows the area and is welcome there!"

"And you think I'm welcome in Cielo Solo? Have you forgotten why I left?"

Juanita was the only person he'd ever told about his last trip to Sonora, and even then he'd revealed as little as possible. The only reason he'd mentioned it at all was to clear the air about his past so she'd stop haranguing him about it. It hadn't done any good. In fact, once he'd told her the truth about Liliana, she'd grown even more convinced that his lingering love for the girl was what kept him so tepid about a future with anybody else.

"Of course I haven't forgotten. And I certainly realize that going back would be...well, difficult for you, Nico, and a mixed blessing for some of the people you left behind. But as long as your grandma still sends you homemade marzipan candy on your birthday when it takes your uncle a whole day to hike to a mailbox, then I'm positive that—"

"That's enough." Nick rarely got truly angry. He could deflect Juanita's comments about Liliana. After all, the Sonoran girl was as much to blame as he was for the circumstances that caused him to leave Cielo Solo. Probably more so. But his precious grandmother was totally guiltless and unconditionally loving. She was also the reason, Nick was certain, that he still had nightmares from time to time in which a giant saguaro would chase him north across the desert, trying to capture him with its huge thorny hands before he safely crossed the border. It never hurt him; it just wouldn't let him go.

"It wasn't fair of you to raise Kelley's hopes," Nick pointed out, his tone growing hard as he pondered yet another concern. He didn't like the thought of Kelley McKinney loose in the desert. If the smugglers and the

scorpions didn't get her, the blazing sun surely would.
She was so open, so innocent in her trust of the desert
and desert people! No matter what kind of schooling
had lifted her to the lofty peak of "ethnobotanist"—
whatever that was—she sorely lacked the street savvy
that had kept Nick alive during the precarious years of
his youth on both sides of the border. "She has no
business going down there, anyway," he told Juanita.
"She's confusing a happy childhood with one dear old
lady with a pathetically primitive life in the desert. And
this whole herbal-cure thing is best left to history, as far
as I'm concerned."

He'd felt a great urge to set Kelley straight on her
romanticized vision of modern-day Mexican herbs and
witchcraft, but he knew he wasn't particularly rational on the subject. If his mother had gone to a
doctor instead of a *curandero* in Los Angeles when
she'd first suffered from stomach pain, she probably
would not have died in the east-side barrio at the age of
thirty-three. And her son would not have returned to
Cielo Solo until he was a man.

"Nico, I'm sorry if I...if it was wrong of me to make
you face all this again. But Kelley seems just as terrific
as the rest of her family, and she's very determined. I
think she's going to go down there with or without
competent help, and that makes me very uneasy. I
honestly thought you'd be a way to guarantee her
safety. On top of that, the reason for her trip
might...well, give you an excuse to go back there
without having to admit how badly you really need to
go. You're so stubborn about it! Besides, if things
don't go well, you'd have, uh, somebody to confide in,
somebody who would understand. And somebody who

could give you an excuse to leave quickly if things got sticky.''

Anger flared through him. "I'll be damned if I'll run away from Cielo Solo again, Juanita! The only reason I can live with the memory is because I was just a kid. To turn tail as a man, with a gentle soul like Kelley McKinney depending on me—'' He shook his head. "That's not something I could handle.''

He didn't like the sudden gleam in Juanita's eyes; she looked like a woman who'd just scored a victory. "Well, then, start packing, Nick Morales, because if you refuse to help Kelley that's exactly what you'd be doing. Turning tail and leaving her in the lurch!''

"Oh, come on!'' His laughter was forced. "Since when is it my responsibility to chauffeur every pretty girl who shows up?''

"Stop it, Nick.'' Juanita's tone was suddenly grave. "You can make all the jokes you want, all the excuses your agile brain can come up with. But the simple truth is that you will *never* be completely at peace with yourself until you go back there and you know it!'' Her voice broke with feeling. "You don't have to stay there forever. Just long enough to tell your grandmother how much you love her...and long enough to make Liliana tell you the whole truth. Even if you find out that you don't want her anymore, Nico, you've got to *know* what really happened!''

They'd had this discussion a thousand times when they were dating, and he couldn't imagine why he'd come back today when any fool could have predicted that Juanita would rehash every one of her old arguments. Then, with sudden perfect hindsight, Nick sheepishly realized why he'd come to see her: he *wanted* Juanita to talk him into going to Sonora with Kelley

McKinney! He hated the idea, but he couldn't get it out of his mind, any more than he could forget the freckle-faced redhead herself. He wanted to see her again, and even though there was no reason why he couldn't just pick up the phone and ask her out, he knew he never would as long as his unresolved business in Cielo Solo lingered between them.

"I don't want to do this, Juanita," he said, the resolution now muted in his tone. "I've got a good life here. There's nothing I need in Mexico, nothing I want there." He met her eyes gravely, almost pleading. "Give me one good reason why I should do this. One good reason I haven't heard a thousand times before."

Juanita faced him squarely, her diminutive stature no impediment to her determination. "You need to go to Cielo Solo, Nick Morales, because your grandmother is eighty-two years old and you love her more than you love anybody on the face of this earth! If you don't go soon, she's going to die before you get there—die crying for you as she has for the past nineteen years—and that's a burden you'll carry with you for the rest of your life."

It was the only reason she'd ever come up with that Nick could not refute.

MAMA LUZ CRADLED the half-made basket with her agile bare feet, freeing both of her strong hands to deftly weave another strand of palm leaf into the smooth upper rim. Her brown, wrinkled face glistened with sweat, and strands of her braided snow-white hair floated around her face to form a wispy halo. Even though it was not yet springtime in Sonora, it was stifling hot by mid-afternoon. She had to squint just to keep her eyes on the arid land that stretched as far as the naked eye could see.

There was no marked path in the shifting sand, but an irregular chain of prickly pear served as a trailhead toward the huge twisted elephant tree half a mile to the north. Beyond the knoll that sheltered the village towered the fifty-foot-tall saguaro that was visible even in a sandstorm. With a trunk that seemed to split into two great arms and smaller limbs that spread out like a dozen fingers, it seemed to beckon to weary travelers in search of rest. No matter how arduous the journey—and travel was always difficult in this remote part of the desert—anybody from Cielo Solo who spotted the saguaro knew he could find his way home.

"How long is Mama Luz going to be like this?" a young voice drifted to her ancient ears from inside the *huiki* where the other women were working. It was cooler inside the wattle-and-daub weaving hut, which was half-buried in the ground to take advantage of the moist earth below the surface. Normally Mama Luz preferred to work inside, but this afternoon she felt too restless to be hemmed in where her eyes could not feast on the life-renewing desert. "My *abuelito* José came back from Pitahaya two hours ago," the little girl continued. "I thought that would make Mama Luz happy."

José's wife, Carmelita, answered softly, "She is very happy that he is home safely, *mi hija*. But she is very sad that he came back without any mail from America. Again."

Mama Luz tried to block out the voices, but she couldn't ignore the dull ache of disappointment that always gripped her when so many months passed without word from Nico. Her son, José, only took the burro to Pitahaya for supplies once every four or five weeks, and she always prayed for something—anything—from the most precious of all her loved ones. The last time Mama Luz had seen her American grandson, he had been a mere speck in the vast desert landscape, dwarfed by the giant saguaro as he headed north to the foreign land where her only daughter had given birth to him. She hadn't blamed young Nico for running away; she'd even forgiven him for being too proud to say goodbye. But that was only because she'd been so certain that he would come back home after he had a few days to lick his wounds! He had, after all, been dealt a pair of grievous blows for a boy so young: first his mother's death, then his sweetheart's crushing betrayal just a few months later.

But days had turned into weeks, then to months, before Mama Luz had received that first brief letter. She would never forget the way she'd felt on that bittersweet day. What joy to learn that Nico was alive! What grief to realize that he'd decided to make his life in America!

She was not the only one who had counted the days for mail from Nico. He had taught Liliana to read, so she was the one who had painstakingly relayed his words to Mama Luz . . . and the one who could not believe that in that whole letter, not once did he mention her name. She was already big with child by then, and kindhearted Meleseo, another one of Mama Luz's grandsons, had repeatedly volunteered to marry her. Despite her constant harassment by Pablo Villalobos, Liliana had ignored Meleseo's offer until the day Nico's first letter came. It was as though all hope died within her then; the very next day she told Meleseo that she would marry him.

Nico wrote again, three or four times a year, but he never came back to his family. Several times he'd invited Mama Luz to join him in America, where her life, he insisted, would not be so hard. There were times when she ached to see her grandson so badly that she gave serious thought to his crazy notion. But she knew—as Nico surely did—that she wouldn't last a year in the hysteria of Los Angeles. What kind of life would exist for her without the desert? What would she do with her hands all day? And what on earth would the rest of the family do without her? Mama Luz had never understood why Nico had chosen such a solitary life for himself. The only truth she knew was that if she waited long enough, prayed hard enough and loved him deeply enough, her beloved grandson would someday find his way home.

"I don't know why she wants a letter so much," the little girl said with idle curiosity. "She can't read the words and she never spends his money, anyway."

Still weaving the basket, Mama Luz closed her eyes, wishing she could explain to the child how much that money meant to her. She now had three full lard cans of it in her indoor kitchen, hidden from the lizards and kangaroo rats. On those days when she didn't think she'd last another hour without word from her Nico, she would caress the crumpled bills as living proof that he had not yet forgotten the old woman who'd so often rocked him to sleep as a child.

"José told me he saw Pablo Villalobos today in Pitahaya," Carmelita revealed to the other women in a confidential tone. "He was drinking with a gravel-voiced *gringo*, and he bragged about his fine new horse."

"Why would an American want to drink with Pablo?" Liliana's mother questioned, her distaste for the man evident in her strident tone. "And how would he get a fine horse?"

Carmelita sounded uneasy. "I don't know. José said he looked very comfortable for a man just out of prison. He asked a lot of questions about how Meleseo died."

Mama Luz couldn't stifle a shiver as she considered Pablo's interest in Meleseo's death. She had never cared for Pablo much, but ever since he'd driven off her Nico, she'd had no use for him at all. She wasn't surprised to hear that he was back in the area; rumor had it that he'd been released from prison about the time Liliana's husband had died last fall. There were some who believed that Pablo had had a hand in that death, but *La zarca*, Cielo Solo's *curandera*, had insisted that she'd done her best to cure Meleseo. If he'd fallen under a spell, she'd told the village, then it was someone else's doing.

"Do you think he will come back for Liliana now that Meleseo is dead?" one of the other women questioned.

"I don't know why he would," another answered. "The baby died when it was only a few months old. He has no claim to any of Liliana's children now."

"I don't think that matters much to a man like Pablo," Liliana's mother replied tartly. "He didn't even know she was pregnant when he came back before; he just couldn't bear the idea that she was going to marry Nico."

Carmelita coughed, then declared in an even softer tone, "You know, Nico has never married. Mama Luz thought he would come back when he found out that

Meleseo had died. I know that Liliana learned to love her husband dearly, but to this day she still won't talk about Nico."

"Oh, forget Nico Morales!" Liliana's mother snapped. "He turned his back on my daughter when she needed him the most! He turned his back on all of us! If Mama Luz really mattered to him, he would have come home long before now."

"Hush now!" Carmelita whispered fiercely. "She may hear us."

"I'm only speaking the truth," the other woman insisted. "Liliana is better off without him, and so is Mama Luz. What kind of a man forgets his own people?"

"He has not forgotten us!" Carmelita replied stoutly, defending her nephew with instinctive family loyalty in the absence of solid facts. "He is a very rich man now. He has a house with water inside and a floor made of wood! He must watch over the men who work for him. He is too busy to—"

"How could he be too busy to see his own grandmother for almost twenty years? Ismael comes back to see me every winter with his American wife and six children, and he doesn't even own his own car like Nico does! That boy could have come home a dozen times by now with the money Mama Luz keeps in her kitchen!" This time nobody interrupted. "The old one can wait forever, but he's never going to come back to Cielo Solo! She'll never see him again."

Mama Luz put aside the palm-leaf basket and rose unsteadily in the dizzying afternoon heat. She had ignored enough hard words about her precious Nico; she could tolerate no more. She smoothed out the sweat-lined folds of her black cotton dress, then proudly bent her ancient frame to scrunch through the doorway of the *huiki* and confront the gossipers face to face.

Utter silence gripped the weaving hut as the other women watched her enter. Hands frozen, each one stopped her weaving; even the child grew still. Carmelita couldn't meet her mother-in-law's eyes, and Liliana's mother had the grace to look ashamed.

Mama Luz stared at the group for several moments while she gathered her burgeoning feelings into coherent thoughts. It was not her habit to berate others in public, but when someone attacked one of her children, it was very hard for her to stay calm.

At last her dark eyes settled on the woman who had spoken against her grandson. "You are wrong," she declared with quiet dignity. "I cannot tell you why Nico's path has taken him so far away from us, but I can tell you that he *will* come home one day." Her ancient voice quavered as she whispered the hopeful words, but no one in the *huiki* would have dared to challenge her fervent belief. "Our giant cactus has stood there for a century," she reminded the women, pointing toward Cielo Solo's distant landmark with a wrinkled, trembling hand, "and I am nearly as old. But it will still be waiting when my grandson comes back to his people, no matter how long it takes. And I will be waiting, too."

Slowly Mama Luz turned to the little girl whose thoughtless questions had started the conversation, and quelled her with passionate eyes. "I will never give up on my Nico, *mi hija*, no matter how many years go by. You are very young, and you think I am a crazy old woman. But I know that some day when you become a grandmother—" she blinked just once to stave off the threatening tears "—then you will understand."

CHAPTER THREE

THE DOORBELL RANG at six-fifteen, signaling the arrival of Kelley's tardy dinner guests. For her brother Jimmy and his wife, Kelley had always joked, fifteen minutes late was downright early. They had both lacked her methodical organization even before they'd had children. Now that they had two in diapers and two in school, punctuality was only a ghost of a memory.

When Kelley opened the door, only brown-haired, round-faced Bobby stood on her doorstep. As always, his blue eyes sparkled and his smile was wide.

"Hi, Aunt Kelley!" he greeted her cheerfully as he charged in and plopped the diaper bag on the floor. The stuffed bag threatened to topple over on her latest botanical acquisition, a large Princess of the Night cactus shipped from a first-rate wholesaler in Arizona.

"Careful, Bob. That's a fifty-dollar specimen there," she pointed out. Kelley took great pride in her cactus collection, but she knew from experience that her nephew was immune to the beauty of her beloved desert plants. She was not surprised that he studied the thorny plant with some disdain. Its long, ridged, blackish-green stems had tiny buds that hinted of the gorgeous floral treat that lay in wait for Kelley in the spring, but it wasn't the sort of plant that would inspire a six-year-old boy to poetic rapture.

"It looks like it's already dead," Bobby observed uncharitably.

"It is not dead!" Kelley protested. "And I think it's beautiful. At least, it will be when it blooms. For one glorious night this cactus will have dozens of fragile white flowers, the prettiest you've ever seen. In the morning they'll all be gone, of course, but—"

"They die overnight?" Bobby was not impressed. "Why did you buy an ugly plant that's just gonna die?"

His mother walked in at the tail end of his question and studied her son with a bemused look as he scampered out of the room. When she burst into laughter, Kelley couldn't help but join in.

"Well, I like your Princess of the Night, Kelley," Bonnie confessed, automatically handing the four-month-old baby she held in her arms to her eager sister-in-law.

"Thanks. I'm glad somebody in your family has good taste in plants. I'll make a point to invite you all over it if ever blooms. I'm sure Bobby would feel differently if he saw the desert in the springtime."

On that note, Kelley turned her attention to her youngest niece. The baby grinned for her aunt and eagerly sucked the warm finger she was offered. "I know it tastes good, sweetie, but it won't make you grow big and strong," Kelley told the infant, dropping a lingering kiss on the little one's cheek before she gently gave her back to Bonnie. "I think maybe you need your mama."

As Bonnie sat down at the table and started to nurse the baby, Kelley wondered, not for the first time, if she'd ever have a child of her own. Her job kept her very busy and intellectually fulfilled, and she didn't look forward to all the conflicts she'd have to face if she ever tried to juggle a baby and a career. Nonetheless, she'd always hoped to start a family of her own eventually. The real problem was finding the perfect husband...one who loved her as much as her brother cherished Bonnie.

Bonnie was no great beauty, but many women would have envied her peaches-and-cream complexion and the natural wave of her dark brown hair. At twenty-seven, she was four years younger than Kelley, but she often complained that she was showing some wear and tear after giving birth to four children. Everybody—except for Jimmy—could see that she'd gained a few pounds with each pregnancy. Kelley, on the other hand, still looked as fresh as a teenager, even in her tight designer jeans and ''Save the Mojave'' T-shirt.

But tonight, Kelley didn't feel particularly fresh. She'd spent the last week trying to track down a guide to take her to Sonora, and so far she hadn't found anybody but Nick Morales whom she'd trust to take her to the state line, let alone into the back of beyond.

Of course, in her more honest moments Kelley knew that she wasn't likely to find anybody who measured up to Nick. The fact that he didn't want to take her to Mexico—and disapproved of herbal medicine, anyway—made little difference to Kelley. He was a man of integrity, of that much she was sure. There was a depth to the man, a quiet kind of caring, that had intrigued her right from the start. It didn't hurt any that he was gorgeous—well, not gorgeous so much as virile and playfully appealing—and that his smile could have added an hour of sunlight to a winter's day in Alaska.

She liked him, pure and simple. And she wanted to see him again.

"What are the chances that you'll get to the desert this spring, Kell?" Bonnie asked, tenderly rubbing one finger over her baby daughter's ear. "In real life, I mean, instead of in your mind."

Kelley knew what she meant. Between her ever-growing cactus collection and the southwestern theme of her interior decorating, visitors often commented that a trip to Kelley's house was like a trip to the desert. The living-room couch was made of buckskin-colored leather, which matched the background of the oil painting of a saguaro at sunset, which monopolized one wall; even the dishes Kelley used were hand-thrown Papago pottery. The sand-and-earth-toned serape that hung over the recliner chair was hand-woven somewhere in Sonora.

"I'm fresh out of leads at the moment, Bonnie," Kelley admitted, "but I haven't given up on the expedition yet."

Before Bonnie could answer, eight-year-old Liz zipped past the grownups with a cheery hello, then joined Bobby in the backyard. A moment later, Kelley's brother ambled into the kitchen with his younger son clinging to his leg. When Jimmy plopped down at the table, little Nathan instantly wobbled over to his aunt and demanded a hug.

"Hey, how's my buddy?" she asked the smiling child. Honoring him with a giggling lift up high in the air, Kelley couldn't help but notice how much he looked like his proud papa. As if the blond hair and blue eyes weren't enough, his black and white jogging suit was a miniature copy of Jimmy's.

"I thought Bonnie said that a friend of Bobby's teacher was going to be your guide," Jimmy observed, joining the conversation without preamble. Having lived in a big family all his life, he knew better than to waste time on amenities when the children were quiet and a discussion was in bloom.

"Miss Martinez was very kind, Jim, but her lead didn't pan out," Kelley answered, automatically opening the bottom drawer where she stored the pots and pans that were suitable for Nathan to play with. She lowered him to the floor and handed him a long wooden spoon before turning back to the stove in hopes that her brother would drop the subject. She didn't want to talk about Nick Morales. His rejection of her proposal was disheartening enough. But what complicated matters was that now—a whole week later—she still couldn't quite shake her memory of his glorious smile and the rich timbre of his heartfelt laugh. Not only had he left her with a vague, unfulfilled longing, but he'd dropped a host of unwanted questions in her lap as well.

Why was he so sensitive about *curanderos*? Who was the girl in the picture and the dear old lady? And why had Nick's voice roughened with pain when he'd tried to convince her that he didn't care if he ever saw either one again?

"Kelley?" It was her brother's voice, soft but insistent. "I said, what happened with Juanita Martinez's friend?"

She met Jimmy's eyes hurriedly, then started setting the table. "I went to see him and he said no. That's all."

Bonnie and Jimmy exchanged one of those knowing looks common to people who've been lovingly married for years; words were often a waste of time when they'd learned to think alike. Kelley thrived on their ongoing romance, but at times she felt excluded by their closeness. She had once adored a man the way Bonnie loved her brother, but Allan had never been able to return the depth of her feelings. A piece of his heart had always lingered elsewhere, perpetually beyond her grasp.

"Juanita said he was a hunk," Bonnie commented enthusiastically. "I think she used to date him at one time."

Kelley didn't answer, but Jimmy picked up his wife's cue. "Well, Juanita's certainly pretty enough to attract a good-looking fellow. Now you don't suppose that my little sister found him attractive as well, do you, Bon? Is it possible that—"

"Is it possible that you'll ever outgrow your need to tease your big sister?" Kelley snapped.

Jimmy stopped abruptly. He and Kelley were very close; it was rare that she pulled rank on him, rarer still that she got angry despite the way he'd always ribbed her about her Irish red hair. "I'm sorry, Kell," he said simply.

Kelley's anger fled as quickly as it had come. She touched Jimmy's shoulder in mute apology, then finished setting the table.

"I'm just so frustrated, Jim," she confessed a moment later. "I've got to find a way to go down there. I owe it to Mama Chayo, and I owe it to myself."

"I know, Kelley," he replied sympathetically. Jimmy, of all her brothers and sisters, understood her love for her "grandmother" best. From infancy, he'd spent more time in Mama Chayo's arms than he had in his own mother's. "I know. But if there's no way to go this year...."

"There is a way. That's what bothers me. Nick Morales—Juanita Martinez's friend—could be the perfect person. He deflected most of my questions about his desert past, but he's got roots in Sonora."

"But he's too busy to take you?" Bonnie suggested mildly.

"No, it's not that. He's got some kind of problem with going back to his hometown. I'm not sure what it is, but—"

"Gee, Kelley, if he's got legal problems in Mexico he's the last person you want to go down there with," Jimmy pointed out.

"I didn't say he had legal problems. I got the impression that his problems were more . . . personal. Besides, he strikes me as a very law-and-orderly type of man."

"Well, I'd make sure before you go with him. If you get busted for *anything* south of the border they just lock you up and throw away the key."

"Come on, Jimmy. That's a bit of an exaggeration, don't you think?"

Jimmy thought a minute, then answered, "I don't know. That's just what I've heard."

Kelley had heard the same thing, but she didn't really believe it. "I suspect that you have to break the law to get arrested in Mexico, Jim, and I'm hardly planning to do that!"

"What if you run across a problem that's got nothing to do with the law?" her brother prodded. "I've heard it said that anything that hasn't been smuggled over that desert border—going north or going south— just hasn't been invented yet. And those drug runners aren't real big on human life, you know. It's not as though you're taking a cruise to Acapulco, Kelley! When you disappear in that wasteland, it's just like walking off the far side of the earth."

This time Kelley didn't rebuke him. He was her brother, after all, settled with a wife and family and prone to be cautious. And he did have a point.

"I'll be careful, Jim, I promise. And I'm not going anywhere with Nick Morales anyway, so whatever his problem down there might be, it has nothing to do with me."

Again Jimmy and Bonnie exchanged a knowing look. Frustrated, Kelley glared at them both. "All right, so I'd like to see him again!" she admitted. "But he doesn't seem to be interested—in me or in the trip. So that's it, okay?"

For a moment silence reigned in the kitchen. Then Jimmy said very softly, "Is it okay with you, Kell?"

She wanted to tell him to buzz off, but he was her brother and he knew her too well. After a futile moment spent trying to ignore the question, she met his eyes. "No, it's not okay," she confessed. "But it's not that big a deal, either. I don't really know the guy; I just think he's good-looking and very, very nice. It's hardly the first time that a man's been indifferent to my interest."

Jimmy congratulated Nathan on his pot-and-spoon drum, then stood up to lean over the counter and watch his sister as she worked. "Kelley, it's been three years since you and Allan broke up," he began gently. "Bonnie and I haven't bugged you much about dating because we never got the impression that you met anybody you cared about one way or another. But this guy—I can't even remember his name—"

"Nick," Bonnie supplied helpfully, earning a glare from Kelley.

"This Nick person—" he smiled gratefully at his wife "—seems to have made quite an impression on you. That's so rare, Kell, that I hate to see you just let him slip away. I also don't like to see you so quick to give up. That's not the big sister who taught me to stand up to Sean Robertson when he used to steal my toys."

Kelley managed to smile. She knew she was a lucky woman; all her life she'd been surrounded by a loving family. Even now that she lived in Los Angeles and didn't get back to Kansas much to see her parents, Jimmy's fortuitous transfer to California had been a godsend. Jimmy and Bonnie were her very best friends... and her model of the kind of marriage she someday hoped to have. Through hellish pregnancies, unpayable mortgages, unplanned surgeries and nights with teething babies, they had never faltered in their devotion to each other. Sometimes Kelley thought their marriage had spoiled her for the real world. Maybe the kind of love she wanted from a man only existed in fairy tales... and in her brother's house.

"Kelley, are you sure that Nick isn't interested in you?" Bonnie asked seriously. "Maybe it's just this trip that he doesn't like. From what you said, the very mention of Sonora set him back on his heels."

"You can say that again," Kelley responded soberly. "Actually, he was very kind to me, but I get the impression that he's kind to everybody—especially friends of Juanita's."

"And that's bad?" Jimmy asked.

"Of course not. I just don't know how I could... well, subtly come up with some other good reason to see him again. He'd be courteous if I asked him out, but I think he'd feel awkward about turning me down. And under the circumstances, I'd really feel clumsy asking. It's not like we met at work or a party. Besides, it's just not my style to be so direct."

Jimmy sat down and studied Bonnie again, as though the very sight of his wife cuddling their baby daughter gave him inspiration. "Okay, let's try something indirect," he suggested, raising his eyebrows at Bonnie in mute request for assistance. "Could you go back and ask another question, Kell? About the desert, even about his work? What does he do?"

"He's a mechanic," Bonnie answered. "Owns his own shop."

"Women!" Jimmy groaned, slapping his forehead melodramatically. "Kelley, didn't it ever occur to you to make an appointment for the man to work on your car? It's overdue for a tune-up anyway; I've been meaning to take it in. There's no better way to let him know you respect his judgment and trust his—"

Jimmy stopped when Kelley shook her head. The whole idea was just too contrived to suit her and Nick himself had already torpedoed that plan. "Jimmy, he says I've got a sticking piston, but he doesn't want to work on it," she explained. "He said he doesn't specialize in imports, but he was able to I.D. my car just by the sound. I just ... oh, I don't know...."

"You don't know what?" Bonnie prodded.

"I just got the feeling that he didn't want my business."

Jimmy contemplated her words for a minute. "Kelley, is it possible that Nick didn't want you to think he was trying to—"

His sentence was cut off by the brisk peal of the telephone. Kelley wiped her hands on a sand-and-cactus-colored dish towel, then picked up the receiver.

"Hello?"

"Hello," a strong male voice echoed across the wire. "May I please speak to Kelley McKinney?" The words were seasoned with the intriguing hint of a Mexican accent, and the unaccountable double time of her pulse told Kelley that this was a voice she had heard before...and had hoped to hear again.

"This is she."

"Kelley, this is Nick Morales," the voice continued smoothly, confirming her first suspicion.

Kelley blanched; she couldn't seem to respond. Her tongue felt paralyzed.

"We met at my shop last week," he explained as her stunned silence filled the receiver. "I'm a friend of Juanita Martinez's and—"

"Yes, Nick, hello," Kelley finally managed to mumble. "I certainly haven't forgotten your name. It's just that I...I wasn't expecting you to call."

"That makes two of us," he answered succinctly. His tone was quite serious; the cheery laughter of their first encounter lingered only in her mind. "Look, Kelley, I'd like to apologize if I offended you when we talked before. Your...suggestion...simply knocked the wind out of me. It's been so long since I've given any thought to going back to Sonora...." He paused for a moment, as if the concept still posed a sizable challenge to him. "Juanita used to harangue me about it all the time but since I stopped seeing her, nobody has...."

His voice faded again, revealing to Kelley that he was just as nervous as she was. She was certain his anxiety had more to do with Sonora than it had to do with her, however. Kelley wished she could have been sure of her own reasons for responding so potently to the sound of his voice. She was bewildered by her excitement; she honestly didn't know if it was Kelley the woman or Dr. McKinney the ethnobotanist who was more delighted that he'd called.

"I realize that I caught you off guard, Nick," Kelley replied, hoping to ease the awkwardness between them. "If I'd had any idea that you had, uh, personal reasons for avoiding the area, I wouldn't have troubled you."

He didn't answer at once, but after an unsettling pause he confessed, "Kelley, my reasons for going back are just as compelling as my reasons for staying away. I've given a lot of thought to this since we talked—to tell you the truth, I haven't thought about much else— and I think I'd like to get together with you and chew on this a little bit more." He took a deep breath, as though he'd reached the top of the summit and it was downhill from that point on. "If you're still interested in going, that is. And you haven't found somebody else—"

"No, I haven't found anybody else. I mean, I'd be delighted to talk to you some more." *About anything,* she suddenly realized. It was such an unprofessional thought that she asked judiciously, "Shall we make an appointment for some time later this week?"

"I was thinking of dinner tonight, actually," he replied at once. "Assuming you're free."

Kelley swallowed hard and turned to face her brother and his wife. Both were listening intently, making no effort to veil their interest in her conversation. They would understand if she ran off and left them here with an unfinished meal, but she couldn't bring herself to do it. Besides, Nick hadn't called to ask her out on a date—not really. It wouldn't be smart to get her personal feelings tangled up in this Sonoran trip, especially before she had a chance to figure out what emotions her erstwhile guide and traveling companion might be harboring for her.

"I'm sorry, Nick, but I have company for dinner this evening," she told him. "Perhaps—"

"Forgive me for interrupting, Kelley." His tone was apologetic but not distressed. "I should have asked if you were busy before I suggested we get together."

"Oh, it's okay, Nick," she assured him, her voice rising as Nathan started banging on his drum. "It's nothing special—"

"Thanks a lot," Jimmy muttered with a grin.

Kelley shot him a quelling look as she realized that both his voice and Nathan's racket might have carried over the phone. "My brother and his family are here," she explained, wanting to make sure that Nick didn't think she had a date. "Maybe we could get together some time tomorrow."

If there was relief in Nick's voice, she couldn't hear it. "I can break away for lunch if we meet near the shop," he suggested. "I don't know where you work, but—"

"I'll come to you," she volunteered, then instantly regretted her eager words. "I mean, uh, under the circumstances lunch with you is business, you see, so there's no problem with—" She stopped abruptly as she realized she was digging a deeper hole for herself; her only hope was that Nick thought it was only excitement about her research that made her sound so giddy.

When Kelley glanced at her brother, he was grinning like a Cheshire cat. Bonnie turned away from the phone and buried her face in the baby's neck. Kelley had a sneaking suspicion that she was hiding a spate of chuckles.

Fortunately Nick didn't seem to find her enthusiasm so humorous. "Kelley, I usually knock off around twelve and head for a little Chinese restaurant around the corner on Seventh Street," he informed her matter-of-factly. "It's very casual, but I can't be fancy in the middle of the day or I'd lose an hour trying to clean up the grease. Since I'm interviewing for a desert-guide position rather than a debutante-escort service, I hope that'll be all right."

His light banter put Kelley at ease. Obviously he didn't have a houseful of relatives eavesdropping on his end of the conversation! Before she could answer, Bobby and Liz came tearing through the kitchen, both hollering about a squirrel they'd seen in the yard.

"That sounds fine, Nick," she said quickly. "I'll meet you at twelve."

"*Hasta luego*, Kelley." His charming accent curled intoxicatingly around her name. "See you then."

"Well?" Bonnie demanded as soon as Kelley hung up the phone. "Do you have a date? Do you have a guide to Sonora?"

Kelley couldn't keep the rainbow of emotions off her face—joy, relief, confusion. "Well, I've got a business date for lunch tomorrow...in a Chinese restaurant on the edge of East L.A."

Bonnie cheered and Jimmy gave his sister a quick thumbs-up sign. "A journey to Mexico begins with a single step," he misquoted cheerfully.

Kelley took a moment to replay the conversation in her mind before she answered, "You might be right, Jimmy. And I get the feeling that Nick Morales has just traded in his work boots for a pair of homemade *huaraches*."

CHAPTER FOUR

NICK BRUSHED A NERVOUS HAND through his thick dark hair as he walked briskly around the corner of Seventh Street and ducked into Lee's China Palace at five minutes to twelve. Despite the fact that he'd chosen a time and place for this meeting that wouldn't interfere with his busy day, an hour ago he'd found himself zipping home to shower and change. In his navy-blue slacks and matching cashmere sweater, he knew he was overdressed for Lee's, but he simply couldn't bring himself to meet Kelley McKinney for lunch in his coveralls.

As he spotted her in his regular booth near the kitchen, Nick felt the frustration that he'd experienced ever since Kelley had left his shop the week before. The gauntlet she'd inadvertently laid down for him made him angry, but the woman herself—bright-eyed, smooth-skinned, quick to smile and laugh—made him feel warm inside. From the moment she'd told him about her Mexican "grandmother," he'd had the odd feeling that he could have told Kelley McKinney his whole life story and she would have understood everything. She would never laugh at the dirt-floored hut that Mama Luz called home; that was the only reason he could even consider this trip to the back of beyond. He would have sold his own soul before he'd have taken a woman to Cielo Solo who might treat his beloved grandmother with derision or scorn.

As Nick reached the table, Kelley's eyes flashed up to meet his; she couldn't conceal her surprise at his dapper attire. "Hi, Nick," she greeted him warmly. "It's really good to see you." Her cautious smile revealed such pleasure that Nick couldn't help but wonder if her interest in him might go beyond her need for a guide to Sonora.

"Nice to see you too, Kelley," he answered honestly. It seemed to Nick that she was also a bit overdressed for this take-out Chinese diner. She wore a tailored silk teal shirtwaist and a single string of pearls. Her fingers, he noticed, were bare of rings, and the polish on her short nails was clear.

As he slipped into the booth facing her, Kelley licked her lips and gripped the red vinyl menu tightly against her chest. "I already ordered," she informed him apologetically. "I didn't plan to, but when I told the waitress that I was meeting someone, she asked who, and...well, she said she already knew what you wanted."

Nick was sure her choice of words was accidental, but it caused him to wonder exactly what it was that he *did* want. An image of Liliana fluttered before him, her dark hair and distinctive Indian features shading the fragile glow of Kelley's green eyes. He could tell she was excited and more than a little nervous about his interview, but he wasn't sure why. Despite her promise to Mama Chayo, this challenging trip was really just a job for Kelley. To Nick, the rough desert terrain posed the least of his problems; it was the other journey, the one inside himself, that was so fraught with danger.

"I always have the house special—a little bit of everything," he quickly explained. "And I've eaten here almost every working day for seven years, so it's got to the point that I only call if I'm *not* going to come." He shrugged and offered her a reassuring smile. "I live alone and I'm not much of a cook, so this way I get at least one decent meal every day."

Kelley seemed to relax a little bit, but her smile, while more cautious than his, was nonetheless beguiling. With her delicate freckled face and curly red hair, it seemed to Nick that she looked more like a cuddly Raggedy Ann doll than a scientist. The first time they'd met he'd been too distraught by her talk of Sonora to take in all of her feminine attributes, but now, with his difficult decision behind him, he knew he was going to have a rough time thinking of her as a platonic fellow traveler on a botanical expedition.

"You must really like Chinese food, Nick," she cheerfully deduced.

He grinned as he followed her inquiring gaze around the tidy restaurant. Tables with bright red tablecloths filled the small space, and a pair of flat brass dragons adorned one wall. It was always busy at this time of day; it was the sort of place where nine-to-fivers came for good food, not exotic Oriental ambience.

"Actually, I like the people here," he admitted. "When I first opened the shop and didn't have a dime, Paul Lee called me one afternoon and said his delivery van wouldn't start—since I was just around the corner, was there any chance I could help him out right away? Well, I didn't have much business yet, so I trotted on down here to check it out. It only took me ten minutes to get his engine running, so I didn't charge him anything, but he was so grateful that he insisted on treating me to dinner." He spread his hands in an expansive gesture. "We've been friends ever since."

Kelley's smile widened. "I wish I had that kind of luck with mechanics. Every time I need any help they charge me an arm and a leg and make me wait till next Tuesday. The last time I had clutch trouble, I had to go back three times just to get my Datsun running as well as it did *before* they looked at it."

Having heard these horror stories before, Nick always went out of his way to make sure that no car would give its owner any more trouble after it left his shop. He thought it was unneighborly to give a man automotive headaches—and unforgivable to leave a woman stranded somewhere because of sloppy work.

Nick told himself, not for the first time, that such courtesy on his part was the reason he had no intention of exploring any sort of romantic relationship with this appealing woman—at least until after the trip. It was a good reason, after all, and certainly a more palatable one than the lurking suspicion that he was reluctant to get involved with anybody before he saw Liliana again. Surely Juanita was wrong, surely he had no lingering desire for the object of his first passionate puppy love. After all this time, he and Liliana undoubtedly had nothing in common. And whether she'd used him or not, whatever she'd once felt for Nick had surely evaporated over time. Nothing, after all, stayed fresh and whole in the desert for nearly twenty years.

Abruptly he noticed that Kelley was waiting for some sort of reply to her last comment . . . something about her car. "I've got a friend who only works on imports," he offered quickly. "Name's Scotty Hayward. His boss won't let him give you a discount, but if he works on your Datsun you can guarantee that sticking piston won't bother you again." He paused, remembering the harsh staccato of Kelley's engine. He'd hated letting her out of the shop without putting it to rights, but he hadn't wanted to give her the impression that he was trying to solicit her business. "I don't suppose you've taken care of that yet."

She flashed him an embarrassed grin. "Oh, I just don't have time to worry about things like that, Nick. Jimmy'll take care of it sooner or later."

"Jimmy?" Vaguely he remembered hearing her mention the man's name, but he couldn't remember what she'd said about him. The truth was, he couldn't remember much of anything Kelley had said after she'd mentioned Sonora.

"My brother. Actually, I have three brothers and two sisters, but Jimmy's the only one who lives in L.A. We're only three years apart and we've always been especially close."

Nick envied her family ties. He had many good friends in the area, but nobody he thought of as family. At times he felt as though he'd been hatched from thin air. "I'm an only child," he informed Kelley. "I've got more relatives in Cielo Solo than I can count, but...I've never been particularly close to most of them."

Another woman, he knew, would have prodded him for more information. But to her credit, Kelley waited patiently for him to continue. When he didn't, she tactfully suggested, "Maybe we should discuss some of the details of our trip. Assuming that we *are* taking one."

He nodded slowly. The decision, he'd realized during the night had actually been made long before he'd called Juanita yesterday to ask for Kelley's number. "When were you planning to go?"

"I need to go in a month or two," she answered promptly. "Not just because spring is the best time of year weather-wise, but also because there are many desert plants that are practically impossible to spot in the sand when they're not flowering. On top of that—and this is the biggest reason—my boss at the institute is leaving in May to go to Washington, D.C. Paul's got a terrific new job, so we're happy for him, but once he goes the man taking over has the power to scrap or refocus all of our projects. And this new fellow shares your view of folk medicine, I'm sorry to say, so he's likely to kill my Opata research before it even gets off the ground. If I've already got the project well under way, there's a much better chance that I'll be able to finish it. At the very least, I should be able to publish a preliminary report on Opata folk healing and that would clear the slate with Mama Chayo."

Nick twirled his water glass in his hand and tried not to think about Kelley's views on folk healing…let alone the domestic aspects of traveling alone with this enchanting woman. Three meals a day sitting close enough to hold hands across the table; nights in motel rooms, nights under the desert stars…nights in Cielo Solo where the fragrance of the nocturnally flowering cacti surrounded the village for six months of every year. Even now the scent lingered in his mind, as clearly as the vision of Liliana wearing the fragile white blossoms in her hair.

Again the two feminine faces blurred in his mind, and he struggled to focus on Kelley. "How long do you plan to spend down there?" he managed to ask.

"The first time, possibly only a few weeks. What I need to do with you is to establish a network of people who will trust me enough to talk and help me make other contacts. Once I have a friendly base down there, I can go back by myself and—"

"Without a translator?" he asked. "As it is my Spanish is pretty rusty, and I sure don't know the scientific names of any of those desert plants. Fortunately the Opata all speak Spanish these days, even in the villages that are still inhabited only by Indians. They live in the river valleys up above the driest part of the desert, so they can irrigate crops that won't grow for love nor money in Cielo Solo. I figure the best route to—"

He stopped speaking as he caught Kelley smiling at him, her green eyes delighting in his words. It was such a cheerful, spunky grin that he felt as though somebody had just opened the drapes to let in a ray of morning sun. "What's so funny?" he playfully demanded.

This time she laughed out loud. "When we last talked, you didn't know a thing about the Opata, Nick. Has something jogged your memory?"

He had to chuckle, too. "You mean like a trip down memory lane . . . or a visit to the library?"

She nodded.

"All right," he admitted sheepishly. "I *did* try to find out a little bit for you. But there's almost nothing in the library about the herbal cures used by the Opata—at least not in the material available to civilian types like me. But I did find an old mining map of the area and I was able to figure out how far it was from Cielo Solo to where most of the Opata live now."

"And?"

"It's close enough that I can probably rustle you up a friend of a relative of a friend who knows somebody who knows something and will find out a little more for a bit of desperately needed cash."

Kelley laughed again. "Were you a company clerk in the Army? You sound like Radar O'Reilly scrounging supplies for a MASH unit."

Nick shook his head. "I'll have you know I was a Jeep mechanic in Nam. If it weren't for my stint with Uncle Sam, I never would have learned enough about cars to get a job as a mechanic, let alone my own shop."

He didn't expect a woman of Kelley's extensive education to be interested in his own blue-collar credentials, no matter how hard he'd worked to attain them. But to his surprise, she asked, "What sort of training do you need to be a mechanic? I don't buy the theory that most men are just born with a natural mechanical gift. I've watched them look under the hood. All they do is poke at a few wires and check the radiator. I can do that myself."

Nick laughed, intrigued by the vision of Kelley bending over an engine in that smooth silk dress. "Well, to tell you the truth, I got my basic training on engines in the Army, then studied at a school for Ford mechanics when I worked for the dealership. I still take a class now and then just to keep up with the technological changes. Nowadays the electronic ignitions and computerized fuel-to-air ratio adjustments are just too complex to figure out by the seat of your pants, and I won't take a customer's money if I'm not sure I can give him a first-rate job."

Kelley looked impressed. In fact, her smile filled Nick with such warmth that he couldn't seem to recall why he'd originally been irritated with Juanita for sending Kelley to see him. "It certainly looks as though you've got a thriving business, Nick. I guess you've come a long way since you fixed Paul Lee's delivery van."

He nodded slowly, unable to conceal his pride. Juanita used to say that if anybody had ever pulled himself up by his own bootstraps, it was Nick Morales, and privately, he had to agree. While he never bragged about his success, he wasn't about to pretend it was just good luck, either. "Actually, Kelley, it's grown so big I really need to hire a fourth mechanic and move to a larger building. But I'm attached to the old place. I've been discussing it with the instructor of a class in small-business management I've been taking, but I'm still not sure if it's worth all the headaches."

Kelley shook her head. "I'm pretty ignorant about finances, but I imagine that the accounting considerations of your business might be as complicated as the mechanical end."

"More so," he agreed. "But fortunately I've always been pretty good at math."

Kelley shuddered. "If I'd majored in math I wouldn't have made it out of junior high. To this day I balance my checkbook at the end of every month with an entry that says 'Gift to Bank.' Once I was overdrawn by eighty-eight dollars and I never did figure out what I did wrong."

Nick laughed. "So much for higher education! Next time you run into trouble, Kelley, give me a call," he offered sincerely. "I never met an account I couldn't balance. You can't be careless about that sort of thing and run a successful business."

"Speaking of business, I guess we ought to discuss your fee," she replied, watching him closely as she spoke.

By the wary look on her face, it was obvious to Nick that Kelley knew she was treading on thin ice by bringing up the subject. What he couldn't determine was the feeling that lay beneath the intensity of her gaze. There was something terribly personal about the way she studied him—something warm, something sensual—that had nothing whatsoever to do with medicinal cures or even her Mama Chayo.

It occurred to Nick quite suddenly that they were both dancing around the truth. This wasn't turning out to be an interview or even a planning session. It was a date! They were both acting terribly professional and dignified, but such platonic restraint didn't change the fact that Kelley was a very appealing woman . . . who gave every sign that she saw Nick as a very attractive man.

He was flattered, but a bit confused. If he wanted this woman and she wanted him, he should have felt happy. He should have felt relieved! But instead he felt uneasy, much like he'd felt last year when one of his female customers had asked him out repeatedly even though he'd kept turning her down because of his commitment to Juanita.

But Nick didn't belong to anybody now; he'd been free and unattached for months. He'd liked Kelley McKinney right from the start, and if the smile on her face was any indication, she was tickled pink to be spending time with him. So why did he feel so guilty? Why did he feel as though he'd just done something wrong?

I love you, Nico. Liliana's voice came back to him, pristine with the innocence of youth. *No matter what happens, no matter how long it takes you to forgive me, I will always love you. I will always be waiting. Always, always, always . . .*

"I realize that you're not particularly in need of money, Nick," Kelley said gingerly, "but my boss has given me the go-ahead for—"

"No." The word was quick, almost fierce in its intensity. He could ignore his guilt about Liliana because most of that disaster had been her fault. But when it came to Mama Luz, he knew his cowardice had been indefensible. "No money, Kelley."

"I beg your pardon?"

Nick shook his head. This wasn't something he could negotiate. "Under no circumstances will I accept payment for taking a trip to see my grandmother. I ought to be paying you for jogging my conscience enough to make me do it. It's a journey I should have made years ago," he finished quietly.

He couldn't quite face Kelley as he murmured that confession; he certainly couldn't explain to her how he felt every time he received one of those letters—painstakingly copied down by Liliana—that conveyed the anguish his long absence had caused Mama Luz. He'd sent her enough money over the years to build a new house and feed half the village, so he wasn't concerned about her physical well-being. But still, knowing his grandmother, he suspected that she probably would have traded every penny for a single glimpse of his face. Just thinking about the long years he'd neglected her filled him with shame.

Mercifully Lee's wife arrived with lunch before the silence grew too long. She was a perky older woman who found it necessary to tease Nick about his suave appearance as well as his "date," assuring Kelley that he only brought a girl "home" to eat with them if she was very special. It was hardly the sort of comment Nick needed at the moment, but he realized that her perception was pretty accurate. Juanita was the only woman he'd ever met at Lee's for lunch before. And he'd always worn his coveralls.

Nick noticed that Kelley had ordered the house special, too, and seemed to dig in with enthusiasm. Belatedly it occurred to him that he'd never even asked her if she liked Chinese food. It wasn't like him to be so discourteous, especially with a woman he wanted to impress.

And I do want to impress her, he finally admitted to himself, suddenly very glad that he'd gone home to change. *So why am I trying so hard to pretend I don't?*

He knew the answer, and he didn't like it at all. He wanted to kiss Kelley's freckles and nuzzle the nape of her neck. He wanted to feel her smooth white skin beneath his rugged hands . . . he wanted to bury his face in that frizzy red hair. He wanted to make her eyes light up when he told funny stories, and he wanted to see her smile when he whispered her name.

And yet the simple truth was that he wanted none of these things as much as he wanted to arrive in Cielo Solo unattached. After all, Mama Luz wasn't the only person he was going back to see. Over the years he'd started half a dozen relationships with girls just as nice as Kelley—girls who couldn't date a man casually, girls who always gave their hearts—only to find himself emotionally hamstrung, sooner or later, by the omnipresent memory of Liliana. He wouldn't go through it again; he wouldn't crush another gentle soul the way he'd hurt Juanita. He already liked Kelley far too much to lie to himself about his feelings.

"Uh, what other details did you want to go over?" he asked uneasily, toying with his chopsticks. "What else do we need to work out today?"

"Well, let's see." Her eyes lit up again as she pondered the upcoming trip, and he realized anew that her natural beauty multiplied by leaps and bounds when she smiled. "As to your concerns about translation," she surprised him by saying, "I'd say my own Spanish is . . . adequate. I studied it at school and I also learned Opata plant names from Mama Chayo, so you don't have to worry about that."

But that's not the only thing I need to worry about, Nick found himself thinking. *There's the problem of how to keep my distance from you, how to behave like a gentleman for days on end, how to pretend I'm the only one who feels this way when you look at me as though . . . as though what? As though I might already mean something more to you than a mere desert guide?* Out loud he said, "I'll need to soup up an old clunker with Sonora plates, one we can afford to have stripped or stolen when we leave it in Pitahaya. We also need to buy or rent a burro to carry supplies from there to Cielo Solo. And though I hate to say it, we should probably travel armed in case we have trouble with the rattlers, coyotes or two-legged predators down there."

"Two-legged predators?" Kelley repeated uneasily. "Why would we have any trouble with the villagers?"

Nick shook his head, appalled at her naïveté. "Kelley, it's not the villagers I'm worried about. You're talking about a part of the world where the Apaches eluded the U.S. Cavalry for thirty years! Anybody who's wanted for anything can go there to hide and never be found. They run drugs, guns, exotic birds and God knows what else through the mountains and down to the flatlands . . . and they aren't polite to anybody they stumble over in the dark.''

The flicker of alarm in Kelley's green eyes almost made Nick wish he hadn't been so blunt. He was forced to realize how much her safety would depend on him.

''I'm aware that, uh, caution is in order, Nick,'' she answered uneasily. ''And obviously you're more familiar with the area than I am. That's why I need somebody who knows the land and has people who can, well, give me the native seal of approval.''

Reluctantly Nick shook his head. He wasn't ready to give this lovely girl any more than the bare outline of his past, but he owed her the truth: he might not be welcome in Cielo Solo even though Pablo Villalobos was still doing hard time.

''Kelley, to be honest with you, I can't promise you that anybody down there is going to be glad to see me except for my grandmother.'' Nervously he fingered his Virgin of Guadalupe medal as he compressed his life story into a few terse sentences. ''My mother took me back to Cielo Solo when I was just a few months old, and we didn't return to the states till I was eight. But we still went back to visit every year or so till I was a teenager, and when my mother died, I went back to stay.''

He studied Kelley's face for several moments, asking himself how Liliana's version of this story would differ from his own. But Kelley didn't probe his painful memories for details, and her guileless gaze conveyed only sympathy and trust. He felt a strange urge to lay all his feelings on the table, but a lifelong habit of keeping such thoughts to himself caused him to refrain.

"I only made it three months," he finally admitted, surprised at his temptation to tell her more. "I left quite abruptly under... well, difficult circumstances which... may have been interpreted uncharitably by... some people who didn't have all the facts."

There were many possible replies Kelley could have made to his confession, but her quiet choice of words took him completely off guard. "I'm deeply sorry about your mother, Nick," she offered in a very low tone. And then, incredibly, she asked, "Was she treated by a *curandero*?"

The surprise surely must have registered on his face; nobody, not even Juanita, had ever figured him out so quickly. But for some reason, Kelley's gentle insight didn't bother him. "Yes, she was," he quietly revealed. "But not in Mexico, Kelley, she found one right here in L.A.! I still don't know just what she died of, but my guess is that it was some kind of stomach cancer. I was too young to insist that she get decent medical care. When she said she was seeing somebody, I just assumed that she meant a real doctor." He shook his head, still haunted by the memory. "If I hadn't been at such a selfish age, I might have noticed a lot of things sooner. I might have... well, I might have done a lot of things differently."

Kelley met his eyes with a warm, healing gaze that softened some of his lingering bitterness about his mother's death. He found himself wanting to believe that if Kelley's Mama Chayo had been the one who had treated his mother, she might not have died.

"Nick, we all make mistakes," she assured him. "If I'd known a few years ago what I know now, I would have done a whole host of things differently myself.

One in particular. But until you've made those mistakes and learned from them, you never know."

"What's your mistake? Your 'one in particular.'"

Instantly the shining beauty faded from her eyes, and Nick longed to retract his question. He hadn't meant to pry; he'd only wanted to draw her out, to find out more about the sensitive human soul that lurked beneath that frilly mop of red curls. But it was obvious that he'd stumbled over some private grief of Kelley's, some old scar that hadn't yet healed. "Kelley," he began, "you don't—"

"I tried to pretend that I was...very special to someone who...always saw me as second best," she confessed with an artificial grin. Despite her forced attempt at levity, it was obvious that her "someone" had hurt her deeply. "Actually, I don't think he really ever saw me at all. He probably just...pretended I was somebody else."

It was a vague, unsettling confession and for one terrible moment Nick thought she was talking about him. But how could Kelley possibly know how often a vision of Liliana clouded his view of her lovely face?

"I'm sorry, Kelley," he murmured sincerely, then added in a half serious tone, "Any man who can't see how beautiful you are must be stone blind."

"No, Nick," she protested quickly, "I'm not a beautiful woman and we'll get along a lot better if you don't try to pretend that I am. On my best days I'm cute, and on my worst days—"

"On your worst days you must be as sensitive to old war wounds as I am, lady!" he cajoled her, instinctively reaching across the table to take both her hands in a soothing gesture. The last thing he'd ever intended to do was to hurt her! "How did some old fool fail to miss your beauty?'' he teased, hoping to recapture the happy smile he loved to see on her face. ''I've had to keep myself on a short leash ever since we met!''

The playful words tumbled out in a rush of reassurance, but they echoed across the crowded restaurant like a schoolboy's confession of love. As Nick studied Kelley's face, he realized that she wasn't at all sure whether or not he was kidding; worse yet, neither was he.

While he debated what to do next, Nick discovered that he couldn't seem to release her hands. His heart began to pound in a slow, erratic pattern as he found himself caressing Kelley's white palms with his own dark fingers.

Repeatedly he told himself that he ought to let her go, but he was mesmerized by the warmth of her skin. It felt so good to pull her toward him; it felt incredibly right. Nothing, in fact, had felt so right with a woman since the last time he'd touched Liliana, a tender kiss by desert moonlight that he still remembered as clearly as he could see the freckles on Kelley McKinney's face.

The sudden memory jolted him, reminding him of why he'd decided to keep his distance from this beautiful girl...the reason he had no business whatsoever clinging to her hands...and no business giving her any false expectations. But he didn't want to let her go, and he certainly didn't want to insult her, so he struggled for a way to pass off the brief aberration as a harmless flirtation.

''Just for the record, Kelley,'' he managed to toss out lightly, ''I joke a lot, but whenever I'm serious, I mean what I say.'' With great reluctance, he released her smooth white fingers and realized, as he did so, that her grip had been as eager as his own. That sweet discovery was almost enough to make him forget Liliana, forget common sense, forget the complications of a spontaneous affair in the midst of a desert survival test and the emotional trauma of his homecoming. Uncertainly he finished his intended compliment. "Take it from me, Kelley McKinney, you are a beautiful woman." *And this time,* he realized uneasily, *I couldn't be more serious.*

For several moments, they stared at each other in awkward silence. It was Kelley who finally broke the impasse. "Thank you for the compliment," she said simply. Her tone was calm, almost indifferent, but her shadowed eyes sent a clear message. *If I'm so beautiful, Nick Morales, then why did you pull away?*

CHAPTER FIVE

KELLEY GLANCED AT HER WATCH for the thirteenth time in thirteen minutes, then straightened the bow tie on her mint-green silk blouse. The dark ribbon matched the forest-green velvet skirt and short jacket... and even the brand-new pair of three-inch heels. She knew she was overdressed for this meeting, but she hadn't been able to resist this last chance to show Nick Morales her most feminine side before they started on their journey. From that point on he wasn't likely to see her in anything but jeans and hiking boots—hardly her most charming apparel.

"You are a beautiful woman," Nick had told her the last time they'd met. But when she'd squeezed his hands, he'd pulled away. Kelley didn't know if it was pity, habit or a tiny bit of interest that had so briefly tugged Nick in her direction, but she wasn't about to pass up any opportunity to subtly encourage him to notice her again.

It had been a month since she'd seen him last. Of course, they'd talked on the phone a few times to shore up the details of their trip, but their conversations had always been brief, pleasant and businesslike. At times, Kelley had hoped that her interest in him had paled; she'd told herself that it was only the journey to Sonora that had kept her so excited. Now, imagining his thick black hair and round, compelling eyes, Kelley suspected that she'd only been lying to herself.

A moment later she was sure of it.

"I guess this is the place," a deep male voice declared from the doorway, intruding on her reverie.

As Kelley turned quickly to face him, it seemed to her that Nick's accent was stronger than usual today... and his effect on her senses was more powerful, too. Her pulse began to hammer out a staccato beat that seemed to grow more erratic when he smiled.

It was the first time she'd ever seen him in a suit, and while it was only a good department-store variety, the cut set off the natural breadth of his shoulders and the coffee-brown shade dramatized his rich dark skin. A waft of leather-scented after-shave drifted in Kelley's direction, and the manly texture of his freshly shaved skin seemed to outline the square jaw and strong chin. For one ludicrous, impulsive moment she was tempted to kiss him.

"Good morning, Nick," she managed to greet him, already feeling unsteady on her feet. "Won't you sit down?"

He stepped gingerly around the sprawling octopus agave that owned the corner by the door and settled down in a soft leather chair. He glanced around the room, taking in the university plaques on the wall, the kachina dolls in the glass case and the picture of Bonnie, Jimmy and the kids that lived on her desk.

"No fan belts," he observed with a grin. "But I like the view."

The view to which he referred was the spectacular collection of southwestern flora adjacent to Kelley's office building. The Botanical Garden—artistically framed by her ceiling-to-floor sunlit window—was only one part of the Institute for Southwestern Studies, wedged in among a western art gallery, a library of local history and a museum tracing native plants, animals and people in the area from the dawn of time.

"I asked for this office just so I could be near the garden," Kelley confessed as she perched on the edge of her desk. "I can't stand to be away from green things for very long."

Nick couldn't hide his smile as his eyes came to rest on her outfit. "I think maybe you got a little too close, Kelley. Either photosynthesis is already taking place or else you're turning into a leprechaun."

Well, you managed to get his attention all right, Kelley groaned inwardly. But her moment of chagrin was mercifully brief. "You look stunning in that outfit, Kelley," he complimented her. "Absolutely stunning."

He sounded awed and perhaps a bit surprised, but his eyes registered such approval that Kelley couldn't help but smile. "Thank you. You're not looking too bad yourself."

Nick appeared uncertain, and Kelley wondered if he, like she, was feeling overdressed for the occasion. Of course in Nick's case, the choice of a suit had probably been a mark of respect for Kelley; he had no way of knowing how informally the guys at work normally dressed. Her boss, Paul Harris, kept a multicolored tie in his top desk drawer and usually dug it out only when he had an appointment with an important Institute guest.

"So, shall we get down to business?" Nick asked abruptly, his brisk tone catching Kelley off guard. "I'm not quite done overhauling the engine on that decrepit old Ford we're taking to Sonora and I want to wrap up

everything else before I go. I assume we're still scheduled to leave on Thursday?''

"As far as I know." It was only three days till
Thursday, three days before Kelley started off into the
desert with the virile man whose eyes now quietly caressed her. It seemed as though she'd waited for months
instead of weeks to see him again. They'd planned
every detail of their trip, yet now, with her clasped
hands just inches from Nick's and itching to edge them
yet closer, Kelley didn't feel at all prepared for the
journey. Nervously she asked, "Are you closing the
shop while you're gone?''

He shook his head. "No, I'm going to leave Jeff in
charge. I can't afford to risk having my clientele drift
away in my absence. Besides, some of my customers
really depend on me, and whenever somebody else
works on my cars I always have to do everything over
later." He stopped and studied Kelley's green eyes for
a moment, then asked pointedly, "Did Scotty Hayward do a good job on that sticking piston for you?''

Kelley shook her head, a bit embarrassed that she'd
let the problem slide. "I haven't called him yet.''

"You haven't called him yet?" Shock vibrated his
deep tone. "Kelley, you won't hurt my feelings if you
find a mechanic on your own, but that sticking piston
is an indication that—''

"Okay, okay!" Taken aback by Nick's vehemence,
Kelley couldn't stifle a nervous chuckle. "I'll take care
of it soon. I promise.''

A swift tap on the door was followed by the arrival
of gray-haired Paul Harris, grinning as he made himself welcome in the room. Dressed in worn jeans, a
short-sleeved plaid shirt and his ubiquitous multicolored tie, he took one look at Kelley and gushed, "My,

my, aren't you dressed up to beat the band!'' Before
Kelley's blush had time to catch up to her freckles, he
pulled up a wooden chair and plopped down next to
Nick.

"Paul Harris,'' he introduced himself, vigorously
shaking Nick's hand. "So you're Kelley's desert rat.''

Kelley knew that Paul meant no disrespect; a ''desert rat'' was a man who was totally at home in the desert, a compliment from a botanist who'd been raised in
the Mojave.

"Well, to tell you the truth, it's been a long time
since I rested in the shade of a saguaro, Paul,'' Nick
confessed, "but I imagine it'll come back to me once
we cross the border.''

"Long before that, I imagine. Kelley tells me she's
going to stop in Tucson on the way down to see Bill
Johanneson at the Arizona-Sonora Desert Museum. I
gather he's been doing similar *curandero* research
among the Tarahumara Indians.''

Nick tensed slightly, as Kelley had noticed he often
did whenever herbal medicine was mentioned. But he
replied pleasantly, "Well, that's not my department,
I'm afraid, but I imagine I can find something else to
do while Kelley studies witch doctors.''

"Oh, no!'' Paul cajoled him. "You can't miss the
Desert Museum. It's world famous—there's nothing
like it in the whole country. You'll find plenty to keep
you busy while Kelley chats with Bill. Aside from the
cacti, there're all sorts of Sonoran animals, and the
view itself is absolutely spectacular. On clear days they
say you can see all the way to Mexico.''

Nick gave Paul the smile he expected, but his grave
eyes made it clear that the last thing he wanted to see
in Tucson was a view of Mexico, clear, spectacular or

otherwise. Kelley had hoped that by now he'd come to terms with this trip and everything it might mean to him, but it was obvious that he still had mixed feelings.

"So tell me about yourself, Nick," Paul asked, his tone blatantly avuncular as he glanced at Kelley, then back to Nick, like a father interviewing a boy about to take his sixteen-year-old daughter on her first date. "Kelley tells me you've got family in Sonora, so you get to combine business with pleasure on this trip."

For the first time since Paul had joined them, Nick glanced meaningfully at Kelley. *Traveling with you is the only part of this trip that I'd call pleasure,* he might as well have declared out loud. She felt a flurry of confusion somewhere in her midriff as he commented enigmatically to Paul, "Most of life's a mixed blessing."

Ignoring this uninformative answer, Paul pressed on, "I hear you were raised in Opata country, so you'll be able to make the connections Kelley needs for her research."

Again Nick shot her a quizzical glance, as if to ask, *How many of my secrets have you shared with this man?*

Quickly she answered his unspoken question by steering the conversation away from his family. "I told Paul that we can count on word-of-mouth connections once we get there." *And that's all I told him,* she insisted with her eyes.

A flicker of relief danced across Nick's face, and Kelley thought she heard the ghost of a sigh before he continued in the same vein, "It's not that far from Cielo Solo to the Opata country, even though the terrain is quite different. Cielo Solo is in the foothills of

Sonora so you'll find lots of saguaros, ocotillos and bur sage. Which, come to think of it—'' he shook his head as though the memory had just hit him ''—gives me hay fever in the spring.''

If Nick realized that neither botanist was in need of a topological description of the Sonora Desert, he gave no sign. Kelley suspected he just wanted to keep Paul from asking any more personal questions.

''Now the Opatas live up a little higher in the thorn-scrub country,'' he continued knowledgeably, ''where the gray thorn and manzanita are thick enough to stop a puma in its tracks. They settle mainly along the riverbanks. Have for centuries. In fact, I think some of the same Indian families have been running those floodwater farms since before the Spaniards came. They lost their language over time and a fair amount of their culture, but the old folks will still tell you proudly that they're not Mexicans, they're Opatas.''

Kelley nodded. Mama Chayo had often made that same distinction.

''That's pretty much the way the Navajos look at being Americans, isn't it?'' Paul asked.

Nick nodded. ''I imagine. Though I don't know that much about the Navajos. I was born in Papago country—in Arizona, that is. Though there were lots of Papagos and mixed Papago folks east of Hermosillo, too.''

Again his eyes met Kelley's, with a look that told her clearly that only in deference to her feelings was he willing to share even this much of his childhood with her curious boss. Yet she saw no resentment in Nick's expression; instead she sensed intimate collusion in the way that the two of them shared silent secrets that Paul Harris would never learn. She couldn't put words to the feeling, but as the conversation continued, Kelley had the inescapable sensation that when Nick had arrived today, they'd been heading in the same direction on two parallel but separate journeys, but now they were a team.

"You were born in Tucson?" Paul probed, oblivious to the undercurrents flowing between Nick and Kelley. "I thought you were—"

"Nick has a lot to do today, Paul," Kelley interjected, hoping to spare him any more discussion of his homeland. "We really ought to get down to the business of my research."

Nick shot her a grateful look, then kept the conversation moving smoothly as they finalized their plans. They'd make the trip to Cielo Solo in three long days, traveling most of the last one on foot. Paul was concerned about Kelley lugging priceless herbarian samples and a plant press around Mexico on the back of a burro, but Nick assured him that burros were sturdy creatures and easy to come by in almost any rural town.

"Wouldn't it be easier to ride good horses to Cielo Solo than hike across the desert?" Paul suggested after they'd gone over everything.

"For Kelley, maybe," Nick countered, "assuming she knows how to ride."

"I do," she declared promptly.

"Well, I don't. The last steed I mounted was a three-foot-tall burro when I was eight, and by then my feet dragged on the ground so I walked as much as rode." He grinned, but the smile didn't quite reach his eyes. "Even if I could ride, Paul, good horses are costly and hard to come by in rural Mexico. If by chance we could ferret out a few to buy or rent In Pitahaya, it would be—" he fidgeted with his tie "—inexcusably pretentious to show up in Cielo Solo in so grandiose a fashion."

Paul looked confused by Nick's observation, but Kelley understood his concern. "It's been a long time since I've gone riding daily," she quickly volunteered, even though she could still handle a mount with expertise, "and I've spent a lot of time hiking in the desert. A pack burro is plenty of horseflesh for me."

Again Nick's intimate gaze brushed her face, thanking her for reading between the lines. But when she failed to look away, his eyes conveyed another message—a slow, sensuous invitation that went far beyond gratitude.

Kelley was certain that if they'd been alone, Nick would have reached out for her hand, and the sensation was so compelling that she almost took a step in his direction.

But reality reclaimed her the instant Paul Harris stood up, signaling an end to the meeting as he reached for Nick's hand. "I guess you understand how important this project is to Kelley, Nick."

Nick nodded gravely. "I'll do my best to help her, Paul," he vowed. "In terms of the research, I can't do much more than point her in the right direction, but when it comes to her safety—" his eyes met Kelley's fiercely for just a moment, promising her something that went far beyond his honorable words to Paul "—I guarantee you I won't drop a stitch."

After Nick shook Paul's big hand, he took Kelley's smaller one and wrapped his fingers around it firmly. His hand was warm and confident, yet there seemed to be a question in his touch...an invitation, perhaps, that spoke more of hello than the obvious goodbye typically associated with the gesture. Still, Kelley could have ignored the seconds that ticked by while he held on, sensuously kneading her fingers; the grip really didn't last that long. But what she could not ignore was the wash of hunger that zigzagged from her sensitive palm all the way down to her new high heels...and lingered within her long after Nick, and then Paul, bid her goodbye and left her alone in her sun-washed office.

And she couldn't ignore the fresh well of hope inside her, either.

KELLEY WOULD SUNBURN terribly in the desert, Nick concluded as he stuffed a frozen dinner into his microwave and grabbed a cola to sip while he was waiting. And she wasn't likely to appreciate the native version of sunscreen—drippy mud slathered all over her delicate face, neck and forearms—so he decided that he'd better make sure to put some heavy-duty lotion on his list of things to worry about. Nick was convinced that Kelley was a nature lover, but so far he hadn't seen any hard evidence that she had the instincts of a desert rat.

"It's a good thing I'm in charge of the car," he mumbled, still appalled at the fact that she'd let that sticking piston go for over a month. "If I left it up to her, we'd never even make it across the state line."

The morning meeting hadn't been easy for him, and he suspected it hadn't been easy for Kelley, either. She'd intervened for him several times when her boss had inadvertently probed into his personal affairs, and her quiet green eyes had reflected her intense interest in the man who would guide her through the thorn scrub of Sonora.

The responsibility weighed on him heavily—not just the question of her safety, but his need to protect her feelings as well. If only she weren't so damned appealing, so fresh, so vibrant, almost innocent in her casual sophistication! It wasn't going to be easy to resist her; in all likelihood, he reproached himself, Liliana wasn't worth it. But Kelley—Kelley who had frankly admitted how deeply a man had once hurt her—she was worth protecting.

Nick stared at the plastic wrap on his fried-chicken pattie and mixed veggies and tried to remember what he'd eaten the night before. All that came to mind was that he'd pulled an entrée from the freezer and shoved it into the microwave—and it, too, had come out five minutes later in this same plastic wrapping, tasting like straw.

He knew that his grandmother would be appalled to see the way he lived. Oh, he had a very respectable middle-class home with a refrigerator that was still on warranty and a three-year-old carpet that ran wall-to-wall. But Mama Luz, who had never had either, would see only what he lacked: cactus blossoms in the windowsill, a passle of children to shower him with hugs and kisses and a good woman to rub his shoulders after a hard day's work.

He pulled open the sliding-glass door and stepped out onto the patio, sitting down for a moment on the wide back step as he sipped on his can of soda. Though he kept the lawn mowed and the hedges trimmed, there was no sense of bucolic beauty in Nick's backyard; the crush of L.A. traffic intruded on the twilight. Only the twisted prickly pear by the fence seemed oblivious to the smog; it was proud and thorny, disdainful of its unexpectedly urban surroundings.

He hadn't planted the *nopal*. In fact, he'd been planning to pull it out since the day he'd bought the house. Nick had always wondered why so many Mexicans felt the need to plant the ugly cacti all over the states as reminders of their homeland; all he'd ever wanted to do was forget that heinous, arid place. Yet four years had passed, and still the cactus grew on the south side of his yard. He seemed no closer to uprooting it now than he was to erasing his memories of Cielo Solo.

His thoughts strayed back to the trip itself...the trip with Kelley by his side. Kelley with a sunburned nose and sand in her carrot-red hair; Kelley amazing the natives with her courageous broken Spanish and delighting Nick with her shy but cheerful smile; Kelley with the courage to brave the remote Opata country but not enough sense to keep her car in good repair in the urban jungle of southern California.

"Can't believe she hasn't fixed that yet," he grumbled again as he ambled back into the house. That unsafe car troubled him a lot more than he wanted to admit. When he was little, his favorite uncle had always insisted that the women of the family take the larger burro—the brown one that didn't kick—when they went out to collect the fruit from the prickly pears in the spring, even though that often left him with the grumpy little one that could only carry half as much. When Nick had asked his Tio José why a man would deliberately choose to inconvenience himself for a woman, the older man had chuckled. "Someday, Nico, when you are a man, you will not need to ask me that question," he'd teased his young nephew. "And now, if I were to answer, you would not understand."

"Now what made you think of that?" Nick asked himself out loud, feeling guilty and helpless as he tried to imagine life with a crochety burro as his dominant means of transportation. Liliana had probably never ridden in a car; Mama Luz had probably never even seen one. Nonetheless, he suddenly decided that it was untenable to let Kelley drive that Datsun with a sticking piston for even twenty-four more hours. Granted, they were leaving town in just a few days, but there was no way of knowing how things would stand between them by the time they came back to L.A. He knew she wouldn't let him fix it for free if he asked her ahead of time, but it wasn't in his nature to come up with a lie. Still, he decided, there had to be a way to put his mind at rest about the car. The fact that he was lonely tonight and would love to hear Kelley's soft voice had nothing to do with his determination.

He was still working on the right approach as he reached for the phone.

IT WAS ONLY eight o'clock when Kelley arrived at Nick's shop the next morning, but the sun was already shining.

"Good morning, Kelley. Thanks for dropping by," Nick greeted her briskly. He was sporting the same mechanic's coveralls he'd been wearing the first time they'd met, and the hairy chest revealed by the half-opened zipper was every bit as charming. He didn't wait for her to get out of her car and come inside the shop; he had zipped across the street the instant she pulled up outside. "I won't hold you up, Kelley, I know you've got a lot to do."

Kelley studied him uncertainly. He'd been just as abrupt last night on the phone—friendly, but decidedly brief in comparison with their earlier conversations. He hadn't told her what he had to give her this morning, but he'd insisted that it was vital.

"Well, you said it was important, Nick. Do you want to go inside to talk?"

"Nope." He opened the Datsun's door for her and held out a hand. As soon as she took hold of his fingers and stood up, he released her, his quickness a disturbing contrast to the slow, sensual way he'd said goodbye in her office. As soon as Kelley reached out to lock the car, Nick cheerfully snatched the cactus-shaped key chain from her hand. "That won't be necessary. I'm taking it in right now."

"You're what?"

Nick plucked another set of keys from his pocket and tossed them to Kelley, then stuck his thumb over his shoulder in the direction of a freshly waxed red Buick. "Square key opens the door, round starts the car. Gas tank is full. She's easy to drive—no quirks. You might want to call me if you're going to come back before three or four, but I'll give your Datsun my top priority."

He was grinning, looking remarkably pleased with himself. The breeze had loosened a forelock of his straight black hair, and the way it hung in his face gave him a boyish look.

"Did I miss something here?" Kelley asked, trying to decide if she should be flattered or offended by the way he'd commandeered her car. "I don't recall making an appointment. You just said you had something to give me—"

"And I do. The keys to my car, my well-maintained, utterly reliable car. Come sundown yours will be the same. No fee, Dr. McKinney; this is on the house."

Touched and bewildered, Kelley protested, "Nick, you don't have to do this."

"Of course I do. Think of it as professional pride. Or even instinct." He softened his words with an impish grin that could not possibly cause offense. "You're a botanist," he offered by way of analogy. "Do you think you could bear to go into an office day after day with a pathetic brown plant drying up in the corner without sneaking it a drink of water?"

"Probably not," she had to admit. "But it doesn't take any time or money to water a plant. Besides, I'm an adult. I can decide when—"

"I know, I know." He folded her fingers over the keys, his warm palm sending streams of anticipation coursing through her body. "Call it chauvinistic if you like, but I just can't stand the thought of you driving this unsafe car in downtown L.A. after dark, Kelley. That's as honest as I can be."

As Kelley's eyes flew up to his, she couldn't seem to speak. It had been a long time since anybody had given her such a generous, spontaneous gift. She wanted to throw her arms around him; she wanted to tell him how wonderful he was. She also wanted to return the favor if there was any way she could.

Before Kelley could sort out her scrambled thoughts, Nick suggested, "If you can't swing by before five-thirty, just go on home and I'll come over later so we can switch cars. I'd just as soon find your place now than the morning we take off for Tucson anyway, since it won't even be daylight when we pull out of here."

"Nick, why don't you plan to bring the car over to my house tonight about six," she offered eagerly, as an idea began to form in her mind. "I'll leave work a little early and get dinner started. Is there anything special you—"

"I don't want anything special," he interrupted. "I don't want you to cook for me."

Kelley couldn't conceal her hurt. She tried to meet his eyes directly but failed. Coolly she backtracked. "I'm a decent cook, Nick, and I know you must be tired of eating out all the time. If you won't let me pay you, it's the least I can do."

"Don't rob me, Kelley," he said bluntly.

This time she did meet his eyes, not in hurt so much as confusion. His voice dropped softly as he started to explain, "I want to give you a present. No strings attached, no debts owed, no expectations to be fulfilled. What I get out of it is the good feeling that I've done something noble and unselfish. If you act as though you have to pay me back, then all I've done is a repair job for a customer who stiffed me when it was time to pay the bill."

Slowly Kelley pulled away, her cheeks hot with embarrassment. For the thousandth time she cursed her fair skin, which showed the faintest blush; she had no protection from her feelings, no privacy at all.

She marched stiffly to the Buick and tried the lock. She knew Nick had told her which key to use, but at the moment she was trembling too much to remember anything but his harsh rejection.

Suddenly she felt his hand on hers as the door popped open. But before she could safely slip inside, Nick's strong arms slipped around her, holding her firmly against his chest.

She'd imagined this glorious moment a dozen times, but never in a parking lot, never on a public street. And never when Nick's sole motivation seemed to be the need to arrest her flight. Still, the masculine power of his touch pierced her shell of calm with rapier-sharp intensity, and she felt helpless, hungry, as she melted into his warmth.

As she cautiously leaned against him, Kelley could feel Nick's heart beating rapidly. A ragged sigh escaped her lips, followed by his strangled moan. The arms that had sought solely to detain her now gentled even as they pulled her closer, and Kelley found her own hands slipping instinctively around his rib cage as she buried her face in his chest.

"I'm sorry, Kell," he whispered, the unexpected nickname shivering huskily down her spine. His fingertips traced nervous circles on her back, then slipped down to grip her elbows with an urgency that his courteous proclamation could not deny. "I meant no offense," he insisted, his accented syllables uneven and slightly hoarse. "I just don't want an enchanting woman like you to cook for me out of...gratitude or pity or obligation."

His warm breath tantalized her ear and the vulnerable patch of throat right beneath it; unconsciously Kelley bowed her head as her pride disappeared. She focused on the zippered neckline in front of her, feathered with dark, curly chest hairs that couldn't be restrained. "I don't suppose it ever occurred to you, Nick, that I might have some other reason for extending that invitation?" Kelley knew she was getting in over her head, but she just couldn't seem to stop the flow of words. "Did you ever consider the possibility that I might have wanted to get to know you better since the first day we met and I've been waiting for an excuse to ask you out?"

Kelley waited for him to summon up a courteous rejection. She braced herself to feel the imminent coldness of air against her skin now inflamed by his touch.

But he didn't let her go; his firm brown arms actually pulled her closer. She could feel his warm breath against her temple, smell the tangy soap leftover from his morning shower. He waited until she bravely met his eyes, and then, ever so gently, he traced the fullness of her cheek with the back of his hand.

"Is that really the only reason you offered to cook for me, Kell?" he prodded. "Would it really make you ... terribly happy to spend some time with me?"

Embarrassed but unable to deny it, Kelley nodded. She bit her lower lip, feeling like a fool. Nick had given her some mixed messages up to now, but he'd never come right out and said that his interest in her might be more than platonic. His concern about the car was touching, but it could have been fraternal. A gentleman like Nick might feel obligated to accept her invitation.

But no gentleman, she deduced a moment later, could fake the quiet joy, the sudden firm resolution, that she read in his haunting brown eyes when she found the courage to meet them. And no man was likely to pretend to tremble ever so slightly as he pulled her closer, brushing her temple with the gentlest of preliminary kisses.

Kelley didn't move, didn't speak, as Nick slowly released her, his eyes now dancing with a mischievous brand of joy that she'd never seen there before. His grin was slow ... uncertain at first. And then it burst wide open, like a wild poppy in the spring, as he gave her a courtly bow and said, "In that case, Dr. McKinney, it would give me the greatest pleasure to spend the evening at your table." He took her hand in a mock-courtly fashion and kissed it softly, his lips warm, inviting, promising far, far more for later that night. He was still grinning when he dropped her hand and said, "I'll be there with bells on at six."

CHAPTER SIX

IT WAS ONLY five fifty-five, actually, when Nick arrived at Kelley's three-bedroom house in West L.A. He was always punctual, but tonight he'd been so early that he had circled the block a few times to avoid crashing in on Kelley before she was ready for company.

There was a possibility, of course, that he'd made a mistake in coming here. Logic dictated prudence with this sensitive woman, at least until he saw Liliana again. But this morning when Kelley had gushed out her great desire to spend time with him—capturing his own feelings in risk-taking words that Nick himself had lacked the courage to voice—all rationality had left him. Liliana was nineteen years and a thousand miles away, a barefoot peasant who had nothing in common with him anymore. He wasn't sure how a man who had started life in the slums of South Tucson could now find himself so at ease with the proud owner of a Ph.D., but from the moment he pulled up in front of Kelley's house, he had a cozy sense of coming home.

Of course, the multitude of cacti in the front yard might have helped, even though her succulent garden lacked the omnipresent prickly pear of the typical Mexican-American homestead. Kelley's exotic cacti were attractively laid out in a free-flowing pattern that somehow generated a sense of grace and serenity from the spiny, warty sticks of brown and green.

She opened the door at once, as though she'd been keeping an eye on the street, waiting for him to arrive.

"Good evening, Nick. Dinner will be ready in a few minutes." Her smile was bright and engaging as she offered to hang up his blue blazer. It was easy to picture her saying, "How was your day at work, honey?"

Instead she asked him, "So did you fix up my car to your satisfaction?"

"Yes, indeed. She's purring like a kitten. I did everything but rebuild the engine." Before she could protest, he asked quickly, "How long has it been since your last tune-up?"

Kelley shrugged, the casual gesture emphasizing her delicate shoulders. She was wearing a rose-colored dress with ruffles around the sweetheart neckline. The hand-embroidered apron, which sported a cluster of barrel cacti softened by a hem of ecru lace, had a big bow in the back, which emphasized her small waist.

Nick refrained from whistling. *Hard to believe that every time I see her she just looks better and better,* he thought to himself. Out loud he said, "I'm trying to decide why they say redheads should never wear pink, Kelley. On you it's just—" he searched for a word and concluded honestly "—perfect."

She smiled almost shyly and licked her lips. "Why, thank you, Nick. That's very kind of you to say." She sounded genuinely surprised at his compliment and more than a little bit doubtful.

Vaguely he remembered a comment she'd once made about a man who hadn't thought she was all that special, and he wondered how deep her scars still ran. He had no use for women who were brazenly vain, but

Kelley was so unaware of her stirring appeal that it was a bit unsettling. Innocence, he'd found, was a state of mind which could linger to almost any age, but once it was shattered, it could never be repaired. Even though Kelley was surely an experienced woman, there was a vulnerability about her that worried him. Not that he'd ever hurt her on purpose, of course.

"I'm making potato gnocci. I hope you like Italian food."

"Sure. I love it." He used his enthusiasm to cover up his surprise. Juanita had once told him, when they were at a classy Italian restaurant, that the only time she'd tried to make gnocci, she had given up after she'd realized how many hours it would take to shape each tiny potato-based noodle by hand. Granted, Juanita wasn't exactly Julia Child in the kitchen, but still, he had an uneasy feeling that Kelley had devoted half the day to fixing him a spectacular meal. "I'm partial to anything that doesn't start out wrapped in tin foil or plastic."

Kelley laughed. "Good thing you weren't here last night. I love to cook, but usually it just isn't worth the trouble to prepare a snazzy meal when I'm eating by myself."

"I know the feeling," he agreed, relieved that she hadn't gone to all this work just for him. "Of course, I couldn't come up with a snazzy meal if my life depended on it, so in my case TV dinners mean the difference between life and death."

Kelley ushered him into her kitchen and asked him to sit down while she finished. When he declined a drink, she asked, "Tell me, Nick, how do you handle food when you're hiking in the desert? Just freeze-dried stuff?"

He chuckled. "Actually, I've never been 'hiking' in the desert. Getting from one burned-out dried hole to another isn't something you do for recreation when you live in Cielo Solo. You do your best to get where you're going between dawn and midday, and if you have to eat more than tortillas you get fruit from the saguaro and the prickly pear."

Kelley stopped her fussing to study him. "You really are a desert rat, aren't you, Nick? You tried to deny it the day we met, but I was certain that you were.

"Kelley, I'm a survivor," he explained. "I don't like the desert, but I know how to get along there. I wasn't much on Vietnam, either, but I managed to get by. Hell, there are times when I can't stand L.A. either, but I do all right."

Green eyes twinkling, Kelley asked, "If you don't like L.A., why on earth do you live here?"

"My business is here."

"I know that. I mean, I can see why you'd choose to stay here now. But why did you settle here in the first place?"

He shrugged, trying to pass off the uneasy feelings her question triggered within him. "It was as different from Cielo Solo as night and day."

"That's all?"

With most women, he would have nodded and left it at that. Nick felt compelled to tell her the truth. "My mother died here, Kell. When I left the service, I couldn't go home to Cielo Solo, so the only other destination I had in mind was somewhere near my mother's grave. I've never had a good reason to move anywhere else."

He couldn't hide the wistfulness of his tone; couldn't shake the memory of the day he'd left the Army, watching his buddies cheer for joy because they were all going *home*. Each man had somebody who was counting the minutes until he arrived—mother, girl-friend, wife, child. But nobody had been waiting for Nick Morales, nobody but Mama Luz, and he'd lacked the courage to go to her. But never had he hungered more for the sight of her beloved, wrinkled face, never had he felt more hatred for Pablo Villalobos.

Kelley's expression softened. "I'm sorry, Nick. I didn't mean to pry."

"I know. It's okay. I've accidentally stepped on your toes more than once, as I recall."

They shared a smile, then enjoyed a companionable silence until supper was ready. Nick didn't have to feign his enthusiasm for the meal; Kelley was a spectacular cook. He offered to help her with the dishes—hoping she'd ignore him—but she just stacked them neatly and suggested that they enjoy dessert outside while it was still balmy.

Her backyard was different from his own. Like the front, it was more of a botanical display than a back-drop for a chaise longue, but every plant, pot and hanging basket was so artistically displayed and lovingly maintained that it made him feel very much at home.

"You've really got a thing about cactus, don't you, Kelley?" he asked her as they settled on the back-porch swing. "You could open up your own nursery just with what you've got right here."

Kelley smiled as though her plants were children. "I'd never part with a single one of them. Some of these are pretty rare and hard to come by legally."

He arched one brow. "Does that mean you came upon them some other way?"

"Of course not!" Kelley was indignant. "I couldn't possibly enjoy having a plant that I knew had been uprooted from the wild. I'm devoted to saving the desert, Nick, and it's desperately in need of protection. Did you know that a hundred years ago the conestoga wagons could hardly find their way around the saguaros that forested the southwest? Now one third of all the cacti in that region are endangered. Organ pipes still grow in only one little corner of Arizona, and some other species can't even be found north of the border."

Nick didn't have much interest in the desert's problems, but he loved to see the vigor that brightened Kelley's eyes when she defended her beloved plants. "Why are they endangered?" he asked to keep her talking. "Off-road vehicles galloping about or Sunday drivers swiping samples off the highways?"

"Well, there's no question that both pose a problem, Nick, along with the idiots who go out shooting saguaros to prove their manhood."

Up till now, Nick hadn't taken Kelley's concern seriously, but for some reason the image of some jerk firing shotgun shells into the giant saguaro outside Cielo Solo made him feel a little anxious. For the first time it occurred to him that the king cactus of his childhood might no longer be waiting just the way he'd left it. Nervously he asked, "Why on earth would anybody want to shoot down a cactus?"

"Why would anybody want to shoot scores of buffalo from a moving train and take nothing but their tongues?" Kelley countered. "People are crazy, Nick, even when greed isn't their motivation."

"I can't argue that." For a moment he was silent, studying the way the moonlight framed the fragile beauty of Kelley's face. Then he draped his arm over the back of the swing, letting his fingers spill across her shoulder. She smiled shyly without guile as he pulled her a little closer. But he knew she wasn't quite ready for him to kiss her, so he clung to the discussion for just a little longer. "Is that a Queen of the Night?" he asked, spotting a blackish-green cactus in a huge pot near the fence.

"Almost," she told him, rocking the swing with one lazy foot. "It's a Princess. She just started to bloom last night. I've been hoping that we might get flowers again this evening."

Nick knew all about nocturnally flowering cacti; Liliana had loved nothing more than walking through the desert after sundown, collecting blossoms and slipping them into her endless black hair. "It's been years since I've seen one of these in bloom, Kell. I still remember the scent. I couldn't smell it until I had the flower in my hand, but I had a . . . friend who could track these down for hundreds of yards just by following her nose."

Kelley met his eyes, questioning the identity of his female friend. But when Nick rubbed his knuckles enticingly along the curve of her jaw, her worry seemed to vanish. Quietly she edged a little closer to his side.

"The Princess doesn't smell like the Queen," Kelley informed him, her voice husky now. "It's got the same gorgeous white flowers, but no aroma. That's why it's just called Princess. You know—always the bridesmaid but never the bride." She sighed unconsciously and added, less to Nick than to herself, "I know just how the poor things feel."

The porch swing came to a stop as Nick gently laid his palm against the back of Kelley's neck. Her skin was warm, inviting. Her own scent, every bit as provocative as a Queen of the Night's, beckoned to him softly. But he wanted to know why a cactus could make her so sad. He wanted to know how she'd come to doubt herself as a woman.

"Tell me about him, *corazón*," he suggested gently, unconsciously using the Spanish word for "sweetheart" as he pulled her closer yet. "Tell me about this fellow who looked at you and was so pathetically blind to the beauty I see before me."

Kelley looked up, surprised by the intimacy of his heartfelt words. "You really do think I look all right, don't you, Nick? That's not just something you say to...to make me feel better."

He smiled and deliberately slid across the swing until their thighs touched. Then he stroked her head until she leaned against his shoulder. "Kelley, I think you look a hell of a lot more than just all right," he confessed, his heart starting to beat erratically as he revelled in the feel of her hand sliding across his chest. *I think I want to kiss you,* he could have added. *I think I want to feel your smooth white skin beneath these rose-colored ruffles, petal soft and just as delicate to my touch.* But it was too soon to reveal the depth of his hunger. He'd let Kelley tell her story; get the other man out of the way. Then it would just be the two of them on the back porch, gazing into each other's eyes. Nick hoped that once she shared the old hurt with him, her former lover would be exorcised forever, and he could have Kelley McKinney all to himself. And that was something, he realized acutely, that he wanted very much indeed.

"He was...a botany professor at UC Santa Barbara, where I used to work," she began slowly, as though words were already difficult to utter while Nick's fingers teased her neck. "I met him right after I got there. He'd been dumped by his fiancée the year before and was still hurting quite a bit. He really needed a friend."

"Mmm." He pressed closer, unable to resist brushing his lips over the delicate skin of her temple.

Kelley drew a shaky breath and continued. "I fell in love with him, though I knew that he needed some time to get over Janice. But when we got engaged six months later, I figured that he'd finally made his choice. After all, she was married by then and he...well, he really did act as though he were in love with me."

Nick slipped his free hand across Kelley's midriff, cradling her with both arms now. He kissed her neck again, then her ear, then warmed his nose in the finely crinkled strands of her hair.

"Nick," she whispered, her hand now trembling against his elbow, "are you listening?"

"Listening," he managed to reply, tugging ever so gently on her red tresses with his teeth. "He acted as though he were in love with you."

He felt her fingers slide over his biceps, then felt the warmth of her hand against his face as he crushed her gently against his chest. She smothered a soft moan, then whispered the next few words of her story.

"When Janice left her new husband, Allan started to hope all over again. He never took her out, never tried to get her back—she still didn't want him—and I'm sure he was never unfaithful to me in a physical sense." She traced Nick's firm jaw with one finger. "But he didn't belong to me anymore...assuming he ever did. He postponed our wedding date over and over again until even his mother told him he was going to lose me if he didn't shape up. I could feel him slipping away from me; I could see Janice in his eyes when we made love." She stopped for a moment and swallowed hard, then met Nick's eyes in the twilight, her lingering pain now mixed with joyful expectancy. "That was the worst of all, Nick. It was the one thing I could never forgive him for. He never called me Janice by mistake, but I know that while I was the one he held in his arms, she was the one he held in his heart."

Nick looked away. It was as though Liliana had suddenly slipped up behind him in her quiet, sunshiny way... slipped up behind him and then wedged herself right between the two of them on the porch swing, like a ghost returning to its favorite haunt.

But Kelley continued to nestle against him, oblivious to the fact that his heart had already moved away. "It was Bonnie who finally made me see that even if Allan married me, I would always be number two in his heart," she concluded, her lips now close enough to kiss. "She kept telling me that I deserved a man who adored me just the way my brother adores her. I finally decided she was right."

It was the time for Nick to say, "You've waited long enough," or "That man is sitting right beside you, Kell." Or a fervent kiss would have sufficed, preempting romantic speeches altogether.

But Nick could say nothing. He still held Kelley in his arms—warm, willing, eager—and his body pulsed with hunger to draw her down flat on the swing. He was fifteen minutes away from her bed, a layer of clothing from a romantic journey to Sonora beyond his wildest expectations... a mere promise away from the beginning of a love affair that might well be his last.

Nick was a man who knew his own mind, and he already knew that few things would make him happier than coming home to this extraordinary woman's cactus garden every night. Surely it was Kelley he'd been waiting for all this time; surely it was the simple fact that he'd not met her yet, and not Liliana's ghost, that had kept him from marrying Juanita.

It had all felt so right, so natural, so nearly perfect. If only she hadn't said, *It was the one thing I could never forgive him for.... While I was the one he held in his arms, she was the one he held in his heart.*

Slowly, achingly, Nick straightened on the porch swing and eased out of Kelley's loving grasp. Instantly she stiffened and her eyes filled with surprise and hurt.

Kelley! he wanted to beg her. *I want you, dear God, oh how I want you! But I owe it to you, to her...above all to myself... to be sure this time. To make sure the wound is healed.*

But he couldn't explain all that to Kelley. Not now, maybe not ever. From the moment he'd arrived at six, everything between them had been perfect and she had every reason to expect him to stay for the rest of the evening... perhaps the rest of the night. But he didn't dare stay now; he couldn't let his hunger outweigh the need for truth between them. He couldn't promise Kelley more than a few short days of romantic pleasure—and the strong possibility of a long, hard fall once they arrived in Cielo Solo.

He slowly got to his feet and slipped both hands into his pockets. "Uh, dinner was wonderful, Kelley. You're a great cook."

Her eyes were huge, wounded, like a doe who's just felt the arrow pierce her heart. "Thank you," she murmured uncertainly, her voice trembling with hurt and disbelief as she realized that he was getting ready to go. "I'm glad you...were free tonight."

He tried to think of a logical explanation for his sudden departure, but no lie would come to his lips. Instead he reached down to touch her cheek again, then stopped himself just in time. A flash of red darted across her white skin as she spotted his aborted caress, and confusion, as well as anguish, marred the glistening green of her eyes. "I'll see you the day after tomorrow then," he finished clumsily. "Bright and early."

Her voice was a whisper of pain as she repeated, "Bright and early." She rose to face him.

Nick tried to walk away. He tried to think of Liliana. But Kelley's eyes were haunted, and his own heart was dragging anchor. He wanted to kiss her but he couldn't, so he patted her on the shoulder instead.

The awkward fraternal gesture only angered Kelley. She turned abruptly to lead him back inside the house. Neither one of them said a word until they reached the front hall, where Kelley briskly pulled Nick's blazer out of the closet and thrust it into his hands.

"Good night, Nick," she declared woodenly, then gathered up his Buick keys from a small table in the hall.

As she stood there, the keys in her hands glittering in the hallway light like the unshed tears in her eyes, Nick dug in his pockets for Kelley's cactus key chain. He could have made the trade quickly, painlessly, but once he'd reclaimed his own keys and dropped hers in her hand, his fingers lingered against her silken palm, and a fresh surge of need scrambled his senses.

If his touch affected Kelley the same way, she gave no sign. She simply snatched her hand away as though it had been burned. Feeling helpless and angry with himself, Nick wheeled away from her and plunged gratefully into the cool brisk night. It took all his strength of will to leave her, but he knew he would have felt even worse if he had stayed.

CHAPTER SEVEN

"TRACKS OF THE BIG CAT again," Mama Luz observed pragmatically as she tugged a fresh blouse loose from the prickly pear that served as a clothesline outside her thatched-roof hut. She studied the ground with a watchful eye, then glanced toward the south, which was most likely the direction from which he'd come. "Has anyone seen him yet?"

Her daughter-in-law shook her head. "No, but José has tracked him to the great saguaro, and he found a dead antelope where we go to fill our buckets from the stream. Paws too big for a puma, he said. He told me to keep the young ones close for a while."

Mama Luz suppressed a shiver. The puma was no braver than the bucks and does he stalked. At night he screamed like a woman possessed or wailed like a child in mortal pain, but the villagers paid him no heed. Like the coyote's howl, his cry was a familiar note in the desert's nighttime song. But the spotted cat that came from the south rarely ventured near Cielo Solo; the last jaguar to threaten the village had come the year Nico had made his First Communion. Double the weight of the puma and three times as cruel, such a killer only ranged this far from the jungle when game was scarce and hunger paralyzed its normal caution.

Carmelita tugged off the rest of the clothes, being careful not to let the cactus spines poke holes in the faded fabric. "I think José is worried about more than the jaguar, Mama Luz."

Quickly she turned to face her daughter-in-law. "Why do you say that?" she queried. José was never one to worry, but he had not smiled enough in recent days. Mama Luz had assumed it was his nagging cough that had robbed him of his laughter...or maybe concern for his family because of the cat.

Carmelita patted a strand of hair that had slipped out of her bun. "José has seen Pablo Villalobos again," she revealed. "He has a new hat with silver on it, and store-bought leather boots. They say he rides to the hills at night on a fine horse to meet a gringo there. In the morning, he always comes back to Pitahaya with even more money than he had before."

"That one," Mama Luz muttered, adding a silent prayer to protect her son from the evil spirits that might well have leaped from Pablo into him. No wonder José's cough was so bad! "I am glad Pablo went to Pitahaya when they let him out of prison. I do not want him here."

"I don't want him here either, Mama Luz, but José says he asked about Liliana again," Carmelita murmured darkly. "He thinks Pablo will come back for her."

"Ha! He is wasting his time. She will never go to him."

Carmelita's voice took on a chilly note. "José is afraid that he may not give her any choice this time."

Mama Luz faced her son's wife squarely, her courage even greater than her fear. "We will not let him take our Liliana."

Carmelita crossed herself, as though in silent prayer. "I do not know how we can stop him," she whispered. "He is so—"

"We will find a way," Mama Luz said stoutly. "Liliana will marry again only if this becomes her wish. And there is no man here she will marry, anyway. This time she will wait for Nico. She knows that he will come."

Carmelita threw up her hands in exasperation. Though she always defended Nico to those outside the family, privately she was not so kind. "Mama Luz, if he hasn't come back for her by now—"

"She belonged to another man until now! Nico has only known for six months that she was free. He would give her some time to mourn for his cousin." She patted her daughter-in-law's cheek with patience born of desert stoicism and hope born of maternal love. "She will not give up on Nico, and neither will I. You wait and see, Carmelita, you wait and see." She squinted toward the north, as though he might appear beyond the king saguaro at any minute. "Any day now, *mi hija*, my Nico will come home."

IT WAS ALMOST EIGHT-THIRTY when Kelley's doorbell rang the next evening. Bonnie had invited her over for an early dinner, so Kelley had said all her goodbyes. She was not expecting anyone to drop by, and since she was getting up before sunrise, she'd already changed into her silky pink nightie and a warm fleece robe of a darker hue.

To her dismay, a quick glance out the window revealed a car in the driveway that bore a striking resemblance to Nick's cranberry-colored Buick.

"Oh, no," Kelley groaned, appalled by the notion of greeting Nick in her bathrobe without so much as a drop of makeup. After their last miserable farewell, she desperately needed some armor to steel herself for their next meeting. At the moment, both her clothes and her courage failed her.

She wasn't mad at him—not really. She knew it wasn't fair to blame Nick for the way she was feeling. At first Kelley had thought that he might have been playing games with her on the porch swing, but later, with a sleepless night to mull over her failure, she'd begun to see that every tender moment between them could have been the product of her own fertile imagination. Nick was a kind and decent man. How could he have turned down her invitation to dinner when she'd nearly come unglued after his first refusal? And how could he have pushed her away while she'd been baring her soul to him?

She had hoped, foolishly perhaps, that they could have gone to Mexico together anyway, pretending that their aborted lovemaking had never taken place. It wouldn't have been easy, but the consequences of calling off the journey were so great that Kelley was willing to swallow her pain and pride. But now—the doorbell was ringing again—she had a sinking suspicion that Nick had already had more trouble with her than he could endure. He'd never wanted to go to Sonora in the first place.

Reluctantly Kelley padded barefoot to the door and gingerly pulled it open.

"Hello, Nick," she greeted him dully.

"Hi, Kelley," he replied. His tone was grave, but for a long moment he just stood there on the porch, making no move to enter, and Kelley wondered if he intended to give her the bad news without bothering to come into the house. She'd seen him in coveralls, knit slacks and a suit; but tonight he wore blue jeans and a Dodgers baseball jacket... and an expression on his face that would make one guess that his home team had struck out.

"I know we're scheduled to leave in a few hours, Kelley," he began slowly, his accent clinging tightly to the l in her name, "but there's something I need to say to you before we go."

Kelley's eyes widened. "You mean we're still going?"

He cocked his head and studied her. "That was my understanding. Has there been a change in your plans?"

"When I saw your car I assumed you'd come to tell me you'd changed your mind about the trip," she confessed.

"Damn!" he exclaimed with a grimace. "Kelley—" He stared at her with perplexing urgency as he jammed both hands into his jacket pockets. "Look, this isn't going to be easy for me. Do you think you could bring yourself to invite me in so I could get it over with?"

Befuddled, Kelley took a step back and Nick eased past her, taking an uncertain spot on the end of her leather couch. He sat in silence for a moment, fiddling with the religious medal at his neck, while Kelley perched uneasily on the edge of her favorite rocker. When he finally looked at her, his expression became even more grave. By the way he took in her discreet scarlet bathrobe, Kelley suspected that he hadn't realized how she was dressed before he'd barged into her house.

"Did I...get you out of bed?" he queried awkwardly.

"Not quite. I just wanted to get as much rest as I could since we...since I expected to get up so early."

This time he glanced away, his eyes drifting through the sliding-glass door toward the Princess of the Night in the backyard. His expression was strained, and Kelley suspected that he hadn't gotten much rest since he'd left her house the night before. She wondered why. She was the one struggling with demolished pride and a broken heart.

Slowly, deliberately, his eyes came to rest on her face. Still, he was silent for a long, tense moment until it was Kelley's turn to glance away.

"Kelley," he said softly, his voice reaching out to corral her gaze, "I want you to know that I've wanted you since the very first day we met."

Though the words were all but whispered, they seemed to echo through the room. Kelley couldn't hold back the fierce retort that spilled from her lips unbridled. "You sure as hell have a funny way of showing your desire!"

"I came here to explain!" he pleaded. "I know you're hurt. I know you're angry. I don't know if it'll help for you to understand what really happened last night, Kelley, but I can't imagine I could make things any worse by telling you the truth! What have we got to lose by being honest with each other?"

"I can't speak for you, Nick, but I certainly have *nothing* left to lose where you're concerned. I made a complete idiot of myself last night...with more than a little bit of help from you, I might add. I know you were just trying to be kind, but your patronizing—"

"Damn it, Kelley, I was not being kind! I wanted you!" he roared at her, suddenly leaping to his feet. "If you hadn't told me about Allan I never would have gone home last night at all!"

Stunned, Kelley pressed back into her rocker and tried to make sense of Nick's words. "I don't understand," she said softly.

He released a great sigh, then turned away from her. He didn't return to the couch; he just paced back and forth on her brown shag carpet like a wolf fighting the bars of a cage.

"There's a girl in Cielo Solo," he finally blurted out. "A woman now, to be accurate. But I haven't seen her in nineteen years, so it's hard for me to think of her as anything but sweet and innocent and hopelessly devoted to me. I've done everything in my power to forget her, Kelley, but I can't." He faced her bleakly; angst, not anger, claimed his demeanor now. "Do you understand? I *can't*. I want to, I've tried to, I've lied to myself over and over again that she's gone, but she's *still there*." He tapped his temple. Then, more slowly, he laid one hand across his broad chest and added, "She's still *here*."

He stopped then, turning toward the backyard, as though it was just too hard for him to look Kelley in the eye. "I thought I'd gotten rid of her last night, Kell," he admitted. "I wanted you so much! But when you started talking about Allan and how his fiancée was always there inside him, always—"

"I understand," she said, unable to bear anymore. But she didn't understand, not really. She didn't understand what it was about Kelley McKinney that always made her come in second best, what it was that made men see her only as an also-ran. But she did know a case of déjà vu when she tripped over one, and Nick couldn't have made his position any more obvious if he'd commissioned a painting of the other woman and hung it on her wall. "I suppose I should be grateful that you had the decency not to use me…and the kindness to tell me the truth." But she didn't feel grateful; she felt wounded and betrayed.

"I wanted to marry Juanita," he charged on, as though he had to finish no matter what the cost to Kelley. "I told myself that I just hadn't found a woman who was good enough before her. But I'll never find a woman much better than Juanita."

"And here I thought I only ranked second," Kelley remarked acidly. "Now I've been demoted to third. Or are there others in this lineup?"

"Damn it, Kelley, hear me out! I loved Juanita! I could have married her. I *would* have married her. But she wanted something from me I just couldn't give her. I was faithful to her; I never let her down. But she wanted something more from me than loyalty, something from inside me that called out for all the world to hear that nobody else even came close to what I felt for her. You're the same kind of woman, Kelley, whether you know it or not, and sooner or later, you'd want the same thing from me. I'd like to pretend I could give it to you someday. There are times—hell, there are lots of times—when you look at me with those soft green eyes and I'm sure that I'd die for the privilege!"

He paused as Kelley gulped and edged forward on the rocking chair.

"But there are other times when I remember," he barreled on, pulling the rug out from under her again, "that I've felt this way before…thought I did. And I don't want to lead you down the primrose path. I don't want to take your body without giving you my heart, Kelley, but until I see Liliana, until I sever whatever tie has bound me to her all these years, I can't promise you a damn thing. I've *got* to go to Sonora free to do whatever it takes to let her go once and for all—'' he clenched the air with his fist ''—or else bring her home with me . . . if that's the way it's meant to be.''

Nick stared at her then, unmoving, while his words whirled around Kelley in the silent room. She wanted to tell him that it was all right, that she understood, that she cared for him enough to wait until he made his peace with Liliana. But she couldn't do it; she couldn't think of a single word that was both honest and safe.

In the end it was Nick who spoke again. ''We're going to make this trip as though last night never happened, Kell. I'm your guide and maybe your friend, but that's it until I see Liliana. I want that clear between us. I want to make sure you understand.''

He was asking a lot of her, but Kelley knew she didn't have much of a choice. She'd never find another guide at this late date, and if she didn't go to Sonora this spring, her promise to Mama Chayo might never be fulfilled. Worse yet—though it broke her to admit it—she just couldn't turn down the chance to spend three weeks alone with Nick Morales, even if it meant watching him moon over this other woman from his past.

Green eyes brimming, she promised shakily, ''I understand.''

He exhaled a deep breath, then swore again in keen frustration. He crossed the room and planted himself in front of Kelley, waiting until she found the strength to rise to her feet.

She didn't want to say good-night; she didn't want him to leave her. She wanted to run her fingers through his thick dark hair and drink in the tangy clean scent of him. She wanted to feel his lips claim hers, just once before they set out together on their desert journey. And she wanted—oh, how very much she wanted!—to hear him whisper *corazón* as his warm, strong fingers caressed her quivering skin.

But he said nothing at all, so she muttered, "Good night, Nick. I'll see you in the morning."

His nostrils flared as he stared at her; his hands clenched and unclenched by his side. In a gravelly tone he said, "Good night then, Kelley. I'll find my own way out."

He turned to go, and even took a step or two toward the door before he wheeled sharply. Kelley had only a moment to gaze up at his blazing brown eyes before he seized her shoulders and pulled her close, his lips finding hers with unerring need and anguish.

Instantly his searing hunger claimed her, and she swayed against him without a second's thought. The heat of his open mouth burned hers with a passion so fervent that Kelley lost consciousness of everything but his flame.

She wrapped her arms around him as he crushed her to his chest. His fingertips slid urgently down her spine then traced a line up her ribs to the sides of her breasts. She pressed against him, her tongue urging his for a more potent kind of union, and he took her at her word.

It was a quick kiss but a potent one that left its brand on Nick's dark face when he breathlessly broke away an instant later. He left Kelley reeling as he slammed out the door, unable to make any logical connection between his tormented speech of denial and the unquenchable flame of his fiery touch. But Kelley knew that this first kiss was a thousand times more potent than she'd ever imagined it might be, and it had shaken her very soul.

She also knew that despite Nick's passionate disavowal of any hope for their future, it had been a kiss that said hello and not goodbye.

CHAPTER EIGHT

IT WAS WITH GREAT RELIEF that Nick drove the renovated Ford sedan into the Arizona-Sonora Desert Museum parking lot three days later. From the moment he'd picked up Kelley in the silent hours before dawn on the day after that searing kiss, gloom had shadowed them across the sun-drenched southwest. They'd been studiously polite to each other, jumping every time their hands accidentally touched, apologizing profusely for unintentional slights even before they could be perceived as such by the other party. After one endless day on the road to Tucson and one worthless night in a hotel room next to the busy interstate, Nick was physically exhausted and emotionally fatigued. And the worst was yet to come; they hadn't even crossed the border yet.

"You know it's a good five or six hours to Hermosillo from here," Nick pointed out as he marched beside Kelley toward the museum administration building. "And that's assuming we can talk or buy our way quickly through customs on the Mexican side of Nogales."

He wasn't telling Kelley anything that she didn't know; it was simply easier to fill the air with casual conversation than it was to study the small, compact hips tightly covered by her designer jeans or the inviting slope of her breasts in the lace-trimmed blue knit shirt. Almost anything was easier than facing the bewildered hurt in her eyes each time he turned away.

It was barely dawn, and the stillness of the desert enveloped the shrub-studded valleys. Streams of sunlight spilled across the easternmost ridges of the hills; the golden mounds were crowned by scattered stands of saguaros, each one towering forty or fifty feet above the checkered carpet of purple lupine and silvery bur sage. The regal cacti cloaked the land like pine trees in a high sierra forest, and privately Nick had to admit that the effect was breathtaking.

"Oh, Nick," Kelley sighed. "And you call this desert ugly!"

Gazing at her unconscious beauty, feeling her awe at the sight, Nick couldn't recall why he'd ever thought the desert ugly. He couldn't even remember why he'd ever wanted to be anywhere but right where he stood at this moment...or with anyone other than the enchanting woman by his side. "Kell, why don't you go on inside?" he urged. "I'll take in the sights and meet you back in the lobby in, say, two hours. That's about all the time we can spare if we want to get to Hermosillo in time to settle in for the night."

A few minutes later Nick was prowling around a natural garden of cacti and succulents from as far away as Cielo Solo's corner of Sonora, experiencing a sense of homecoming as he spied one spiny plant after another that he hadn't even thought of in nearly twenty years. Even the birds brought back memories—redtailed hawks with their spiffy cinnamon pantaloons, and the striking magpie jays, which boasted royal-blue tails almost four times as long as their bodies. His grandmother had always kept one in her kitchen when he was a toddler; he remembered pulling its tail and receiving a sharp rebuke from Mama Luz . . . and from the bird, as well.

He was disappointed to find the jaguar cage empty; it was the only Mexican big cat he'd never seen. He still remembered one time when his Uncle José had hustled him indoors as a jaguar's thunderous roar had echoed on and on in the night, so frightening, somehow, compared to the puma's shrieks that he'd grown up with.

He found a pair of wolves in the section of the park called "Mexican Pine Woodland," where black bears slept in caves, and ravens shrieked from the treetops. This was the high desert country where the Opata lived, the green coves nestling far above the saltbrush flats that most folks had in mind when they spoke of the drylands of Mexico. He sat down next to the handsome tawny wolves, saddened, for some reason, to read on the placard that only fifty of them remained in his homeland. He found himself studying the endless stretch of saguaro-starred hills that surrounded the museum.

I've missed the saguaros, he realized with sudden dismay. *I always said I hated this damnable desert, but I've missed the coral snakes and the javelinas and the tiny elf owls blinking at me from their holes in the king of all cactus.*

Above all, Nick realized, he missed Mama Luz; missed her with a fierce intensity that now, surrounded by the land from which she drew her strength, threatened to overwhelm him. Suddenly he was grateful to Kelley, and even to Juanita, for making him take this painful prodigal journey. As a donkey-eared jackrabbit raced down a nearby slope, Nick longed to follow him southward . . . then realized that there was no longer anything to keep him from doing exactly that.

He was already halfway home.

AFTER TWO HOURS of comparing Tarahumara and Opata *curandero* notes with Bill Johanneson, Kelley and the effervescent museum ethnobotanist found Nick studying a giant cactus diorama in the administration building lobby. The live plants fit into the artistic mural so well that she had to take a second glance to be sure what was real and what wasn't.

"Are you a cactus fancier, Nick?" Bill asked after Kelley had introduced the handsome, middle-aged man to Nick.

She cringed as she waited for Nick's answer; the only worse question Bill could have asked was how Nick felt about herbal medicine.

But to her surprise, Nick offered Bill a noncommittal smile as he asked, "Are these raised in a nursery or scalped from the wild? Kelley tells me there's a big problem around here with poaching endangered species."

Kelley knew Nick well enough to detect the note of disbelief in his tone, but she knew he wasn't casting aspersions on her botanical expertise. He'd told her before that he simply found it hard to believe that anybody would break the law to own a thorny cactus.

"Kelley's right," Bill assured him. "And if you look at nursery-grown plants and compare them to the ones you see on the hills, you'll be able to pick up the difference right away. A plant that's survived a dozen years in the desert looks like it. Its skin is tough, blotched and scarred. A lot of times the stem is crooked or missing a piece. But a nursery-bred plant has delicate skin and grows up straight—you know, like a perfect tree on a Christmas-tree farm.''

Nick shrugged. ''Sounds like the hothouse kind would be prettier and a lot less risky.''

''I guess that's a matter of taste,'' Bill replied. ''But the problem is, cacti take so long to grow that regular nurseries can't begin to meet the demand. It takes a saguaro, for example, ten years to grow three or four inches. Most operations are quite reputable, of course, and resent government inspectors casting aspersions on their operations. But some nurseries buy wholesale from the sort of dealers who smile enigmatically and answer no questions.'' He lifted his eyebrows to emphasize his point. ''And every now and then somebody will just park a truck on a street corner and sell cacti from the back to anybody passing by with a buck.''

Nick studied the diorama thoughtfully, then commented, ''I'm surprised anybody would make much money on such small plants.''

''Well, the key word is volume, Nick. The professional smugglers already have routes set up for drugs, birds, jewels, you name it. There's even a few groups into cattle rustling! They just move cacti as one additional source of money,'' Bill explained. ''They send out people to obscure Mexican villages and offer to pay the locals a handful of pesos for every plant. They're useless to a peasant who doesn't have two centavos to rub together, so everybody—men, women and children—goes out and cleans off the landscape for miles and miles around. It doesn't take too much of that sort of work to doom a species to extinction.''

It was then that Kelley noticed the lines of tension around Nick's firm mouth, a new kind of tension that seemed to go beyond his frustration with their aborted romance. She doubted it was the imminent doom of the Mexican cacti that troubled him, and his next words proved she was right.

"You say, just any village where there are cacti might be approached by these people?"

"Any village in the desert. Every convenient source of marketable cacti between Hermosillo and the border has been pretty well wiped out. The smugglers are going farther into the Sonoran foothills all the time."

"And what happens to the locals after they've... given the smugglers what they want?"

"Usually nothing much, if they just go about their business," was Bill's noncommittal reply. "Actually, it's the people on this side of the border who usually have more to fear."

"How's that?" Nick asked, still showing a remarkable amount of interest in a topic that Kelley had assumed would bore him.

"Well, we have an international treaty with Mexico prohibiting the transportation of endangered species across the border, but a greased palm here or there usually takes care of that on the Mexican side. But here in Arizona we've got an official patrol of cactus cops who pursue these smugglers quite vigorously and bring them to trial."

"That's terrific!" Kelley interjected.

"Terrific when they succeed. But as I mentioned before, these professional smugglers aren't just little old ladies wending gardening trowels. They've killed off several potential witnesses who would have guaranteed their convictions, and shot down one of our cactus cops during an arrest." More quietly he added, "John Lyle was a professor of mine at the University of Arizona. He tripped over a group of men uprooting a forty-three-foot-tall saguaro down by the border. It only takes an hour, you know, with the right equipment and planning.''

"What on earth would you do with a forty-three-foot-tall saguaro?'' Nick asked abruptly. "Isn't that a bit hefty for a typical backyard?''

"Sure, but it's very showy in a resort hotel. You'll see them all over Arizona and Sonora, too, in any city big enough to have a resort community. Of course, most of the time these guys manage to cut off a main taproot so the plant is doomed by the time it's replanted, though they get their money anyway because it takes a saguaro two or three years to die. And even if it survives the transplant, it usually gets stuck in the middle of a golf course or somewhere with completely different climatic conditions than it needs to survive. A saguaro will drown in the water a lawn needs to flourish. After all, nature designed it to last several years, if need be, without any water at all.''

Kelley wasn't sure why Nick's interest in the subject had become so intent, but anything that got him thinking about Cielo Solo was sure to depress him, so she quickly tried to wrap up the conversation.

"Thanks so much for your time, Bill,'' she told the other botanist. "I'll be sure to let you know what I find out in Sonora.''

"It's been a pleasure, Kelley,'' he replied. He shook hands with Nick and turned to go, but Nick stopped him as Kelley reached the door.

"Bill—''

"Yes?''

"Your friend...the botany professor from the college...what else were you going to say about him?''

The smile on Bill's face vanished. "I told you that John came across four guys digging up a saguaro. Turned out they were part of a massive smuggling ring bringing up guns and drugs from Mexico as well as cacti." He shook his head, grief evident in his quiet eyes as he revealed, "The day after he volunteered to testify, his wife found him in his study . . . shot through the head."

On that sober note, Nick and Kelley headed back toward Tucson. Nick was unusually quiet as he hunched over the rag-wrapped steering wheel of their old black clunker, all but ignoring Kelley's feeble attempts at conversation until they reached the outskirts of the city.

"It's been a long time since I left Sonora, Kell," he finally declared without preamble, his voice low and strained. "A lot may have happened since I've been away."

"I'm sure it has," she responded mildly, not quite certain what was troubling him now. "Some good, some bad. But—"

"You're missing the point," he interrupted. "The last time I made this trip, I was seventeen years old. The only thing I was afraid of was whether or not my friends were going to laugh at me. Now it was never very safe down there—between the wolves and the sidewinders and the likelihood of dying of thirst—but for all I know, there could be other dangers by now, as well. Cielo Solo's only criminal is in jail, thank God, but that doesn't mean that there won't be others of his ilk wandering around."

For the first time Kelley realized that it wasn't just locals in general he'd been worrying about when he talked to Bill; it was his own family in Cielo Solo.

"I don't think there's much you can do about smugglers operating near your village, Nick," she tried to console him. "You heard Bill say that as long as nobody opposed them there wouldn't be a problem."

"And I suppose that if *you* saw somebody digging up an endangered cactus, you'd raise no opposition?"

Although his tone reflected more anger than fear, Kelley felt an unaccountable ghost of warmth as she realized that it was her safety that was troubling him.

She gave him a grateful, indulgent smile. "Nick, I appreciate your concern, but I'm a big girl. I live by myself in L.A., for heaven's sake. Now if I can handle that, I'm sure I can survive whatever new experiences Cielo Solo has to offer."

"Oh, you can?" he challenged her, unappeased. "You think that living in that mansion of yours qualifies you to cope with squalor and crime and—"

"Nick, it's hardly a mansion!" Kelley interjected. "It's just an ordinary middle-class home."

"It's a *mansion*, Kelley!" he insisted. "So is my little house. At least it would be in Cielo Solo."

This time she didn't smile. In fact, for several moments Kelley didn't do anything but stare at the dashboard as the first turnoff for South Tucson came into view. Nick had been moving away from her steadily since the night of that searing kiss, and if she didn't find a way to close the gap soon, they'd be crossing the border in separate cars.

"I think it would be smarter for me to check out the area alone first," Nick announced with feeling. "It's not too late for you to go back to L.A., you know." He switched on the turn signal and pulled into the right lane. "You could fly from here, Kell. And if everything checks out in Cielo Solo, then—"

"What are you doing?" she demanded, afraid he was taking off for the airport at once. "I thought we were going to drive straight through to Hermosillo."

"So did I, but I think a slight detour is in order. It's important for you to understand just what you're getting into tomorrow, Kelley, and they say a picture is worth a thousand words."

She studied him uncomfortably. "What picture did you have in mind?"

His neck reddened as his expression took on a note of shame. "I thought you might like to see where I was born."

Kelley was surprised, but answered softly, "Of course I'd like to see it, Nick, if you'd like to show me."

He met her eyes with a sorrow that Kelley remembered from the first day they'd met, when he'd lovingly caressed his battered old photo of Cielo Solo. "I don't particularly want to show you, Kelley," he admitted reluctantly. "But I think it's something you need to see."

With that revealing comment he pulled off the freeway into an area of town that looked as though it should have been reserved for industry, but for some reason was struggling to pretend it was a residential area. The term was one a city planner would have used quite loosely, because nothing about the scene before her caused Kelley to believe this was somewhere that anybody would want to live.

They bounced along a potholed back alley for half a mile, then lurched over a rocky dirt road to a handful of dilapidated houses clustered by some oak trees. Drying clothes fluttered from branches between trash-filled yards; boarded-up windows sported obscene graffiti in English, Spanish and indecipherable gang codes. Several half-dressed brown children stared soberly as Nick slowed down in front of a tar-paper shack with two front steps where there should have been three. Wordlessly the children stared at the car as it crawled to an uncertain stop. Then an old woman opened the screenless screen door and bustled them into the house.

"Look at it, Kelley," Nick instructed her. "Look at this dump and imagine four families crammed into two bedrooms, a kitchen and a tiny front parlor. One bathroom, when it works. No heat, and even in Tucson, it's been known to snow in the winter."

Kelley stared at the house but said nothing. It was hard to imagine the Beau Brummel she'd had to dinner growing up in this pathetic slum.

"I was born in the back bedroom. I don't mean I lived here after I came home from the hospital—I mean my mother *gave birth* to me on a flea-infested mattress on the floor." He gazed at Kelley as his point sank home. "She was so excited because the house *had* a floor, Kelley! It was the first time in her life she'd ever had running water, glass windows or even a throw rug made out of rags!"

She looked away, suddenly remembering Mama Chayo's early stories of her life in Mexico, stories of a primitive world that had seemed no more real to Kelley at the time than the pictures of African tribes she'd seen in *National Geographic*.

"This is heaven on earth compared to housing in Cielo Solo, Kelley. And Cielo Solo is posh compared to an Opata Indian village!" Gently he tucked one finger under her chin to make her face him. "Do you understand where you're going, Kelley? This isn't just a backpacking trip into open country untouched by man! You're traveling back in time to a place where people have nothing to lose. And whenever a man has nothing to lose, he's bound to be dangerous.''

Kelley's eyes swept over the pathetic shack as she struggled to think of an answer, but no words found their way to her lips. All she could think of was what it would be like to give birth to a baby in this hovel, alone and frightened on a filthy floor. ''Why did your mother come here, Nico?'' she asked him shakily. ''Why on earth did she take a chance on this awful dump?''

''In the first place, this dump is a *palace* compared to our house in Cielo Solo,'' he growled. ''In the second place, this is where my father promised her he'd be waiting as soon as he could send her a little cash. He told her that he loved her, then left her with nothing but an address, a promise . . . and an illegitimate baby on the way.'' His mouth tightened with remembered bitterness and grief as he finished hoarsely, ''She was only sixteen at the time.''

Kelley couldn't look at him. There were tears in her eyes.

''My mother wasn't much older than you are now when that *curandera* killed her,'' Nick revealed, pain clouding his husky tone. ''Which might not have been so bad except for the fact that she never really lived, Kelley. She never really lived at all!'' He gripped the steering wheel until his knuckles grew white. ''She told me once that I was all that made her life worthwhile.''

He sighed deeply and turned away, as though the sight were just too much for him to handle. It was too much for Kelley, too, and she trained her eyes on the ratty plastic remnants of the old Ford's seat covers, understanding for the first time why Nick felt the need to strip down a car with Sonoran plates so it wouldn't stick out like a sore thumb in Pitahaya.

His voice was still quiet but more composed when he spoke again. "I didn't come here to depress you, Kelley. My point is that from Tucson to Cielo Solo is no further than it is from San Francisco to L.A.—and yet we might as well be shuttling to the moon or taking a submarine journey to the lost city of Atlantis." Urgently he met her eyes. "We're going to a different world, Kelley. At best it's going to be grim and at worst it's going to be dangerous. I'll do everything in my power to protect you, *corazón*, but if you don't want to get into trouble, you've got to leave your rose-colored glasses behind."

On that note he revved up the engine and pulled away from the hovel, his steering sharp and hurried until long after they'd pulled back into the paved alley. Kelley didn't know what to say that might comfort him, but despite her promise to keep her distance, she just couldn't feign indifference to his worry or to his grief.

She waited until they were back on the interstate heading south before she braved the silence to reach out for his hand. To her surprise Nick gripped it quickly, gripped it hard, as though he'd been waiting for her to make that very gesture.

They were halfway to the border before he let her go.

CHAPTER NINE

IT WAS DUSK by the time Nick and Kelley settled into a charming mission-style hotel in Hermosillo. They were both too tired to consider dressing up for dinner, but after they'd eaten some marvelous *flautas* and *chiles rellenos*, they succumbed to the time-honored tradition of an evening stroll around the local *zócalo* with the rest of the tourists.

Though American businessmen had helped the construction industry to boom since Nick had last bought a bus ticket from Hermosillo to the border, he was glad to see that some things about the old colonial city hadn't changed. The proud adobe cathedral, where mass had been celebrated for hundreds of years, still dominated the center of town. And whitewashed homes with red tile roofs and luxuriant gardens still gave a weary traveler the illusion of a sparkling oasis in the middle of Sonora's sea of sand...as long as he paid no attention to the beggars, street urchins and omnipresent pigs and chickens that roamed the dusty streets.

"Oh, Nick, it's simply beautiful!" Kelley sighed as she studied the brilliant lights and enthusiastic street vendors.

One of them took advantage of her momentary hesitation and instantly started waving clothes and artifacts in her face. "You wan' dress, *señorita*?" he urged her in broken English, then looked at Nick expectantly. "Pretty, pretty, like *señorita*, no, *señor*?"

"She's pretty enough just the way she is," Nick replied in Spanish. Then he tried to drag Kelley away before she weakened, but it was a lost cause.

"I know we're not here on a vacation," she pleaded, fingering the soft turquoise fabric the vendor had thrust in her hand, "but do you suppose I might pick up an embroidered dress or two?"

Nick gave her an indulgent smile. Kelley might be a scientist heading out for the boonies in her blue jeans, but her woman's heart could still be set aflutter by the sight of a good bargain. "Buy whatever you want, Kelley," he teased, "but remember you'll have to carry it on your back for the next three weeks."

She laughed. "Maybe I should just look tonight and make my purchases on the way home."

He tossed a casual arm around her shoulder and gave her a light, teasing shake. "I knew you'd see it my way."

He hadn't really meant to touch her, but then again he'd given up trying *not* to touch her ever since that soul-bearing scene in South Tucson. It had embarrassed him to let her see the darkness within him; yet somehow he felt a little lighter now, a little more at peace. Juanita hadn't been too far off the mark when she'd pointed out that Kelley could make his prodigal-son journey a little bit easier.

She glanced up at him, green eyes laughing, as his hand lingered on her shoulder. Nick knew that he owed her some consistency, at the very least, but half the time he couldn't seem to remember why he'd decided to postpone their inevitable romance. Kelley wanted him; she couldn't begin to hide it. And he...well, there wasn't much point in pretending that he didn't want Kelley McKinney more than he'd ever wanted any soft, supple female in his life. He loved her sharp wit, her compassion, her compelling blend of no-nonsense scientific thinking with her undeniably feminine appeal. And he loved the curves that beckoned to him from those tight jeans, the memory of the soft scarlet robe she'd been wearing the night he'd kissed her…and the silken nightgown he'd caught a glimpse of underneath. And, beyond the burgeoning hunger and the growing respect he had for this delectable woman, he *liked* Kelley McKinney. He just plain liked her a lot.

"If you really have your heart set on making a purchase," he suggested mischievously, "why don't you buy a sun hat?" He plopped a garish one on her head that said I Love Hermosillo on it. "Even with that number twenty-nine sunscreen you've been slopping on since we crossed the border, you're likely to burn without more protection when we set out on foot across the desert."

Kelley grinned. "That's a wonderful idea, Nick, but I think I'll pick something a little more subtle." She traded the garish hat for another one while the vendor all but salivated in praise of her beauty. "At least it's something I won't have to carry." She spent the next ten minutes trying on wide-brimmed straw hats with every kind of ribbon, flower and embroidered accessory, ultimately settling on one that that had a single saguaro stitched onto the crown.

Nick was about to start bargaining with the sparkling-eyed vendor when she cried out in spontaneous Spanish, "*¡Eso es!*" She gushed out a litany of praise for the hat in what had once been Nick's native tongue before she turned to him saucily and preened, *"¿No te lo gusta, Nico?"*

"Sure, Kelley. It's just fine," he answered meekly, disappointed that she'd revealed her interest too keenly for him to negotiate a good price... not to mention embarrassed to discover her fluent command of the language he now spoke so poorly after so many years of disuse. All day long Kelley had thanked Nick for interpreting for her, but it was suddenly obvious that her own Spanish was much more than adequate; it was vastly superior to his own.

"And you, *señor*?" the grinning merchant cajoled him in clumsy English. "You no want handsome hat for hot, hot Sonora sun?"

"No lo necesito," Nick grumbled. He knew the vendor was probably just practicing his English, but nonetheless he was offended that the man didn't respond to his Spanish automatically, as he would surely have done with a fellow Mexican.

"But is so hot in desert!" the man insisted, plopping a huge peasant's sombrero on Nick's head. "Ah, but this you already know, *señor*! You come Mexico before!"

Nick shot him a curious glance. "How can you tell?" he asked, wondering if there was still a layer of Cielo Solo dust that shone through his cosmopolitan demeanor.

He receive a wide grin. "You talk Spanish good for *gringo*!" the salesman praised him, patting the hat on Nick's head. "Your woman, she talk good, too!"

Kelley couldn't stifle a giggle, but Nick wasn't sure that his clear identity as a foreigner in his grandmother's homeland was particularly funny. Still, he knew he'd need the hat so he bought it anyway, then shelled out a few more pesos for a pair of cool cotton pajama-type pants.

I'd like to see a tourist wear these in Hermosillo, he wanted to joke. *Only a man like my uncle would realize they're the best defense against the desert sun.*

But the cheerful vendor one-upped him yet again. "A very good choice, *señor*! Yes, *señorita*?" He winked at Kelley. "Now he look almost handsome like real Mexican!"

This time Kelley laughed out loud, and Nick couldn't help but join her.

"Was he pulling your leg?" she asked a moment later when they were out of earshot.

Nick shook his head. "I don't think so, Kelley. As far as he's concerned, I'm as American as you are." And once again his hand closed around her warm fingers; it felt too good to pull away. Nick knew that he was heading for another rough night with Kelley just a closed door away from his bed; the barriers that he'd so carefully erected between them were rapidly tumbling down. Deliberately he strove to keep the conversation light. "Besides, in Spanish you don't pull somebody's leg; the expression is to 'pull your hair.'" Chuckling, he seized a red lock to emphasize his point.

Kelley smiled as she brushed against him accidentally, and he had to fight the urge to pull her into his arms. For a moment he thought she might be fighting the same battle, but after a quizzical glance that probed the depths of his inviting expression, she started to walk again, chatting about the local sights.

Nick followed her lead as they prowled through the shops and stands for nearly an hour, but every now and then he found their fingers interlaced as they checked out hand-blown glass vases, leather purses and painted clay bowls. When they stumbled across some hand-woven palm mats like the kind Mama Luz used to make, Nick felt a strange sense of pride, as Kelley oohed and aahed over the fine workmanship of the ancient craft.

"Look, Nick!" she cried out a moment later, tugging on his sleeve as the first bass notes of the preg-nant-looking *quitarrón* crowned the perfect night. "Mariachis! Now I know we're really in Mexico!"

He smiled at her enthusiasm . . . and her naïveté. Granted, the strolling musicians in traditional *charro* dress—black bolero jackets with matching high-waisted trousers that boasted silver *conchas* marching down the sides—were as characteristic of Mexico as cactus and tamales, but Nick had seen them at enough weddings and parties in L.A. to know they could be found north of the border for a price. "I hate to disappoint you, Kelley, but mariachis have been known to perform in the United States. In fact, there are groups in Califor-nia that don't sound too much different from these fellows."

"Well, those must not be *real* mariachis," she sniffed. "I've heard Mexican music at *Cinco de Mayo* parties before, and it was nothing compared to this."

As he reached for Kelley's hand, the stirring beat of the music intensified his need for her. "Yes," he ad-mitted, tucking a loose frizzy curl behind her ear. "I can't say that mariachi music has ever touched me . . . quite so deeply."

Quizzically her eyes met his, challenging the hidden meaning of his words. It was the sort of moment when she could have turned away or moved closer yet, and he honestly didn't know which action he'd prefer.

But Kelley, it seemed, knew exactly what she wanted. "You're playing with me, Nick," she chided him softly. Then, to his dismay, she deliberately disengaged her hand from his and stepped away. "Maybe you don't mean to, maybe you don't even know it, but you've been giving me mixed messages all day, and I'm not sure I can handle it much longer."

He jammed his hands into his pockets like a chastened schoolboy as he pondered her words.

"Nothing could make me happier than to hear that you've changed your mind about Liliana, Nico—" she spoke his Spanish name as though it were a caress "—but if you meant what you said the night before we left L.A., then I don't think it's fair of you to touch me at all."

It wasn't a threat or a bribe or a challenge, but a simple statement of the truth. Nick knew it was time to reach out for Kelley or push her away, and he acknowledged that up until now he'd been doing a little of both. He'd been unintentionally cruel to Kelley almost since the beginning, and the pain in her eyes made it clear that she'd endured just about enough.

Suddenly Nick knew that he couldn't bear the limbo much longer, either. Whatever lay in store for him in Cielo Solo was part of his past; surely it was Kelley McKinney who would be the heart of his future! At least it might turn out that way if he just gave her half a chance.

Her eyes did not flicker as Nick took a step closer; she did not move as he touched her face with one hand. Ever so slowly he slipped his fingers deep into her tangle of hair as his thumb stroked her tender white throat, then skated gently along the delicate curve of her jaw. Kelley closed her eyes as his free hand slipped around her back to pull her closer. Hesitantly her fingers touched his shirt at the waist.

And then, in spite of the hearty *quitarrón* and the trumpet's song and the chaotic street full of people, Nick lifted Kelley's chin until their lips were close enough to touch. And this time, she did not pull away.

IT WAS A SWEET KISS, a kiss of promise, a different kiss from the angry protest against his feelings that Nick had bestowed upon Kelley a few days before. Every nerve in her body, every ache in her heart, responded to his warm, gentle touch. By the time he released her, Kelley knew that Nick had won the battle of her soul.

His eyes met hers for just a second, sad, relieved, as though he were anxious for a private second kiss to follow up the first. But he let his hands drop to his sides, then slip silently into his pockets, as he said very gently, "I'm going to start at the beginning, Kell. I'll tell you everything I can about what I'm feeling, and maybe you can help me make some sense of this mess. Fair enough?"

Kelley's heart was still pounding from the heart-stopping kiss, but she managed to nod and give him a shaky smile. "Fair enough."

"Am I allowed to touch you while I'm talking?" he asked, risking an impish grin. Her answering smile gave him leave to do as he liked; he slipped his arm around her and tugged her close beside him as he began to walk.

"I was seventeen when I saw Liliana—really saw her—for the first time," he began almost nonchalantly as they strolled along the north side of the plaza. "I'd met her as a child, of course, but when I arrived in Cielo Solo that summer, everything was different. Of course, my mother had just died and I knew I was going back to Mexico for good. Still, I think that I was just at an age where the sun seems to rise and set on true romance. Besides, Liliana had just come into bloom."

He smiled at Kelley wryly, but without great pain. "The irony of it all—considering how desperately I wanted to make love to that girl—is that I treated her like a queen, Kelley. I was almost glad that the circuit priest only made it to Cielo Solo once every six months or so, because I was afraid to touch her. It was as though, even married, sex would desecrate her pristine perfection, her..." He stopped and looked uncomfortable as he caught Kelley's steady gaze. She was prepared to listen to a lot of seamy details about his past, but she hadn't counted on a litany of this other woman's virtues.

"Kelley, I'm just telling you this because it's important for you to understand that I never touched her. I left her pregnant, but the baby wasn't—could not possibly have been—my child." He studied her a moment, then added quietly, "It was a little girl, and she died when she was three."

Kelley couldn't help but feel a moment's sadness for the death of a child so young. Yet another part of her was relieved to learn that she wouldn't have to contend with Nick's long-lost son or daughter in Cielo Solo—or even a child he felt he should have raised.

"I'd been there for three months when this piece of slime called Pablo Villalobos—" his grimace said it all "—bushwhacked me one night just outside the village."

"Did you know this man?"

"Sure. I grew up with him. I mean, he lived in Cielo Solo when I did, as a kid. But he was a few years older than I was and had always been pretty wild. He'd moved on shortly before I went back that spring, but I'd heard a lot of rumors that he'd been seeing Liliana a few weeks before I showed up. I asked her about him once, and she said he frightened her. She also muttered something about the fact that she'd once thought he might be falsely maligned and misunderstood, but she'd learned otherwise and never wanted to see him again. By that time she was crying, so I started to comfort her and never mentioned him after that."

"You were . . . surprised when he accosted you?"

"To say the least. His behavior was a lot rougher than I would have expected. I mean, he was always a bad apple, but it was clear that over time he'd turned rotten through and through. Still, I didn't mind getting beaten up nearly as much as I choked on what he had to say."

As they turned the corner and drifted out of the main plaza, Kelley glanced up at the iron gates of the nearby houses and wondered why they were so heavily barred. Even the adobe walls that surrounded each yard were topped with shards of broken bottles embedded in cement. Normally she wouldn't have left the security of the center of town at night in a foreign city, but Nick seemed to know where he was going and it wasn't the right time to interrupt him. Besides, it was incredibly good to feel his arm around her as they strolled together that she didn't want to say anything that might cause him to take it away.

"He told me that Liliana was his woman—in every sense of the word. He said I'd moved in on his territory while he was away on a 'business trip' and I'd have to pay for my transgressions. If I ever so much as looked at Liliana again, I wouldn't live to enjoy the memory."

His biceps tensed. "At first I was too angry to be frightened. I told him that even if he had been involved with Liliana at some point, it was all over now and she belonged to me. I told him that we were getting married. I even went so far as to say that this goddess loved me and I considered myself the luckiest man on earth." They rounded yet another corner, edging ever farther away from the plaza noise and confusion. "I don't know what I expected him to do, Kell. Back down, challenge me, suggest we put it to Liliana?" He chuckled without mirth. "The last thing I expected him to do was laugh."

"Laugh?" Kelley echoed.

"Laugh. Howl, in fact. He laughed so hard he couldn't keep hitting me, even though he had me pinned. He must have laughed for five full minutes, while I just lay there on the ground, open-mouthed, while he spouted bits and pieces of lies about Liliana."

Nick's grip on her shoulder tightened almost painfully as he continued. "He said she was dirt. Scum. He'd taken her the first time he'd asked, and there were dozens of guys before and after him. He said she was pregnant with his child, and she'd only trapped me into marriage because he'd been gone so long she was afraid something had happened to him and she had to have a father for the baby so nobody would think she was a..." He stopped and lowered his voice. "So she wouldn't end up like my mother," he finished painfully, unable to meet her eyes.

In a gesture of comfort, Kelley slipped her arm around his waist and gave him a comforting hug. With every sentence he was painting a clearer picture of why it was so hard for him to forget his past. She only wished there was something she could say to soften the galling memory.

"He pointed out that she ran her scam on me because nobody else in the village would have been naïve enough to fall for it...or stupid enough to take the risk of crossing Pablo," Nick admitted painfully. "On top of that I was an American, more or less, which meant I'd turn out to be a rich husband, to boot."

For several moments they walked in silence. Kelley knew Nick had more to say, but she didn't want to prod him. Instead she tried to enjoy the beautiful evening, but it wasn't easy once she remembered how far they were from the center of town, not to mention the fact that Nick had decided that the legal complications of carrying a gun in Mexico outweighed the likelihood of their need for one.

She grew even more uneasy when Nick dropped his arm from around her shoulder to lean against one of the wrought-iron gates. For a moment Kelley felt naked, unguarded, until he reached out to take her hand, pulling her closer. He didn't kiss her; he just caressed her with his eyes, then slowly slipped his free hand through her hair.

The tenderness of the gesture stripped Kelley of any defense she might have mustered. Instinctively she lifted both hands to cup his square jaw, then slowly stood on tiptoe to soothe his lips with hers. His answering kiss was soft but hungry. As his hands slipped down her shoulders to electrify the bare skin of her arms, she found his gentleness even more compelling than his passion.

Kelley lost all sense of time and place as she wrapped her arms around his neck and eagerly pressed herself against him. At once Nick's fingertips slipped from her arms to the sides of her breasts. His thumbs had just begun a tempting exploration when their two new hats collided, sending both fluttering to the cracked and weedy pavement. Kelley would have ignored the minor interruption—her need for his touch was already too great to ignore—but the sound caused Nick to jerk himself upright while he struggled for self-control.

"Corazón," he moaned, cradling her face against his chest, "we're putting the cart before the horse. Not only are we on a public street corner—" despite his words he bent down to tease the inner curl of her ear, then took her sensitive lobe between his teeth for a brief, erotic nip "—but I promised to tell you the entire story. If I stop now, I may never find the courage to dredge up these old feelings again."

Kelley was breathing hard by then, and wasn't at all sure she could listen to another word about Liliana. But if Nick realized how close to the brink she was, he'd lose what was left of his own hair-trigger control.

Burying her face against his shirt, she forced herself to say, "Go on with your story, Nico. I'm listening."

"What...what was I saying, Kelley?" he asked, slowly rubbing her back with his warm, gentle hands.

"You were telling me about your feelings."

"Feelings?" he moaned, his strong arms pressing her closer yet. "My God, woman, if you can't tell what I'm feeling, then—"

"Your feelings *then*. The night that Pablo came after you."

"Aha! Pablo," he managed to repeat, tracing the ridges and valleys up the trail of her spine. "The night he told me that Liliana was only using me, I was—in a word—crushed," he finally admitted, his voice soft but tense in the silence of the night. "I hotly denied everything, of course. In my infinite teenage manliness, I suspect I even cried. He'd worked me over pretty thoroughly, and I remember thinking that if I'd been in L.A., I might have checked in with a doctor, but a *curandero* was the only medical care available in Cielo Solo or even Pitahaya. So I decided I'd be better off on my own. I had only two choices: run away in pain and shame, or ignore the bastard and pretend that nothing had happened."

Kelley snuggled yet closer to him, drawing comfort from his warmth and masculine strength even though her more sensual needs could not be met. She slipped her fingers through his thick hair, tracing slow, provocative circles against his scalp. He groaned, then nuzzled her cheek as his hands reached the end of her spine and lingered on her hips.

"So you ran," she finished for him. "There was nothing else you could do."

"Yes." His fingertips slipped under the hem of her shirt, etching trails of desire on the bare skin of her back. "But first I decided that I couldn't possibly go without confronting Liliana. I just couldn't imagine that I could be so wrong about her, mainly because...well, this may sound silly, but Mama Luz really liked her." Hungrily he kissed the top of Kelley's head, then her forehead, her nose and the hollow of her throat. "She approved of the match. And even though she'd always desperately wanted me to come back to Cielo Solo, I don't think she would have used Liliana to manipulate me. It's just not her way. Besides, I'd already decided that I was home to stay even before I got involved with Liliana.'' He released a great sigh, and if he hadn't been holding her so intimately, Kelley would have wondered whether it was Mama Luz or Liliana who accounted for his nostalgia.

"At first she denied Pablo's accusations," he went on, "and insisted it was me that she loved. But eventually she confessed that she was carrying Pablo's child. Naturally, I went stark raving berserk. She kept changing her story, so I couldn't quite tell if he'd seduced her or taken her by force, but it was certainly clear to me that I'd been lied to, used and humiliated. So—'' he sighed again, then kissed Kelley on the forehead almost platonically ''—I just took off. Even though I was hurting like hell, both inside and out, I knew I couldn't share my shame with anyone.'' His eyes were dark but trusting in the street lamp's dusky glow. "And I never have," he admitted slowly. "Until now.''

There was nothing Kelley could say to that, so she gently kissed him, just once, on the mouth. It was a different kiss than those they'd shared before; it sprang from mutual trust and succor, not barely banked passion or escalating need. The enormity of Nick's unexpected gift of trust overwhelmed her, yet the sadness of his lost years with his loved ones hit hard when he added hoarsely, "You know, as a man, it doesn't seem all that traumatic, Kelley. Just sounds like a lousy excuse for cutting myself off from Mama Luz. I didn't even have the guts to face her before I left.'' His expression darkened. "I haven't seen her since—not once in nineteen years. Juanita used to warn me that my grandmother might die before I got back to Cielo Solo. That terrifies me, Kell. It really does.''

Kelley slipped both hands around his waist and pressed her nose against his neck once more. "We'll be there late tomorrow, Nick," she assured him. "If anything were wrong with her, wouldn't you have heard?''

Slowly he nodded. "Liliana would have written to me. She writes all the letters for Mama Luz because she's one of the few people in the village who can read—and that's only because I taught her.''

There was a lot Kelley could have said about Liliana—and a lot she didn't dare mention, even now. But she couldn't let Nick's long confession go by without any sort of a comment, so cautiously she asked, "Do you think . . . are you afraid . . . that she really did love you, Nick?''

"Yes," he said simply, again resting his chin on her head. "As the years go by, I'm more sure than ever that she did. I think it's highly unlikely that she ever slept with anyone but Pablo, and I think he may very well have forced himself on her and she lied about it to protect me from him. At the time I thought I was strong and powerful, but looking back on it, considering how green I was, I think he would have killed me if I'd challenged him again before he went to prison.''

Kelley shivered at the thought, and uttered a silent prayer that this terrible Pablo person would stay locked up forever. "Nick," she whispered against his rugged neck, "I can't say I understand everything you've been through—nobody can really walk in somebody else's shoes. But thank you for giving me a glimpse of what you're going through. If there's anything I can do make it easier, let me know.''

To her surprise, he grinned. "You could wear a paper bag over your head till we get there, Kell. That's about the only way I'm likely to resist the temptation," he growled huskily. "Assuming you do still want me to...resist." He drew out the last word until the sultry syllables reverberated through her heart.

A new coil of desire wrapped itself around her. Suddenly she didn't want Nick to resist the temptation; she couldn't even remember why he should. What was Liliana anyway? A memory, a ghost of a teenage love. He would see her tomorrow and say he was sorry; she would forgive him and say what's done is done. And then he would belong to Kelley forever.

Of course, he may find out that his love for her still lingers, she reminded herself stoutly. *He may find out a lot of things you'd really rather not know.* Bravely she asked, "You don't...really think you're going to...just pick things up where you left off with Liliana after all this time, do you, Nick?"

He shook his head and dropped a kiss on her nose. "Of course not."

"She might be married by now," Kelley pointed out with relief. "She might be very happy without you."

Nick ruffled Kelley's hair and honored her with a grin. "Now that's a fine suggestion from a totally unbiased observer."

"Really, Nick!" she protested. "It's not all that—"

"Hey, I know she's not married. Her husband died last fall. Didn't I mention that?"

"No," Kelley answered a bit more coolly. "I don't think you did."

Sensing her apprehension, he said "It's not that big of a deal, Kell. I got word last autumn, and I didn't jump on my pony and go galloping down here, you know. Although I think Juanita thought I would. That's when she really started hassling me about going back to my roots.''

"I didn't think Juanita knew about Cielo Solo," Kelley retorted stiffly. "You just said you'd never told anyone but me."

Nick rolled his eyes. "I said I'd never told anybody else the story of that last terrible night with Liliana, Kelley. And I haven't. If I'd even gotten that far with Juanita, she might have been able to live with what I had to give her. She knew that there was a woman and a problem I'd never faced, that's all. But it wasn't enough for her. She wanted more." He paused for a moment. "And she deserved more, come to think of it. She's a fine woman, Kelley. Almost as fine as you are."

In a matter of seconds Kelley whirled from apprehension to joy once more. She knew what Nick thought of Juanita; she thought pretty highly of Bobby's teacher herself. To be so favorably compared could only do her honor. It was almost enough to make her forget that Nick hadn't yet said she was a finer woman than his precious Liliana. Almost, but not quite.

Kelley was about to answer when Nick abruptly clapped his hand over her mouth in a clear warning gesture. A moment later she heard what had alarmed him—the sound of footsteps, a great many footsteps, shuffling stealthily as though not to be heard.

Kelley knew she should have stopped Nick from strolling this far from the center of town. They were utterly alone, utterly defenseless. Adrenaline flooded her system; ropes of fear corded the muscles of her arms. Nick's grip on her waist grew tense and protective as the footsteps grew closer and closer and then, quite suddenly, stopped.

CHAPTER TEN

FOR A FULL MINUTE the silence was deafening; only the distant squeak of a horn and baby's squall rent the fabric of the night. Kelley was still clinging to Nick, but in terror now, and his fear for her was even greater than his concern for his own safety.

And then, without so much as a pitch-pipe note of warning, the street burst into song.

At first Nick couldn't discern what was happening. Bass tones were dancing up and down the scales; guitar strings echoed rhythms of passion and young love. A vibrant tenor voice was filling the night sky with his passion for *La Negra*, a gorgeous girl with rich dark skin and flashing eyes.

"Oh, Kelley!" Nick burst out, nuzzling her forehead and laughing in relief. "It's a mariachi serenade!"

He felt the tension drain from her body as she collapsed against him. "Why did they sneak up on us like that?" she demanded indignantly, fighting to catch her breath. "Why didn't they just keep playing all the way from the center of town?"

"Well, for one thing, the whole group doesn't perform at a private event like this. See?" He led her around the corner for a better look. "It's just a trio. And it's supposed to be a surprise, *corazón*. They slip into the neighborhood secretly when everybody's asleep. While the whole family enjoys the music, the young man steps out of the shadows so the girl knows who's come to call—though she ought to be able to guess, since the serenade is more or less a public announcement of their engagement. The man arranges everything with her family ahead of time so they can have food ready for the trio and all the neighbors."

"They have an impromptu party? At this hour of the night?" Kelley sounded incredulous.

"At any hour of the night. This is pretty early, as these things go. Nobody minds being awakened for this lofty occasion. It's a tremendous mark of respect for a young man to hire mariachis."

"I'm sure that the girl is honored!" Kelley teased. "Why, I'd have been tickled pink if one of my boyfriends had ever done something like this. But my dad would have had my hide, and the neighbors would have called the police."

Nick laughed out loud, grateful that this was one act of lunacy he'd never even considered committing on Liliana's behalf. "Well, tell your dad to relax. It costs over a thousand dollars to bring mariachis over the border for an evening! A fellow would have to be stark raving loony over a gal to shell out that kind of money and risk getting arrested just to let the whole world know he was a besotted chump." He shook his head as the music changed to a more lilting, tender melody. "Now they're singing *La Mañanitas*, Kelley."

"The Mexican birthday song?" she asked.

"Oh, it's much more than a birthday song. It's the quintessential Mexican love song for a cherished person of any age, sex or relation. If I wanted to tell a special lady that she walks right next to my heart, this is the only song I'd sing."

Instantly he regretted his choice of words when Kelley asked, "Have you ever sung it for anybody?"

Again he laughed, but he couldn't meet her eyes. "With a voice like mine, I'd only sing for my worst enemy. Besides, I'm not much into silly sentimental gestures. Especially at three hundred dollars an hour. That's the price of a new set of radial tires."

The zest in Kelley's green eyes faded a bit. "Well, since I'm never likely to hear a mariachi serenade except by proxy, do you mind if we wander back to town at a leisurely pace so I can hear them sing?"

"I don't see why not."

They tried to be unobtrusive as they sauntered by the lovesick young Romeo—he couldn't have been more than nineteen—and the glowing Juliet who grinned at him so beguilingly from the balcony. Neighbors were already slipping out to watch. A few of the men were even adding their own yelps and traditional *gritos* to the professionals' music. Feeling spunky, Nick couldn't resist calling out a couple of very authentic *ajuas* himself.

"Don't tell me you learned to yelp like that in the Army," Kelley teased him, looping her fingers through his as they walked along. "That's surely an inherited skill."

He laughed as he pulled her closer, reveling in the natural ease with which they reached for each other now. "Actually, it's handed down from generation to generation, like the family whistle code Mexican men use to announce themselves. I can't say I've had much occasion to *echar gritos* in recent years, but it's something you never forget." He paused for moment, then chuckled before he confessed, "You should have seen me when I was twenty, Kelley. I had those Spanish wolf calls honed down to a fine art.''

''Come on!''

''Really! After that mess with Liliana I went through quite a few years when I needed to... well, to prove myself as a man. In lots of different ways.'' He wasn't proud of it, but it seemed important, somehow, to confess all of his past shortcomings to Kelley tonight. ''I guess that's why I enlisted—that and the fact that I was hungry and couldn't figure out how else to get a job.'' He shrugged his shoulders as he ushered Kelley into their hotel, which had black velvet paintings of jaguars and matadors on the walls. ''Actually, I came back to the States and went into the service for all the wrong reasons, but it turned out to be the smartest thing I could have done.'' He met her eyes and added thoughtfully, ''And I guess I decided to come to Mexico with you for all the wrong reasons, as well, Kelley. But maybe this'll turn out to be pretty smart, too.''

A sunbeam of hope lit up her pretty face as she whispered, ''I hope so, Nico. I really do.''

She squeezed his hand, then led him toward the stairs. He followed her mutely, knowing that a monumental decision was about to be made. They'd crossed a line tonight; or rather *he* had crossed a line, reached out for Kelley in a way he'd been afraid to do before. They were closer than they'd ever been, and it seemed to Nick that the ground rules he'd laid out for them in California had become obsolete. They'd also become nearly impossible to adhere to.

He was silent as they walked down the hall to Kelley's room, which was adjacent to his own. Memories of her unspoken invitation earlier in the evening suffused him now, along with the remembered sensations of her warm curves in his arms. If they'd been in a hotel room or on a private beach during those few urgent moments on the corner, he knew he'd no longer be debating the right and wrong of making love to Kelley tonight. He'd already have claimed her as his woman.

So why was he holding back? Did he really owe so very much to Liliana? Or was it Kelley herself, so vulnerable and yet so strong, who forced him to triple check his own values at every step of the way?

"No matter what happens in Cielo Solo, Nick, I think you'll be glad you came," Kelley assured him, misreading his apprehension as he made no move to follow her through the door she'd just opened. "Even if your worst fears are realized tomorrow, it'll be over with and you can put it behind you, one way or another."

Riveted where he stood, he took a sharp breath and faced the harsh truth of her words. "I wish I could say you were right, Kell. I wish I could tell you that I'm so full of you tonight that how I'll feel tomorrow doesn't matter." He struggled for a teasing grin and failed. "The best I can do is say that I wish it were true."

"So do I." Her tone was low, husky, as she moved closer to him. Uncertainty shadowed her gaze.

Nick ached with frustration as he studied Kelley, her lips full and inviting, no more than a kiss away from his own hungry mouth. How keenly he remembered the fire in those inviting lips . . . and the unspoken promise they'd already made in the moonlit magic of Hermosillo! Liliana seemed very, very far away.

At last he moved toward Kelley, ever so slowly, and laid one warm hand on her cheek. She closed her eyes as his hand slipped lower, her delicate neck fitting neatly into the V between his fingers and his thumb…the thumb that washed softly over her lips and teeth, then trailed across her collarbone until it dared to whisper under the lacy collar of her shirt.

"Corazón," he murmured, "I know I'm going to feel guilty if I stay…but so very, very sorry if I leave."

Stay with me, her green eyes begged him. *Forget her, forget the past. All that matters is right here, right now, and the fact that I want you.*

But somehow, before his lips could follow his fingers, a ghostly shadow from Kelley's past stole across her face, and ever so subtly, she moved away.

It wasn't a physical withdrawal; he could still feel the heat of trembling skin and the throbbing pulse in her neck. But the hope in her eyes had faded, and the pain he read there reminded him all too vividly of the evening he'd spent on her back-porch swing.

Finally he leaned down to kiss her, not in invitation, but in bittersweet regret. Kelley understood the gesture, and tenderly patted the hand that lingered on her throat.

"When you're ready, Nick, you know I'll still be waiting," she promised him unsteadily. "But I can't be Liliana's understudy. Do you understand?"

He nodded slowly. "I understand, Kell. I hate it, but I know you're right." He leaned forward and took her face in both hands to kiss her firmly, as if a simple goodbye peck could not possibly suffice. For a moment he pressed against her like a lover, letting his tongue claim her parted lips with a fresh wash of desire that strove to tell her what she would miss during the long sleepless night.

Against his own best instincts, Nick tugged Kelley closer. She didn't protest, her hands grasping his shirt with barely arrested passion.

Nick never knew how he found the strength to finally release her, but somehow he managed. "You're a rare and precious flower, Kelley," he ground out in a strangled tone, "and you deserve to be more than a lady in waiting." He kissed her once more with fierce, aching passion then pried her hands loose from their potent grip on his shirt.

Nick was trembling as he broke away, and he was certain that if Kelley reached out for him one more time he'd never find the willpower to leave her room tonight. With both hands Kelley covered her face, struggling for control, but mercifully, she did not try to touch him again.

Nick knew he couldn't leave her like this; he had to let her know that his restraint was for her benefit as much as for his own. Again he reached out to touch her, his fingers branding her throat once more with his barely quelled desire. "Next time it will not end like this," he promised. "Someday, *corazón*," he vowed, "you'll be my Queen of the Night."

IT WAS THE bloodcurdling roar that awakened Mama Luz; not the comforting howl of the coyotes starting off on their nightly hunt, nor even the demonic shriek of a prowling puma. She was so accustomed to these desert sounds that she always slept right through them. But the eerie rumble of the jaguar nagged at her subconscious mind and alerted her to danger.

She shook off the ghost of sleep, realizing that she'd dozed off again while in prayer; the rosary beads still lay in her hands. Her nightly prayers were always the same: prayers for those who were still with her, prayers for those who had gone on before...and prayers for

Nico, who was still among the living and yet, at times, seemed already dead.

Why do you not come to me? her heart cried out to her grandson, as it often did when the night was still. *I am old; my time is short. Do not let me die without seeing your beloved face; do not let me die before you cleanse yourself of your guilt and grief! Surely you know that I have forgiven you.*

The jaguar's roaring stopped for just a second, as though the spotted beast were tired and needed to draw a great breath. But his rest was brief, and a moment later the haunting rumble echoed once more from the canyon walls . . . for hours and hours, it seemed, without ceasing.

Mama Luz tried to ignore the threatening sound as she struggled to go back to sleep, but she could no more shut out the jaguar's roar than she could silence the tears in her heart.

"I'M GOING TO DRIVE today," Nick informed Kelley as they rumbled out of Hermosillo at dawn the next day. "This blacktop is only for show—it peters out in five or ten miles, and then we're on our own to Pitahaya."

He seemed pumped up, edgy, determined to get on with his mission as soon as possible. The shadows under his eyes assured Kelley that he'd slept even less than she had, a situation that she desperately hoped they'd be able to remedy tonight. Even if they couldn't sleep together—protocol in Cielo Solo might well forbid it— once Nick saw Liliana, surely everything would be okay between them, and that, Kelley was certain, would make all the difference in the world.

Today he was wearing his new sombrero, but it didn't do much to change his image as a tourist. Nor did the white cotton pants he'd bought the night before, though they outlined the firm muscles of his thighs so nicely that Kelley knew she wouldn't mind if he wore them all the time.

She was busy taking note of the homes along the highway—shacks made out of empty tin cans filled with mud—when Nick swerved sharply to avoid an ocotillo-stem fence that had spilled forward onto the road.

"And you think you can navigate this primitive terrain better than I can?" Kelley scoffed as she righted herself, sliding one hand over his thigh in a gesture that gentled her teasing.

"That's what you're paying me for, lady," he joked, weaving his fingers through hers as he slipped them to a safer spot on his knee. "A native's-eye view of the land."

"I'd hardly call this collection of potholes the *land*, Nick," Kelley said with a grin, realizing how much she enjoyed traveling with him now that they were openly sharing all their feelings. "It's an accident waiting to happen."

"It already has happened," he pointed out, gesturing with his chin, Mexican style, toward a pile of rocks near the side of the road. "That, my dear, was used as a jack by a driver who swerved to miss a goat or ran over a piece of jumping cholla that pierced his bald tires."

"I can see somebody using a pile of rocks as a jack, Nick, but why are they still there?"

Nick shot her a mock superior glance, then squeezed her hand. "Who do you think is going to move them, Kell? The government highway-maintenance crew?"

Kelley shrugged, feeling foolish. "Hermosillo is just so beautiful, Nick. The streets are so pretty—"

"Yes, I found the pigs particularly breathtaking."

"Nick!"

Nick laughed at his own pun. "Go ahead and make your point," he urged.

"My point," she began, levelling him with the pretense of a withering glare, "is that our hotel was more charming than anything in L.A. It's hard to believe that the roads this close to such a city could be so inferior to California highways."

He grinned. "If tourists with big bucks made regular runs to Pitahaya, Kelley, then somebody would probably form a local pothole-repair committee. But as it is, only a fool would traverse this road in anything but a junk heap like this one. And even so, chances are good we'll start the hiking part of our journey before we get halfway to Pitahaya."

Nick's prediction turned out to be excruciatingly accurate. They'd bounced along for less than twenty happy-go-lucky miles when Nick rounded a curve at a decent pace only to find a half-starved cow blocking the road three feet in front of him.

"Nick!" Kelley cried out instinctively as Nick swerved to avoid hitting the animal. She fell forward, banging her head against the dash just as some metal part of the car grated loudly over stone.

"Damn!" he swore as the car heaved to a stop. "Are you okay?"

Kelley nodded, glad that Nick hadn't been traveling very fast. She only had a slight bump on her head.

"Are you sure?"

"I'm sure. If I were hurt I'd tell you, Nick," she assured him. "I'm not proud."

Nick took a deep breath, then leaned across the seat to kiss her on the cheek. "I'm really sorry, Kelley. I've been so careful! For hours I've been steering around those rocks and ruts and now that damn cow—"

"Nick, it can't be helped," Kelley said, amazed at the animal's total indifference to the calamity she'd precipitated. The scrawny creature stared blankly at the black clunker straddling the sandy shoulder of the road, then shuffled a few feet to the right and started grazing. "We're not hurt and neither is the cow. So let's just go on our way and forget about it."

"Forget about it?" he parroted, frustration vibrant in his tone. "I suppose we should also forget about that grating sound we heard as we scraped over that massive rock?"

"Grating sound?"

"Yes, grating sound. The sound a mechanic often hears when a tie-rod's been bent or mangled."

"A tie-rod?" Kelley repeated uncertainly. "Is that something...important?"

He sighed melodramatically and rolled his eyes. "Good thing you hired a mechanic as your driver, lady. You might as well get out and talk to the cow. This might take awhile."

Kelley did as she was told, partly because she didn't want to get in Nick's way while he was fixing the car and partly because she was curious about the cow, who was busy munching on some grass she'd found growing between two small paloverde trees.

"So what's your story, old girl?" Kelley asked, wondering if the cow would let her get close enough to pat her. "How come you look so skinny?"

Her words were lost in the sound of a hammer pounding away at some portion of the car—rhythmically enough that Kelley was sure that repair, not revenge, was Nick's motivation. A moment later an anguished cry came from beneath the car and the hammering ceased abruptly.

"Nick!" Kelley shouted, racing back to the car. "Are you all right?"

He had crawled out from under the car and was lying on his back, mouth twisted in pain, moaning. Blood was running down on his chest from one of his clasped hands.

"Nico! What happened? What do you want me to do?" Even as the words gushed out, Kelley knew what he needed. Something to stop the bleeding, something to stop the pain.

She ran to the trunk of the car and unearthed a clean washcloth from her backpack. Nick didn't say much as she quickly wrapped it around his bleeding thumb, but at least he'd stopped moaning.

"Nick, get back in the car," she urged him. "I'll drive. I think we're still pretty close to Hermosillo."

"Forget it," he snapped, sweat beading his upper lip. "Nobody can drive that car. The tie-rod is beyond all hope."

"I don't care. I'll push it if I have to. You've got to have help!"

Just when her panic was about to escalate, Nick gently laid his good hand on her wrist. It was a quiet, soothing gesture that instantly drained away the worst of her fear.

"Kelley—" his eyes met hers as he managed a sickly smile "—it's not that bad. Sorry I shook you up. It was just a surprise, that's all." He unwrapped the blood-drenched washcloth to show her his hand, which was still red and now swelling. "Finger wounds bleed a lot, but they're usually not that serious. See? It's just a small cut. Probably doesn't even need stitches.''

The gash was two or three inches long, and Kelley had no doubt that it needed stitches very badly indeed. Still, she realized, her hysteria would be of little help to Nick. More calmly, she asked, "When did you have your last tetanus shot?"

He paused a moment, then answered, "Last year, I think. Maybe the year before."

"Or maybe the year before that? You really don't remember, do you?"

He ignored her as he wrapped up his bloody thumb again. "We were planning to start hiking in a few hours anyway, Kelley. We've got plenty of water in the car. Let's just hoist our packs and start moving."

"In which direction?"

He glared at her. "The direction we were going. It's not that far to Pitahaya."

"Is there a doctor in Pitahaya?"

Again he shrugged. "Beats me. We'll worry about that when we get there."

"I think we better worry about it now. If you stayed here while I went for help in Hermosillo—"

"Kelley, if I were at *death's door* I wouldn't let you hitch a ride to Hermosillo!" He swore in frustration— or maybe pain—then tightened the washcloth around his thumb again. "Let's just get moving, Kelley. No point in standing around in the sun."

Ignoring his words, Kelley found some Bactine and washed out the wound. But when she tried to wrap it up, she realized she needed to find a way to hold the skin together until Nick could get some stitches. An ordinary bandage just wouldn't do. "I know you're leery about this sort of thing," she suggested gingerly, "but Mama Chayo taught me that her people used prickly-pear skin as a bandage, with the pulp doctored up as a poultice. If I—"

"Not a chance." He cut her off briskly as he struggled, one-handed, with his backpack. This time his smile was clearly forced. "I'd sooner die."

"Oh, come on, Nick!" she pleaded. "It's just cactus flesh. You told me you eat the fruit of the prickly pear. It can't hurt."

"Kelley." His tone was black. "I said I'd sooner die."

On that grim note, they started out across the sand.

CHAPTER ELEVEN

BY THE TIME they reached the outskirts of Pitahaya, Nick was sweating profusely from the early afternoon heat as well as the pain. He was in good condition, and normally a two-hour desert hike wouldn't have fazed him, but the steady throbbing of his thumb made it difficult to carry on a cheerful conversation. He'd done his best to assure Kelley that there was nothing to worry about, even if there wasn't any competent medical care to be found in Pitahaya, but he knew she'd seen through his subterfuge.

"It doesn't look quite like downtown L.A.," was Kelley's only comment as they passed the familiar roll-down metal doors of a grocery, a liquor store and a *jerbero*, where healing herbs and magic potions could be purchased without a prescription. There was no pharmacy in sight, but Nick was relieved to discover a small government-run clinic. It was a rather primitive clapboard building, but the sign out front was freshly painted, and the empty waiting room was scrupulously clean.

So was the nurse who greeted them with a merry grin. Her nametag said Rosa Sumaran and her trim white uniform and matching squishy-soled shoes would have done her proud at any hospital in L.A.

"How may I help you?" she asked in slow, careful Spanish, as though she assumed that neither of the foreigners would be fluent in her tongue.

At the moment, Nick wasn't sure he remembered any Spanish at all, so he just unwrapped the makeshift bandage and showed her the three-inch gash along his thumb. It was Kelley who explained what had happened while Rosa prepared an ice pack and called the doctor. He was a handsome young man, black-haired, clean-shaven, with a firm handshake and a genuine smile. Although he spoke no English, his educated, articulate Spanish quickly put Nick at ease.

"We don't get too many visitors here," Dr. Ramirez commented cheerfully as he anesthetized the torn thumb. "Especially stragglers from St. Patrick's Battalion."

"Stragglers from *what*?" Nick questioned.

The doctor laughed. "St Patrick's Battalion. A group of Irish soldiers in the war between your country and mine in 1848." He winked at Kelley. "You know this story?"

Kelley looked bewildered. "No. I know that President Polk ignited a war over Texas and California so the United States could run a railroad to the Pacific. But as to Irish soldiers . . ." She shook her head.

"They were forced to stay together," he explained, "and were treated abysmally by the U.S. Army. By the time they got to Mexico, those redheaded, freckle-faced lads could see that they didn't have much to gain by fighting." He asked Rosa to hand him some instrument with an untranslatable name, then continued with his tale. "Well, one night when this group was exhausted from battle and freezing to death, the ladies in the nearest village discovered that all those soldier boys were Catholics. 'Why are we fighting our own kin?' they asked. So while the menfolk cleaned their weapons, the women crept out to the Irish camp with warm *tamales* and serapes.'' He winked at Kelley again. ''And stayed a while, I'll bet, to keep the boys company, though nobody ever admits to that.''

The thought of keeping Kelley warm was enough to stir Nick despite his pain, and he realized that he would have liked the doctor a lot better if he'd been old and bald. Nevertheless, he didn't think Dr. Ramirez was flirting with Kelley, a suspicion that was confirmed when he suddenly flashed his patient a smile and a bottle of pills. ''All finished. Take these every four hours until you don't need them for the pain.''

As Nick glanced down at his hand, he realized that the doctor had deliberately told his story to distract his patient until the stitching was done. That kind of bedside manner was a skill that medical schools couldn't hand out along with a degree.

Before Nick could thank him, Dr. Ramirez quickly gave him a tetanus shot while he finished his story. ''In the morning the skirmish was over. The entire battalion had mutinied in the night. The U.S. Army never found the men, because they promptly married the village girls and settled in Mexico. To this day you'll meet a redheaded Mexican now and again, or even one with freckles. It's my personal opinion that we owe this gift to the Irish.''

Kelley laughed out loud, then thanked the doctor for his story and his help.

''I can't tell you how glad I am to know you're here,'' Nick said. ''The last time I came through Pitahaya my only choice was a *curandero*. I'm glad that folks in this area finally have another option.''

At once the doctor's demeanor sobered. "Not an option that they've got much interest in," he admitted sadly. "You saw how crowded my waiting room is. And it's not that Pitahaya is a healthy town. The local *curandero* has people waiting in his neighbors' houses up and down the street." He shrugged unhappily. "Everybody goes to him first. Nobody comes to see me until he's emptied his whole bag of tricks, and by that time, it's often too late to do much good."

Kelley looked uneasy, and Nick had to admit that his personal triumph on this issue was dwarfed by the doctor's sobriety. It was one thing to win a point from Kelley—another thing to realize the pathetic implications of the strength of *curanderismo* in these remote villages.

"The Mexican government has done a wonderful job of putting up these clinics all over the country," Rosa pointed out, "but in many rural areas the people ignore them. And in one village, the *curandero* got everybody so worked up that they burned down the clinic and stoned the doctor to death. And that was only a dozen years ago!"

Kelley flushed, and after a strained silence she asked Dr. Ramirez, "I don't suppose you know too much about Opata medicine as opposed to regular Mexican *curanderismo*."

One eyebrow lifted skeptically. "Not really, but I doubt that it's much better. Why do you ask?"

She looked embarrassed. "I'm here in Sonora to do research on the Opatas' herbal medicine, Dr. Ramirez. Not the mumbo jumbo and superstition—just the plants."

"Are you a doctor?" he asked with renewed respect.

"No, a botanist."

Dr. Ramirez nodded. "Of course. Well, I wish I could help you, but I haven't had the time or—quite frankly—the inclination to learn much about *curanderismo*. I've got my hands full just trying to heal people and trying to teach them a little bit about preventive medicine and sanitation."

He handed Nick some odds and ends to change the dressing on his wound and prevent infection, then said to Kelley, "I wish you good luck on your research, *señorita*, but if you should have any need for a doctor while you're with the Opata, I urge you to send somebody for me. Don't take your chances with a *curandero*."

"You make house calls?" Nick asked, not certain if the joke translated well into Spanish. He expected the doctor to respond in kind with a suggestion that he might do anything for such a pretty lady, but to Nick's surprise the other man answered seriously, "I will go anywhere I am needed, *señor*. Anywhere they will let me heal people with real medicine instead of hocus-pocus."

Nick thanked him again, then ushered Kelley toward the waiting room. To his surprise, another American—a hard-looking fellow with bleeding hands and wrists—was making crude English demands on Rosa.

"I haven't got all day, sister!" he growled. "Can't you see I'm covered with jumping cholla spines? Hustle your fanny in there and get the doc!"

Rosa flinched as the man grabbed her arm, and Nick felt his protective instincts flaring. Normally he felt kinship with a fellow American in a strange land, but this bastard wasn't a tourist, a scientist or even a native son returning to his homeland... which only left some sort of business as justification for his time in this one-horse town. And there was nothing in Pitahaya worth buying or selling that could possibly be legal.

To Nick's relief, Dr. Ramirez spotted the situation from his vantage point in the main room of the clinic, and called out to his nurse, "Would you come here for a moment, Rosa?"

The pretty young nurse all but ran to his side, and the doctor laid a protective hand on her shoulder as he whispered, "Go stay in my office until he's gone." Then, in a low warning tone that carried only to Nick's ears, he said, "I can handle Rinsland; he has been here before. You will be wise to go out the other door." He glanced at Kelley, then at Rinsland, then back to Nick in a clear unspoken message: *Keep your woman away from this man if you hold her dear.*

"Thank you, we'll do that," Nick told him softly, grabbing Kelley's arm as he did an abrupt about-face to lead her out the way the doctor had indicated. He kept her moving after that, so quickly that she didn't even notice the wooden burro cart parked at the rear of the clinic.

But Nick did. He noticed the cart and he noticed the cargo inside, and he didn't want to think about Kelley's reaction if she'd seen what he had.

The cart was stacked to the top of its rickety walls with hundreds of tiny cacti.

LESS THAN TWO HOURS LATER, Kelley found herself once more on foot with Nick in the vastness of the Sonoran desert. They both realized that it would be impossible for them to reach Cielo Solo tonight, but after looking over the town's pitiful accomodations, they'd decided they'd rather take their chances with the desert's wildlife than the kind found in Pitahaya's only "hotel." Nick insisted that he felt fine now that he'd been stitched back together, and his eyes looked so much more clear and vibrant that Kelley was tempted to believe him.

They'd made arrangements for the car to be towed in and repaired before they returned to Pitahaya in three or four weeks. In the meantime they'd purchased a burro for transportation. He was a shaggy little fellow with enormous ears and an abrasive voice that reminded Kelley of a rusty hinge creaking in the wind. She dubbed him Maleta, Spanish for suitcase, which seemed only appropriate for a creature covered with notebooks, stacks of tiny paper bags for carrying herbarian samples, and her ungainly plant press. On top of that, four gallons of water—not nearly enough in the event they got lost and spent more than a couple of days in the desert—heavily burdened the small pack animal.

"Are you sure he's stronger than he looks?" Kelley asked, already feeling guilty as she watched the diminutive equine heave and sigh.

"Yes, he's fine." Nick scratched Maleta just behind the ears. "I'm the one with the problem."

Kelley cast a worried eye in his direction. "Is your thumb bothering you, Nico?"

He shook his head. "Not much. It's this damn bur sage. I told you I was allergic to it." He glared at the gray-green leaves, shaped like tiny gardener's trowels, which sprawled between the beavertail and rainbow cactus all around him. "I'll be rubbing my eyes till we get to the Opata country. Everything I've ever taken for it makes me sleepy."

"Have you ever tried wormwood or agave?" Kelley asked, knowing she was treading on thin ice. "Mama Chayo used to—"

"Kelley!" he warned, indulgent disapproval in his tone. "If we're going to start swapping native cure-alls, then it's time for me to cover your face with a mud pack. You look just as red as you do when you're embarrassed, and I think that means you've had entirely too much sun."

Kelley groaned.

"What's the matter? You don't like my idea?"

She shook her head. "It's a lousy idea, but I may not have any choice. I left the sunscreen in the car."

Nick rolled his eyes. "Use the water sparingly, Kelley, but take off your backpack and make some mud."

His tone was so serious that Kelley had to ask, "You are just pulling my hair, aren't you, Nick?"

He grinned at her discomfiture, but nevertheless he did look concerned. "You didn't bring me along as a fashion consultant, Kelley. I'm in charge of desert survival."

"But, Nick—"

"Just do it, Kelley." His eyes were laughing, but his tone was stern. "Just do it for me."

After that he seemed pretty cheerful as he walked beside a mud-faced Kelley in the springtime heat. Assured that Nick's injury was minor, she was actually enjoying the sense of being loose on foot among the saguaros, blending into the landscape like the roadrunners and jackrabbits that occasionally darted past her feet.

But her pleasure vanished the instant she spied a brightly banded snake dashing across her hiking boot.

"Nick!" she squawked, jumping toward him. "It's a coral snake!"

Instantly Nick grabbed her. "Did it bite you? Did it touch you at all?" He said the words as though he were ready to cut open her skin and suck the venom out with his mouth.

"No," she gasped in relief. "He just crossed my boot and—"

She stopped, outraged, when Nick began to laugh. He pointed toward the tip of red slithering under a turpentine bush and asked, "Is that it? Your terrifying coral snake?"

Kelley straightened indignantly. "I know it's little, Nick, but that has nothing to do with the intensity of the venom. I read that—"

"Did you read how to tell a harmless *coralillo* from a coral snake?" He smiled while he asked the question, then laughed out loud again. This time she realized that relief, rather than ridicule, marked the tone of his voice.

"I know they've got red and black bands around their bodies."

"And tiny white stripes, too. But this fellow has a completely different pattern from a coral snake: red, black, red and no white at all. The bands don't even cross his belly. He's utterly harmless." He grinned at her. "And kind of cute, actually."

"Cute?" she retorted, deciding that he'd had enough fun at her expense. "How do you tell a cute whatever-it-is from a deadly coral snake?"

"*You* probably don't," he suggested indulgently. "And I'm not at all sure I can explain it to you any better than that. But there are a lot of coral snake lookalikes in the desert—milk snakes, shovelnoses, even file tails look similar in the dark.''

Kelley put both hands on her hips. ''And I suppose you can tell them all apart.''

He shrugged. ''Of course. I was an eight-year-old boy here, Kelley. I never went anywhere without a toad or a snake or a lizard in my pocket. In fact, just a few minutes ago I picked up a—''

''Nick!'' she warned as he held out his balled-up good hand, then opened it to reveal an empty palm. ''That wasn't funny,'' she insisted, unable to mask her smile.

He laughed and moved closer to ruffle her hair. ''Seriously, Kelley, you're wise to assume everything's dangerous here unless I tell you otherwise. There's a cute little gecko lizard that lives out here and squeaks in the most entrancing way—if you're a kid, that is— that bears an unnerving similarity to a baby gila monster. The gecko is harmless, but the gila monster's as poisonous as the beaded lizard, so you've got to learn the difference.''

''Why didn't we have this reptile lesson before we left L.A.?'' Kelley asked, growing increasingly uneasy as she realized they'd be sleeping on the ground tonight.

''Because you've got me; you don't need a field identification book. It's all coming back to me, Kell. I told you it would.''

She smiled but made no comment. What a contradiction he was! He insisted that the desert held no warmth of homecoming for him, yet it was obvious that with every step closer to Cielo Solo he was more at ease with the land of his youth.

Kelley tried not to think about what would happen once they reached their destination. Instead she focused on a vision of a tiny Nico Morales, barefoot and shirtless, giggling as he tickled a spotted lizard and hopped after a spadefoot toad. To her surprise, the vision moved her deeply. It was not until he spoke again that she realized why.

She wasn't thinking of Nick as a child. In her mind's eye she was seeing his son. Her son. Their baby.

She brushed away the foolish notion along with a ludicrous tear, then focused determinedly on Nick's recitation of desert animal life as they continued walking. He kept her entertained for about an hour, then gradually grew silent as the sun started to lower in the sky. It seemed to Kelley that his expression was entirely too grave, and his steps grew ever more slow and ponderous. Finally she asked, "Are you sure that you're okay, Nick?"

"I'm fine." His tone was grim. "But I'm not so sure my people are. Have you looked at the saguaros, Kell? On the way to Pitahaya I was hurting too much to notice, but out here it's obvious that this area hasn't had more than a drop of rain in two or three years."

Kelley knew what he meant. In Tucson the taut skin of the saguaros made them look sleek and fat, but here the accordion pleats hung in heavy folds. "I'm sure that Cielo Solo has weathered dry spells before, Nick," she pointed out gently. He made no comment, but his eyes were trained so intently on the landscape that Kelley had to ask again, "What is it, Nick? What's wrong?"

He fanned his sweaty face with his hat as he replied glumly, "I can't find the saguaro I'm looking for, Kelley. Cielo Solo's 'lighthouse,' as it were. We're still half a day out but I ought to be able to spot it by now, especially when we're on a rise. I know we were heading in the right direction when we left Pitahaya, but none of this looks familiar anymore." Impatiently he tugged on the medal at his neck. "Of course the land is so damn chongered up that I can only guess what might have been here before."

"Chongered up?" Kelley echoed. "What do you mean?" She stopped abruptly as her glance fell on the ground beneath her feet. Concentrating on her heavy pack, Nick's enticing walk and the swaying load of the burro, Kelley hadn't really noticed too much about her surroundings since they'd left Pitahaya. Now, quite suddenly, she realized that the rocky ground was a maze of tiny divots where small plants should have been. The crazy quilt of cactus that had recently cloaked this area had been ripped out by its roots, leaving the impression of a moonscape with hundreds of eerie holes in lieu of natural vegetation.

"Nico," she said slowly. "Nick, what on earth—"

"Rape. The land has been raped." His terse tone stunned her. She'd expected sympathy, perhaps, since Nick knew that cactus devastation mattered to her; indifference, maybe, since Nick claimed to have no use for the desert. But anger—no, outrage—was a response she hadn't counted on.

"It's probably Rinsland, that bastard in town!" he all but snarled. "His burro cart was full of cacti. Full of my—" He broke off abruptly and increased his pace. "He had no right," he muttered darkly. "No right at all."

Confused by his comment about Rinsland, Kelley asked, "You saw uprooted cactus plants in his cart, Nick? Why didn't you say something? We need to go back and report him."

"To whom? The local gendarmes? Forget it, Kelley. If Dr. Ramirez can't have him arrested, what do you think we can do? Unless we've got a kidnapping or a murder to report, the Mexican cops couldn't care less. They've got enough to worry about."

"But Nick, it's illegal to collect endangered cacti from the wild. You heard what Bill said about—"

"About the botany professor who got killed because he stuck his neck out for a saguaro?" Nick stopped, wheeling to face Kelley so abruptly that poor Maleta smacked his soft nose into Nick's hard thigh. "You can't do anything for the desert, Kelley. All you can do is risk your life getting tangled up with that guy. He probably can't make a living just smuggling cactus, you know. He's probably running drugs or guns or cramming desperate illegals into the trunk of his car and abandoning them somewhere in the desert. Why do you think Dr. Ramirez sent Rosa to his office and hustled us out the back door?"

Kelley was silent, trying to assimilate his words. He was right, she knew, but the whole thing was just so...wrong. So seamy.

"It isn't right, Nick. If this guy really is involved with so many other terrible things, that's all the more reason he should be apprehended."

"Believe me, Kell, nobody would be happier than I would to see Rinsland put away. But let somebody else do it...a professional who knows how to deal with his type. Somebody who can find enough evidence to link him to a crime."

"Isn't this enough evidence?" she demanded, gesturing to the desecrated desert in outrage. "It'll be years before new plants ever grow here again! And if he's doing this sort of thing all over this part of Sonora—''

"Kelley, you *think* he's responsible for this, but you can't prove it. Besides, he doesn't do the digging himself. He probably even has a Mexican go-between contact for the plants. The locals are the ones who go out collecting, for five or ten cents a plant, and none of them are going to risk their family's safety by doing anything to cross a guy like Rinsland."

"But this is their home! How can they do this?"

"Kelley!" This time Nick's anger seemed to have turned on her. "Cacti is the only thing Sonoran peasants have a surplus of, except for sunbeams. It's of no use to them whatsoever, but a handful of centavos can mean the difference between a baby starving to death and struggling through one more year. What would you do in their position?"

She didn't answer right away. Put so starkly, the tiny cactus plants didn't seem quite so vital. Still, she couldn't help but ask him, "Doesn't it make them angry to see their beautiful home torn up like this? Doesn't it make *you* angry to see what they've done to your home?"

Nick studied the ground and took a very long time to answer. "I don't have a right to be angry. I don't have a right to call this home." He took a deep breath, then finished, "To tell you the truth, for a while there, in Arizona, I did feel like I was coming home. I even got a little bit excited. But ever since that vendor in Hermosillo spelled things out for me, I've felt even more out of place in Mexico than I'd expected to."

Kelley slipped her hand into the crook of his arm. "I know you're not entirely at ease here, Nick, but that doesn't mean that this part of the world isn't still terribly important to you. Otherwise I don't think you'd be so upset that Rinsland violated your desert.''

A slow, sunny smile washed the weariness from his face as he pondered Kelley's words. He traced one sensitive ear with a strong, warm finger, then gently tugged on a lock of red hair. "Oh, there's something in this desert that's still terribly important to me, Kelley,'' he confessed. "Something with green eyes and red hair and a lot more courage than common sense. But Rinsland hasn't violated it yet, and I intend to keep it that way.''

He leaned down to kiss her, and the sweet kiss lasted far longer than the moment called for. Kelley couldn't stop herself from savoring the flavor of his hunger as he took her in his arms. It felt so right to lean against him; so natural to listen to the matched thudding of their hearts. Last night she'd revelled in Nick's embrace, but the public streets had dampened her ardor. Tonight there would be no one to get in the way.

Nick did not break off the kiss until Maleta's switching tail slapped his injured hand. Even then his eyes did not leave her.

"We're going to be alone out here all night, Kelley.''

"I know." Her voice was no more than a sigh.

"I'm not sure I know the right answer to how we ought to spend this time together.''

"Neither am I.''

Still holding her gently, Nick looked far away, where the distant hills were already washed in the first shades of an orange and purple sunset. "The only thing I'm sure of, *corazón*, is that whatever our decision turns out to be, we need to make it together, and we need to make it sanely—" the magic of his touch rebuffed his logic "—in the light of day."

"NICK, DO YOU SMELL that aroma?" Kelley asked as they made camp shortly after dark. "Is that the Queen of the Night?"

He sniffed the air, then shook his head. "I'm sorry, I don't smell anything. I never could until the flowers were practically under my nose. Liliana always—"

"If you don't mind, could we get through just one evening without discussing her? I don't suppose you realize it, but she's been with us on every date we've ever had."

Nick didn't reply. He couldn't deny that Liliana had always been with them, any more than he could pretend that every business meeting and casual meal, even their phone calls, had been preliminary steps in the inevitable dance of love. And Liliana, always, had been waiting for him . . . watching from the shadows.

"Once you've smelled it you're not likely to forget the scent," he informed Kelley, deciding that the tantalizing scent of the nocturnally blooming cactus was a safer topic than Liliana. "If you want to go look—"

"Of course I want to go look! I've seen a Queen of the Night, but I've never been lucky enough to catch one in bloom. If you want to scout around—"

"If *I* want to scout around? Lady, there are centipedes out there the size of my arm and *coralillos* and scorpions and heavens knows what."

"Nico!" she chided him. "You're supposed to be the expert here. The rough-and-ready tour guide. At least that's what you're getting paid for."

He laughed. "If I'm getting paid to go hunting cactus flowers in the dead of night, maybe we better renegotiate my contract."

"Fine," Kelley readily agreed, hopping to her feet as she dusted off her jeans. "But let's go hiking first and negotiate later. Whatever that scent is, somebody ought to bottle it and sell it on the open market."

"Is that what you're going to do if I reveal this desert secret to you, Dr. McKinney?" he teased. "Or maybe pluck it from its roots to zap it into your plant press?"

She grinned. "There's hope for you, Morales. You're starting to think like a botanist."

"Lord help me," he groaned, getting up to follow Kelley.

Her excitement was contagious, her beauty irresistible. She'd spent a lot of time getting the mud off her face, but she still had one beguiling streak on her forehead. There was a bounce in her step as she all but skipped over the desert sand, and joy lifted Nick's heels an inch higher than usual, as well. The saltbrush and creosote were really too thick here to do much skipping, but Nick could hardly bring himself to restrain her enthusiasm. He loved to see her happy, and he loved to see her breasts sway ever so lightly when she walked.

In fact, by this time he realized that he loved just about everything about his Irish leprechaun. He was smitten, badly smitten, and he was glad that he'd given up trying to conceal his true feelings from Kelley. He knew it was dangerous to forget the reasons he needed to keep his distance, but tonight, for some reason, he couldn't bring himself to care.

"Kelley, slow down!" he ordered when her quick pace caused him to trip over a spiny branch of a creeping devil. "I'm the guide, even if I am bringing up the rear, and I'm telling you this is not a good pace for night hiking."

She chuckled. "I thought you didn't hike in Sonora. I thought—"

She halted abruptly as the distant snarl of a big cat rent the silence of the night. Instinctively Nick grabbed her from behind and they both stood perfectly still as the demoniac call was repeated three or four times. Even when silence reclaimed the foothills, the eerie echo persisted in his mind.

"How far away do you suppose he is?" Kelley whispered.

"Three or four miles by the sound of it," he assured her, neglecting to mention how fast a puma could run in the night. "But pumas are scared of people, Kelley. We've got nothing to fear."

"No?" she challenged him shakily. "Then why are you holding on to me so tight?"

He grinned and dropped a slow, thorough kiss on the side of her neck. "I like holding on to you. I like it a lot."

For a moment she leaned back against him, arching her neck so he could continue his sultry seduction. Still standing behind her, Nick slipped both arms around her waist until they met just below her breasts. He kissed her neck again, then spread his hands until the tips of his fingers slipped up ever so provocatively to cup her woman's fullness.

"Oh, Nico," she breathed, lifting her arms above her shoulders to cradle his head and give him greater access. "We decided not to do this." She trembled as his palms brushed across her nipples for the very first time. "Didn't we?"

His own arousal threatening to undo him, Nick pulled her closer as he groaned, "Does that mean you want me to stop?"

She didn't answer, but she made no move to block his hands as they tantalized her curves. She was breathing hard as she repeated, "You said we needed to decide together in the light of day." His hands froze as she finished shakily, "It's already dark, Nico."

He heard the hesitation in her voice, and a bell of warning started ringing in his head. It was bad enough if one of them was unsure; if they both had reservations, logic cried out for them to hold on to reason for one more night.

Somehow Nick managed to release her, but he hadn't taken a single step away from Kelley before a coyote serenade began to rock the night.

"Tell me you're scared," he whispered. "Tell me you want me to hold you. Tell me—"

Abruptly she turned around, her eyes huge in the moonlight as she asked boldly, "Are you sure, Nick? When you look at me, is Kelley McKinney really all you see?"

"Yes," he said simply. It was the truth.

"And tomorrow—when you see Liliana for the first time in nineteen years—will I still be the only one you hold in your heart?"

He struggled for an answer that was honest and safe, but such a paradox did not exist, so he compromised. "I think so, Kelley," he murmured. "But I can't swear it. There's just no way for me to know."

For a moment he held her compelling gaze, then broke away when the coyotes once more began to howl.

It was an eerie sound, but as Nick listened to the or-
chestrated voices, he realized that he'd missed this
·mighty desert serenade, missed it terribly, and he very
much wanted to share it with Kelley.

But Kelley was in no mood to share anything with
him. Crushed by his last response, she turned back toward a likely specimen of *la reina de la noche* and asked
bravely, "Shall we . . . carry on?"

Nick didn't want to carry on, at least in the way Kelley had in mind. He wanted nothing more in this world
than the right to pull her closer and finish what they'd
started.

For an instant Kelley didn't move, as though she
were contemplating the same intoxicating notion, but
when Nick made no move to stop her, she started to
walk again, picking her way through the bur sage with
greater care than before.

"That's it," Nick declared a few moments later.

"What?"

"That's it. Queen of the Night in bloom. I can smell
it now."

"Oh, Nico!" she gasped. "How far would you guess
it is?"

"If I can smell it, we're pretty close. Just flash the
lantern till you see white flowers."

It only took a few seconds for Nick to spot the spin-
dly cactus, waving its long, white blossoms at him as
though it were an old friend. He wondered why the
sight of it should make him feel nostalgic.

"Kell," he whispered. "Over here on my right."

In an instant Kelley was on her knees beside the
Queen, drinking in its scent like a supplicant before a
statue. Her beauty, her womanly innocence, magne-

tized Nick. He watched her smile like a mother cradling a child.

"She's so exquisite, Nico," she breathed, using a feminine reference to the plant like his grandmother always did. "There's nothing quite like her, is there?"

Quietly he knelt down beside her, unable to keep from slipping both arms around her waist. "No, there isn't," he concurred. "She is without question the most beautiful sight I've ever seen."

Slowly Kelley turned to meet his gaze, realizing that he wasn't talking about the cactus. At the same moment, Nick was struck by the thought that nothing else mattered now. He'd wanted this woman north of the border, no less than he wanted her south. He wanted her more than he'd ever wanted anything in his life.

To hell with Liliana, his eyes promised her. *Tonight there's only you and me.* This time he didn't give Kelley a chance to escape; he wrapped both arms around her and clung to her fiercely as his lips found hers. Instantly her mouth opened to him, her tongue as warm and searching as his own, her eagerness calling out to him in the quivering arms entwined around his neck.

Without hesitation his healthy hand crept up from her waist to claim the valley between her breasts, and the tiny gasp from Kelley told him that her fierce desire mirrored his own. He pressed against her, suddenly starved for her loving, and he would have pulled her down to the softness of the desert sand but for the sudden rustling in the nearby brush and sage.

Abruptly she stiffened, fear, not regret, taking hold of her lithe form. "What do you think it is?" she whispered, as though some hidden lizard or snake were watching.

"Anything," he answered honestly, suffused by a sobering memory of the red velvet ants and giant orange centipedes they'd spied earlier in the day. Prodded by the sound, reason reminded him that the ground was littered with jumping cholla stems and countless tiny thorned relations. This was not the place to give in to his passions . . . if, indeed, he was reckless enough to give in to them tonight at all.

By mutual consent they rose and headed back to the campsite, not touching, not speaking, as the time for sanity returned.

But Nick knew he was long past reason; his decision was firmly made. Yet he knew that he couldn't press Kelley when she was the one with so much more to lose. Tonight he ached for her with every fiber of his being—more, it seemed to Nick, than he had ever ached for Liliana. But he couldn't vouch for his feelings in the morning, when dawn could replace his nocturnal joy with guilt and shame.

She was silent as they returned to their makeshift campsite. She didn't touch the plant press or even her canteen; she just set the lantern down next to the matched pair of sleeping bags that were still rolled up in the sand.

As he watched her quiet grace, she unrolled hers first, and checked it for tiny crawlers. Then, before Nick could stop her, she opened his bag too, shook it out, opened the zipper and laid it flat. A moment later she'd zipped the two bags together. Taking off her boots, she slipped inside.

Trembling with the need to hold her, Nick longed to ask if she was afraid of the puma they'd heard in the distance; longed to ask if her sleep might be troubled by lizards and snakes. But when she patted the flannel lining softly, he knew there were no more questions that Kelley needed to ask him…and none left that she would make him answer. At least not tonight.

He didn't say a word as he climbed into the sleeping bag beside her. Her eyes were shining with unspoken love for him; her lips moist and parted with desire. In the twinkling silence of the night, he simply laid one gentle hand on her face in mute invitation, then waited while she snuggled closer.

Her breath was sweet and warm against his neck; the lash of her tongue unbearably erotic as it teased the inner secrets of his ear. He felt her silken hands slide over his shoulders, pulling him closer; then her fingers urgently plucked at his medal, his curly chest hair, and the buttons of his shirt.

Overcome with a wave of tenderness that surpassed anything he'd ever felt before, Nick closed his eyes and buried his face in Kelley's crinkly red hair. "Oh, Kell," he whispered, the words as soft as a Sonoran breeze at sundown. "I want you so much!"

Her answer was a sweet, hungry kiss that promised him everything he'd ever longed for. Quickly now, she wrapped her arms around him, pressing her body along his entire length with an urgency that belied the patient distance she'd struggled to maintain all day. In that instant the mood between them changed; the kindling laid by the evening's furtive touches burst into full flame.

Nick crushed Kelley to his chest, his knee covering her thighs as he surged yet closer. He rolled halfway on top of her, his hands slipping swiftly over the softness of her T-shirt as she moaned her pleasure, revelling in his brazen touch. Urgently he pushed the hem of the shirt up around her neck, then trapped one turgid nip-ple with his thumb and index finger, teasing it ever so provocatively while he plundered her mouth with his tongue.

He cursed his bandaged hand as he struggled to unzip her jeans, but suddenly Kelley was helping him, shedding her own clothes and all but tearing off his drawstring cotton pants as she feverishly cried out his name. When there was nothing more to keep his burning flesh from touching hers, he took her mouth again with a fierce, possessive kiss. He covered her bare breasts with the palms of his hands and rolled them in tantalizing, erotic circles.

He knew he should have waited longer before he straddled her, but they had started and stopped too many times already, and her urgency only heightened his own frenzy. This was Kelley, *his* Kelley, and nothing that happened between them could ever be wrong.

Her warm, searching fingers skied down his back to cup his hips and pull him closer; she arched to meet him as he pinned her in the bag, trembling with volcanic desire as she wrapped her legs around him, wordlessly urging him to meld their two bodies into one.

"Oh, Nico," she moaned, her fingers fiercely entwined in his hair. "I want you now. Don't make me wait another second!"

He didn't. While the coyotes sang their love songs and the cactus blossoms did their part, Nick claimed Kelley as his woman, and she clung to him as though her life had just begun.

CHAPTER TWELVE

THE LYRICAL CALL of a canyon wren signaled the on-set of dawn for Kelley. Wrapped in passion, sur-rounded by joy, she knew it would be a pristine morning even before she opened her eyes and spotted Nick a dozen yards away on the top of a bushy knoll.

Her desire for him flared anew as she remembered the power of their merging. She could still feel his arms around her, still feel the tenderness of his kisses, the fierce passion that had taken her by storm. Any doubts she'd had about their future had vanished in the night. Misty purple fingers of sunrise only hinted at the promise of the new day, but Kelley's heart was already bathed in brilliant sunshine.

But when Nick turned to face her, the sky seemed to turn gray. His beautiful brown eyes were full of sor-row, she was certain, full of regret. Regret for the night that had been the absolute zenith of her life.

A rapier thrust of pain stabbed Kelley, hacking down the foundation of her short-lived hope. Behind the grief came the anguish of her own myopic folly. Nick had warned her. Oh, how many times, in how many ways, had he warned her! Yet she'd pushed ahead blindly, letting her love for him and her naive faith in their future short-circuit all her common sense. How could she have lied to herself? How could she have pretended that she'd fill up Nick's heart so completely that there wouldn't be room left for the memory of a woman who'd held him spellbound for nineteen years?

She wanted to close her eyes and weep—or run blindly back to Pitahaya so fast that she'd never have to see him again. But Nick was hiking toward her now, mouth straight and severe, and there was nothing to do but face him with all the courage she could muster.

"Good morning, Kell," he said gently, sitting down on the sleeping bag a few inches from her side. "I finally found the landmark saguaro I was looking for. With any luck at all, we'll reach Cielo Solo in a few hours."

Kelley swallowed hard. "That's great, Nick," she lied. "I guess your instincts weren't too off base after all."

The dark look he shot her told Kelley that he'd misinterpreted her comment, but all he said was, "I told you it would all come back to me sooner or later. I've been up for hours now, listening to the night sounds and watching the sun get up." His expression softened. "I know where I am, Kelley. I know I'm almost home."

She wanted to say she was glad for him; she wanted to rejoice that he was finding some inner peace. But the look on his face was anything but peaceful. Anguish laced his tender touch as he took her hand and laid it softly against his unshaven face, then turned to kiss her palm.

"Kelley, I won't insult you by apologizing for last night. I wanted you, you wanted me, and it was—" he shook his head as if the memory still awed him "—it was beyond words, *corazón*. It was . . . nearly magic."

Sudden tears flooded Kelley's eyes. How could he be so sweet and push her away at the same time! And he *was* going to push her away. She could see it in his eyes.

Before he got the chance, Kelley sat up and threw her arms around him. She kissed his stubbly cheek and pressed her face against the warmth of his neck. She tossed away her pride and let her love for him triumph over fear. "Don't tell me you still have doubts about her, Nick! Talk to her, apologize if you were wrong, but let it be. It's over! It's in the past." She pulled back to watch his face, then kissed him once, in tender pleading, before she wept, "*I'm* your future, Nico, not Liliana. Surely you know that by now! Don't throw it all away out of guilt for something you probably didn't even do!"

Nick hugged her tightly, rocking her softly in the still morning air. Far away, as if in a dream, Kelley caught a glimpse of a pair of white-tailed deer grazing on the sparsely bushed hillside, and above them a red-tailed hawk circled low, then glided down to the comforting arm of the saguaro that cradled its bulky nest. The sight was so perfect, so serene, it was hard to imagine that any human discord could ever destroy it.

Yet Nick's next words did exactly that.

"Kelley, I want you," he vowed. "You know that. And I think I'm going to want you for a very long time." He kissed her ear, then her temple, where his warm lips lingered as his tone grew soft. "But it'll never be quite right between us if I leave this job undone. Whatever happens, I've got to see this through. I've got to see Liliana, spend time alone with her, follow this trail wherever it leads."

Kelley pulled back from him sharply, tears clouding her vision of the man she'd so foolishly allowed herself to love. "Where do you expect it to go, Nico? Back to your old life in Sonora? To her bed on a dirt floor in South Tucson? Or to your world in L.A. where she'd stick out like a sore thumb for the rest of her life?"

"I don't know, Kelley! I just don't know! Can't you understand that?" His voice was raw, aching, and though she tried to pull farther away from him, he still gripped her shoulders with loving strength. "I don't want it to go anywhere. I just want to leave her here this time when I go back home! I don't want my conscience crippled by the thought of her for the next fifty years!"

"And how long will I burden your conscience, Nick?" Kelley demanded. He looked so stricken, so surprised, that it took all her strength of will not to crumple back against him. "Will you even remember my name a month from now?"

He kissed her then, as if to silence the hurtful words. But it was an angry kiss, and it lacked the potent mystery they'd shared the night before.

"It's too late for that!" Kelley cried out as she pushed herself to her feet.

"Kelley, come on!" Nick pleaded, visibly shaken as he jumped up after her. "Don't punish me for telling you the truth! Would you rather I lie to you?"

"I'd rather you stop lying to yourself, Nick, and then you could be honest with me! There's no point in postponing the inevitable. You've already made your choice." Before he could defend himself, she finished stoutly, "And I've already spent far too much time as Liliana's understudy. If I can't have the starring role, I want no part of this play."

SEVERAL HOURS LATER, Nick stood looking up at the giant saguaro for the first time in nineteen years. It had grown another arm or two—one of them seemed to be beckoning to him—and two branches near the bottom had collapsed against the trunk. Still, it was the cactus of his dreams, the one that had always called to him, and he would have known it if he'd stumbled across it in Yellowstone Park or New York.

Kelley stopped to stand beside him in its spike of shade. It wasn't that hot yet, and neither one of them was all that tired, but the saguaro was a signpost, a turning point in their journey, and it seemed too monumental to pass by without a reverent pause.

Kelley said nothing as she studied the massive cactus. In fact, Kelley had said very little since their early-morning spat, and Nick couldn't really say that he blamed her. From her point of view, he was either a cruel bastard or an unscrupulous playboy; either way, he'd taken her sincerest offering of love and suggested he might take her up on it if he didn't get a better offer by nightfall. He'd opted for the truth, knowing that honesty was the best policy, but now, in retrospect, he realized that he might have dealt their fledgling relationship a blow from which it could never recover.

"Please don't give up on me, Kelley," he implored her, gazing beyond the saguaro to the bushy knoll that was all that stood between the two of them and Cielo Solo. "And don't make me regret that I told you the truth. I know you're angry, but these next few minutes are terribly important to me."

When Kelley didn't answer, Nick took her hand, but she allowed the healing touch for only an instant before she stepped away. He stared at her, feeling hurt and helpless, but Kelley looked singularly unrelenting.

Across the desert stillness came the sound of voices—village voices—children laughing, women chatting, a man calling out a command. *Is that my uncle José?* Nick ached to discover. *My grandmother, my aunt, one of a dozen cousins whose faces I'll never forget?* Trembling in dread and anticipation, he took confidence from the certain knowledge that he was finally going to make things right.

"I won't embarrass you in front of your family, Nick," Kelley said quietly, her eyes meeting his for just a second. "Quite frankly, I'm still too mad at you to feel very supportive, but I'd never do anything to hurt you on purpose. Any hard feelings we might have between us will be kept under lock and key as long as we're in the public eye; that much I promise you."

Deeply moved by her compassion, Nick reached out to rub her shoulders, tense with the sting of his betrayal, and was rewarded with a poorly stifled sigh. "And any hard feelings that we might have between us will be cleared up as soon as I see Liliana, *corazón*," he vowed. "That much I promise *you*.

Kelley blinked and looked away, but she didn't try to dislodge his hands. He lowered his head to kiss her cheek, and for just a moment, it seemed to Nick that she took comfort from his loving gesture. Then she tugged on the burro's lead a little harder than necessary and took a step past the saguaro, expecting Nick to follow.

For a moment he stood rooted, unable to take the last few steps of this awesome journey. First he looked at Kelley, then at the knoll beyond her, where the answers to his past and the key to his future surely lay. And then he looked up to the very top of the fifty-foot saguaro, which had waited so many years for his return.

Nick felt a sudden urge to respond to the unspoken greeting, to shake the hand of the sentinel that had guarded his hometown and kept his people safe while he'd been away. He took a step closer, to touch the wind-scarred skin of the giant...and to reclaim his place in this remote corner of the land he called Sonora.

As soon as he laid his hand against the dull-edged spines of the towering saguaro, Nick knew that he'd come home.

Mama Luz was just pulling down the flat *comal* from the wall to start her midday baking when the first shrill voice reached her ears. *"¡Alguien viene!"* she heard Liliana's oldest son holler as the children gathered near the prickly-pear fence that marked the gateway to Cielo Solo. "Somebody's coming! Somebody's out there... coming this way!"

As always, the words pierced her grandmother's heart with a flare of short-lived hope. It was rare that they had a visitor to the village, especially one who was unexpected. Each time it happened she allowed herself one glorious moment of relief, one peaceful glimmer of the sunshine she knew that she'd feel in her heart on the day that Nico would come home. Ever since Meleseo had died, she'd been sure that her grandson would join them soon. *Why not today?* she asked herself. *It is long past time for him to come.*

"It is two men...or perhaps a woman and a man," sharp-eyed Carmelita declared as Mama Luz hurried to join her by a clump of teddy-bear cholla. "Both wear *pantalones*, but the little one is not so strong as the first. That man knows the desert. He moves as though he knows the trail.''

''Impossible,'' Liliana's mother pointed out, wrinkling her nose in disbelief. ''If he knew our land, then we would know him.''

''Then he must be one of our own,'' José concluded, joining the others as they stood and watched. He smothered a cough, then suggested, ''He has been gone awhile, perhaps.''

Carmelita nodded in assent, then laid one hand on her husband's arm. ''Who is still gone besides Nico? Your cousin Javier lives in Tamaulipas, and his wife died many years ago.''

José nodded, then glanced at another man who said, ''My oldest boy is not due from Chihuahua until summer, and Lorenzo Barajas is too old to move so fast.''

''Look,'' Mama Luz whispered, her eyes still trained on the pair. ''They are stopping.'' Although she had waited like this many times before, only to be crushed with disappointment, she couldn't still the beating of hope in her chest. Nico would be a man by now; at a distance, he would not look much like the young boy she had loved. Still, if this traveler would just come closer, perhaps, perhaps, perhaps . . .

''Listen!'' José gasped in wonder as a familiar sound skipped across the desert landscape. ''That cannot be!''

It was a whistle, like the call of a gilded flicker in flight, the Morales men's message code to one another since time immemorial. Every family in the village had a whistle of its own for the men to use for quick and safe identification in any uneasy setting; but Mama Luz knew that nobody from Cielo Solo would ever use this sound that her beloved late husband had taught his boys but another Morales man.

"Nico!" Mama Luz gasped as the low whistle came again, certain that her failing ears had not deceived her. *"¡Es mi nieto! ¡Les dijo que iba a venir!"*

If she'd been blind she would have been certain now; but her eyes did not shortchange her, nor did her ancient legs as she began to run for the first time in years. Her long braids flapped loose as tears crept from her blinking eyes, then began to stream down her face and into the brisk morning wind as she stumbled across the desert sand.

"Mama Luz!" Carmelita called out after her. "Don't be crazy!"

José's urgent tone seconded his wife's. "Come back here before you fall, Mama! It can't be Nico! And even if it is..."

She could hear no more, because her ears—indeed every one of her senses—were now trained on the two desert travelers who seemed to be crawling toward her so slowly that it looked as though they had come to a stop. Yes, they *had* stopped. Stopped completely. The burro had even ceased to flick his tail.

Now the man in front was staring at Mama Luz as though she were a vision in a dream or a nightmare that had no end. He stood as still and strong as the huge saguaro that guarded the hilly space behind him, signaling to all who would intercede that he was finally safe within the walls of the family fort.

And then, as she had dreamed it a thousand times, a boyish gasp of hope and joy broke forth from the young man, and the stranger shed his heavy burden— the one on his back and the one in his heart—and ran the last few yards to catch her fiercely in his arms.

WHEN NICK THREW DOWN his backpack, Kelley started
to cry. She hadn't planned to, hadn't really intended to
feel anything beyond the hurt and anger that had
gripped her since Nick's excruciating rejection at dawn.
But the minute his ancient grandma had started to run
across the sandy desert floor, her pain had disappeared.

Oh, Nico, forgive me, Kelley whispered in her heart.
I finally understand.

And she did understand, in a way she never had before. It wasn't Liliana, the other woman, who had
gripped her sensitive lover with such fierce guilt for all
these years. It was this woman, this dear old lady with
snow-white braids and tears streaming down her face,
whom he'd so cruelly betrayed; this one to whom he
could never justify his long abandonment. Once he
made his peace with her, Kelley was certain, his Liliana guilt would disappear.

Nick and his grandmother clung together without
regard for the cacophonous crowd that had gathered
around them. The sobbing old woman clutched his
head, stroking his thick black hair and his unshaven
face, patting his shoulders over and over again as
though she couldn't believe the solid muscle that now
proclaimed him a man. Nick hugged her so hard that
Kelley was afraid the dear old thing would break, but
she held her tongue and tried, without success, to block
the outpouring of emotion on her own face.

By now the group was starting to gather around
Kelley, too. Still leading the burro, she stood perfectly
still about ten yards behind Nick, and tried not to stare
back at the awestruck children who surrounded her. It
was clear by their wide eyes and disbelieving smiles that
they found her somewhat of an oddity, which Kelley

suspected had more to do with her red hair and mud-streaked white skin than the fact that she'd arrived with Nick.

She tried to smile back, to show she was a friendly oddity, but the sudden change in Nick's demeanor had thrown her off-balance, as had her own profoundly emotional response to his homecoming.

Finally Nick released his grandmother and turned to greet the cluster of relatives who appeared ecstatic to welcome him home. Everybody seemed to be bubbling a greeting of some kind in rapid, jubilant Spanish. Two or three of the men shook his hand, and one who looked like an older version of Nick embraced him with both arms. A couple of older women kissed him, weeping, and one kept patting Mama Luz on the arm as well.

The hubbub continued for so long that, despite the extraordinary circumstances, Kelley was beginning to feel that common courtesy dictated that it was time for Nick to introduce her to his people. Just as her patience began to pale, he turned to Mama Luz, who was still nestled in the crook of his arm as she hugged him, and gestured toward Kelley.

"Come on over and meet everybody, Kell," he called out to her in English, his eyes red with hay fever . . . or emotion. His glance fell upon Kelley tenderly, as though he guessed what she might be feeling. "I didn't mean to ignore you, *corazón*."

"It's okay, Nick," she breathed as she hurried toward him, her eyes telling him more than her nearly inaudible words. "*Everything* is okay, Nico. Everything is okay between us now."

He swallowed hard, as though he understood her double message, but he couldn't seem to speak as he reached out to Kelley with his free hand. As she clung to it, savoring the warmth and eagerness of his grip, Kelley wanted to throw herself into his arms as Mama Luz had done, to tell him that she loved him and wanted nothing more than to celebrate their first perfect night together all over again.

She couldn't remember a single reason she'd ever been angry with Nico, couldn't think of any reason she couldn't forgive him for whatever thoughtless words he'd uttered in the midst of his anguish. Of course he'd been tense and guilty just hours before his homecoming! The last thing he'd needed was her self-indulgent fury! She vowed to make it up to him in the quiet of the night; she vowed never to be angry with him again.

She had just nestled against his side when a silent dark-eyed peasant girl slipped through the milling crowd. Though she looked decidedly unpretentious, the people parted as though she'd waved a magic wand before her. Even Mama Luz, who hadn't eased her fierce, protective grip on her grandson since the moment he'd arrived, now slowly released him as she caught sight of the long-haired girl who padded softly, barefooted, to Nick's side.

A hushed silence seized the jovial group as they stared at Nick, then at the village newcomer, as though they were watching a climactic scene on a stage. Kelley didn't have to ask who the dark-haired woman was . . . nor did she have to ask what place she still held in Nick's heart. He dropped Kelley's hand as he turned to greet her rival.

Heedless of the door he'd slammed in Kelley's face, Nick stared at Liliana for a full thirty seconds, absorbing every nuance of her cautious smile, her brimming eyes, her shapeless dress of faded blue, which somehow struck Kelley as the perfect fashion choice for this occasion. She wore a Virgin of Guadalupe medal just like Nick's, and Kelley couldn't stifle a terrible jolt of apprehension that the two amulets were a matched set with significance far beyond the religious one.

Even in Kelley's fault-seeking eyes, Liliana looked unimpeachably sweet and cheerful and just plain nice. She didn't want to ask what impression Liliana was making on Nick as they stood face to face for the first time in nineteen years; she couldn't even find the courage to meet his eyes. But Liliana did, and whatever she read there must have given her hope and courage, because the instant Nick reached out in her direction, she plunged into his open arms.

CHAPTER THIRTEEN

NICK DIDN'T REALLY KNOW how he ended up in Mama Luz's dear familiar hut, nor how at least twenty other close relatives managed to fit in with him. But shortly after Liliana had joined the throng just outside the village fence, he and Kelley had been herded inside the tiny house that seemed to have shrunk quite noticeably since the last time he'd been home.

The four corner supports were still crooked paloverde trunks held in place by the surrounding sun-dried adobe; the tiny window hole was still blanketless this time of year. The hard-packed dirt floor was freshly swept and the heavy thatching of the roof was in no greater disrepair than he remembered, but the brightly colored lizards that lived up there seemed to have multiplied.

What troubled Nick most about the hut was the fact that Mama Luz still lived in it after all these years. What had she done with all the money he'd sent her? Thousands and thousands of dollars—enough to buy a veritable mansion in Mexico's depressed economy! Nick didn't care how Mama Luz had spent the money, because he'd only sent it to assure her of his love and to ease her burden. But if she'd never gotten it at all, then *somebody* had stolen those hard-earned dollars from his ancient grandmother, and that was an unforgiveable injury he would have to redress.

A ghost of suspicion crossed his mind as Liliana waltzed across the room with a bowl of soup, warming him with a smile as his Aunt Carmelita came to sit beside him.

"She has been waiting," Nick's *tía* told him, settling down in a rickety saguaro-rib chair. "She thought you would come as soon as you learned that Meleseo had died."

Nick wasn't quite sure how to answer his aunt. It was hard to decipher all the subtle nuances of the unfamiliar Spanish; he wasn't even sure whether she was talking about Liliana or Mama Luz. He had no good excuse for his long absence anyway, nor even a rational explanation for why he'd come back at all.

"You have been well?" he asked instead, bluntly changing the subject. "My uncle has been good to you?"

"He has been *here*," she answered pointedly. "We are all good to each other... *here*."

He felt a gust of shame—or maybe homesickness. But he'd thrown away the communal warmth of Cielo Solo long ago, and he knew he was asking too much to expect to rediscover it now. "I'm sorry, *Tía*, but I—"

He couldn't finish the sentence before the next relative arrived, a white-haired sister-in-law of his late Aunt Raquelito, who seemed to remember baking Christmas *buñuelos* for Nico as a child. He had no recollection of her cooking and much difficulty understanding her raspy voice, but he nodded politely and thanked her for whatever kind things she'd done for him.

He was relieved when his Uncle José wandered over a few minutes later and took the chair his wife had recently vacated. José—who was Nick's godfather as well as his favorite *tío*—had never been particularly talkative, but he and Nick had never needed many words.

José stifled a spasm of coughing, then welcomed Nick with his eyes. "It has been too long," he remonstrated gently. "You should come more often."

Nick grinned. "Thanks, I think I will."

José smiled back, then gestured toward Kelley with his chin. "So this is why you live in America? Our women are not good enough for you now?"

From some other man the words would have been hard and biting, but he knew that José loved to tease. "I had to check out every woman in both countries before I found that one," he admitted, his tone a mixture of laughter and honest love. "There are no others quite like Kelley."

José glanced from Kelley to Liliana but mercifully left his question unspoken. Nonetheless, after they'd chatted for a while, he asked a question that was quite alarming. "Mama Luz has told you that Pablo is back in Sonora?"

"Back?" A stab of panic shot through him. *What have I got Kelley into?* his conscience demanded. "I thought he was in jail."

José shrugged. "He was in prison, but now he is free. I have seen him several times in Pitahaya." Before Nick could digest this information, his uncle tacked on in a cautious, warning tone, "And every time he speaks to me, he asks about Liliana."

Nick felt sick and confused, as though somebody had just kicked him when he'd reached out for a hug. José made no effort to coddle him, however; he just said, "I thought you should know, Nico," then walked away.

From that point on Nick felt like an out-of-town usher at a friend's wedding, greeting scores of well-wishers who all seemed to know more than he did about what was going on, even though he was the guest of honor. Several times he tried to catch Kelley's eye—certain she had to be feeling a bit bewildered by all the fuss, not to mention seething over Liliana's greeting—but it was a hopeless undertaking. Whichever relatives weren't surrounding Nick were barricading Kelley, and it seemed as though the whole village had conspired to keep them apart for the rest of the day.

At the moment Kelley was smiling, artificially, perhaps, but giving a grand show of delight at all the attention. But she'd done her share of crying when they'd just arrived, and Nick didn't think she'd been shedding only tears of joy. For just a moment, right after he'd greeted Mama Luz, he thought he'd caught a glimpse of understanding in Kelley's eyes, a sense of regret for the hard words she'd flung at him that morning. But when Liliana had arrived, claiming his full attention, that painful reunion had all but eclipsed his fragile bond with Kelley.

But it wasn't because he still wanted Liliana. Even as he'd taken her in his arms, felt her familiar body close to his again, his heart had been saying, *It really is over. Liliana is my yesterday; Kelley McKinney is my tomorrow.*

Unfortunately, that simple knowledge wasn't enough to put his guilty mind at rest. If Meleseo had still been alive—or if Pablo had still been in prison—maybe Nick could have left Liliana in Cielo Solo without another thought. But one glance at this pathetic shack forced him to face anew the simple reality of how different her life would have been if he'd married her and taken her with him to the States. Worse yet, one look at her clear gray eyes and he'd known without a doubt that Pablo had lied to him. This guileless young woman was far too decent—not to mention naive—to even consider the blatant deceit he'd ascribed to her.

And to think I left her alone to face that bastard, he reflected grimly. *Alone and pregnant and aching with a broken heart because I turned my back when the chips were down.* Just the thought of it turned his stomach and made him feel like less of a man.

"Are you hungry, Nico?" she asked him now, her gentle smile so full of joy that it rubbed salt in the wound of his guilt. "And your friend? Would she be hungry, too?" From another woman, those words would have held curiosity, condemnation or spite. But from Liliana, there was only honest concern for a stranger. Any friend of Nico's was obviously a friend of hers.

"I don't know, Liliana," he answered kindly. "Maybe you should ask her. She speaks Spanish very well."

Nick knew it was unfair of him to make Kelley face Liliana on her own, but on the other hand, he reasoned, if Kelley could just see what a decent woman Liliana was, she might be able to understand his dilemma. And once she got to know Liliana, he was certain that Kelley would realize that the other woman was no threat to her.

He watched in silence as Liliana approached his vibrant redhead. Kelley had worn a plastic smile on her face as she'd smoothly answered all the curious but friendly questions of everybody else in the house. But the smile paled when Liliana bent down to talk to her, and as soon as Liliana moved on again, Kelley's eyes met Nick's accusingly.

I've got to talk to her alone, he realized quickly. *I've got to let her know that she's the one I want. I've got to let her know that everything with Liliana is...*

Is what? he had to ask himself. *Is up in the air? Still unresolved, especially now that Pablo's back?*

A moment later somebody handed him a plate of unmashed beans and a flour tortilla, and a voice in his memory told him to tear off a triangular piece of the flat, round bread, then fold over a corner to brace the mock handle of his spoon. Kelley, he noticed, did the same without instruction from anybody, and he suspected that her Mama Chayo had taught her far more about Mexico than he'd imagined.

"It is decided," Carmelita declared the next time she wandered by, her eyes still dark and accusing. "Your friend will stay with us, and then Mama Luz will have you all to herself."

Nick did not miss her subtle reprimand. Any moment he expected somebody to ask, *How could you stay away so long? And how could you bring another woman with you when you knew Liliana would be waiting?* He had no answer, so to forestall the questions he said, "Whatever you think would be best, *Tía.*" He hoped that Kelley wouldn't mind being housed in a separate hut. In all honesty he had to admit that he did feel the need of some privacy with his grandmother. There were things between them that needed to be said before he went back to the States, and they would be hard enough to reveal even without an audience.

"I think it would be *best* if you remembered that you are a Morales, Nico. Your mother broke Mama Luz's heart when she went away, and you did the same after all your grandmother did for you." The tight bun at the back of her head dramatized her stern expression. "We are glad you have come home, but do not think that a quick visit will ever make up for all the time you have been away. You are now a man, not a child, and you have much to answer for."

He suddenly felt trapped, lonely, amidst the celebrating crowd, but there was no way he could escape the throng, even after Carmelita flounced away. When he saw Kelley edging toward him minutes later, his relief was great.

"Oh, Kelley, am I glad you're here," he admitted, reaching for her hand. "If I ever needed a friend—"

He broke off suddenly as he glanced at her face, which looked anything but friendly. Tension tightened the alabaster lines of her normally cherubic cheeks, and her eyes were dark and hostile.

"Excuse me for interrupting the festivities," she said coldly, "but one of your relatives seems to feel that I'm spending the night at her house. Is that what you want me to do, Sonoran guide?"

Despite the controlled tone, her anger filled him with anxiety, and he tightened his grip on her fingers. *I want you, corazón,* he longed to tell her. *I want to spend the night with you under the stars. I want to smooth away your tears and heartaches; I want to kiss your tense angry mouth with tender passion until you smile again.*

"Kelley," he said quietly, "I know what you're thinking and—"

"You don't have the slightest idea what I'm thinking, Nick." Despite her decorous low tone, her emerald eyes all but shouted her hurt and rage as she jerked her hand away from his. "And trust me, you don't want to know!"

"MY DAUGHTERS USED TO SLEEP in this bed," Carmelita informed Kelley as the older woman plopped Kelley's backpack down in the corner of the adobe kitchen that served as the guest room in her clean but tiny home. "I had four girls. You will meet three of them. My baby, Ana, died of bronchitis when she was twelve."

Kelley wasn't quite sure how to respond to this piece of unsought information, so she said simply, "I'm sorry, *señora*. It must be very hard to lose a child." *It's hard enough just to lose a man*. Then, after a moment's awkward silence, she added, "It's a very nice bed. After a night in the desert, I'm sure I'll sleep very well tonight."

Fortunately Carmelita didn't ask Kelley anything about her night on the desert with Nick, but she did pose a question Kelley had already been asked more than once in the past few hours. "Why does a pretty American girl want to travel through this dry land? Did you come just to meet Nico's people?"

Are you his woman? she might just as well have asked. But she didn't, so Kelley let it slide. Kelley didn't know the answer to that question anyway; she'd changed her mind half a dozen times since sunrise.

"Actually, I'm here to study desert plants," she explained as straightforwardly as she could, knowing that the idea of studying the Opata from an anthropological point of view might well be offensive to a woman whose life-style was nearly Indian itself. "A very special friend of mine taught me a lot about the Opata way of healing, and I'd like to learn more."

She must have struck just the right chord, because almost instantly Carmelita began to talk about the Opata cures she was familiar with, offering to introduce Kelley to Cielo Solo's own *curandera* and to spread the word among all her far-flung friends and relations that a friend of Mama Luz's American grandson needed a favor. Her spontaneous generosity was so determined that Kelley had to push away a nagging suspicion that Nick's aunt might be entirely too happy to see her leave Cielo Solo, or at least kept too busy with her own affairs to pay much attention to Nico's. After all, the whole village seemed more than ready to start planning a wedding for Nick and Liliana.

Still, Carmelita's enthusiastic promise to find an Opata *curandera* was the brightest spot in Kelley's day. It was late and she was very tired by the time she finally went to bed, but there was no sign of Nick, despite his promise to join her after the hullaballoo settled down. She even went to the doorway once when she thought she heard his voice outside in the sleeping village, hours after her host and hostess had said goodnight.

Too restless to sleep, Kelley leaned against the adobe wall and listened sadly to the sound of the coyotes howling and gazed up at the clear desert sky. It was a scene of peace and beauty, and she tried to draw the serenity into her heart.

She might have succeeded if she hadn't spotted two figures heading over the knoll that led to the giant saguaro. A woman, lithe and graceful; a man, firmly built. Something in the way he walked was unbearably enticing...and painfully familiar. Kelley couldn't hear their conversation, but when a joyful laugh rang out across the desert, she knew for certain that it belonged to the man she loved.

The woman moved closer to her partner and lifted her face toward his as they walked away from the village. Kelley battled with a pain in her lungs as she watched Nick step a little closer, his head inclined as though to ponder every word. As the twosome disappeared over the bushy knoll, Kelley was grateful that it was too dark to see if he reached out for Liliana's hand.

"IT'S A BEAUTIFUL NIGHT," Nick told Liliana as they slipped over the rise which concealed the village and drew closer to the privacy of the great saguaro. "I'd forgotten how clear it is in the desert. Where I live there's so much—" he struggled to translate "smog" into Spanish and gave up the task "—dirty air that it's hard to see the stars."

Liliana clucked sympathetically. "It must be a terrible place to live. Is there nowhere else that you can be happy?"

Nick smiled, touched by her concern. "Oh, it's not so bad, Lili. Actually, except for the smog and the cars, it's a great place to live. And if it weren't for the cars, I wouldn't have any way to make a living, so I guess I can't complain."

Liliana nodded. "You wrote to Mama Luz that you learned about cars in the Army. You are very good at fixing them now? You make enough money to . . . feed yourself well?"

He shrugged, suddenly embarrassed by the incredible difference between her world and his. They drifted to a stop next to a rotting cactus skeleton that served as Cielo Solo's version of a park bench. The ribs of the once huge saguaro were still long and firm, and a couple of "boots"—scabbed-over wounds where birds had once hammered out their homes—stayed rigid in the decaying structure. "I've learned a lot," he admitted. "I was lucky."

Liliana tossed back her head. "You were never lucky, Nico, even as a boy. You always did your best, but bad things happened to you anyway. I'm glad you are happy now."

Happy was not exactly the way Nick would have described himself this evening. Relieved, exhausted, worried...but overall, his life in L.A., even before Kelley, had been a good one. Only this one nagging doubt, this lingering guilt, had kept him from savoring life to the fullest. "Liliana, there's really only one thing that...makes me unhappy these days," he confessed. "It's been nineteen years since I ran away from Cielo Solo, and I've never really been certain that I—" he swallowed hard "—that I did the right thing."

Slowly she turned to face him, surprise and a curious sort of pleasure coloring her plain but friendly face. "Thank you, Nico. Thank you for that."

"For leaving?" he asked in dismay.

"No. Of course not. I'm just grateful that...you've thought of me from time to time. And had enough faith in me to wonder...just a little bit...if Pablo had shamed me with his lies."

Nick was gripped by sudden nausea. "I'm the one who shamed you by believing him. The minute I saw your face today, I knew I'd made a terrible mistake. I loved you, Lili, and I turned my back on you when you needed me most. I'll never be able to forgive myself for that."

To his surprise, Liliana laid a tender hand on his shoulder. "Nico, I forgave you for it long ago. It was my fault, not yours. If I had trusted your love for me enough to tell you the truth myself—before Pablo had the chance to dirty my name—I think we could have worked it out.'' Then she set him on his heels by saying, ''But it was as it was meant to be, Nico. If it weren't for you and Pablo doing what both of you did, I would never have married Meleseo. And he turned out to be—'' pain darkened her cheerful tone ''—the man who truly owned my heart.''

For the first time Nick was certain that Liliana had not spent the last nineteen years pining for him. No matter what circumstances had forced her to marry his cousin, clearly their love had flowered over the years and they'd been very happy. It was Meleseo's loss, not the loss of her adolescent lover, which had cut her heart so deeply.

Though Nick had to admit that he was relieved to learn that Liliana was not spearheading the communal village effort to marry off the two of them at once, he felt the need to express some words of sympathy regarding her still-painful loss. He was struggling for some soothing, appropriate reply when Liliana's nostalgia abruptly vanished.

''He did not die of sickness, Nico!'' she blurted out in a voice laced with fear and anger. ''He was cursed!''

''Cursed?'' Nick echoed, trying to recall a concept of life and death so far removed from his own. ''You mean that somebody wanted him dead?''

''Not just any somebody. The same somebody who wanted *you* dead! When you first left I was so afraid that Pablo would put a curse on you, Nico, but I do not think he had enough money to pay a *curandero* then. Now he does.''

As incredible as Liliana's assertion struck him, Nick knew that she and probably the rest of the village firmly believed that Pablo could kill him with a curse. The notion didn't trouble him, but her reference to Pablo's newfound wealth did. "How do you know he has the money now?" he asked gently.

At once she lowered her eyes, but he couldn't tell if fear or shame caused her to tense all over. "Now Pablo has more on his side than money, Nico. *La zarca*'s cousin is married to his brother's son."

Nick remembered *La zarca*, "the blue-eyed one," well. The vicious old crone had been taking money to "heal" folks or make them sick since he'd been a child.

"She says she did not cast a spell on Meleseo, but I do not believe her. It would have been too hard for a *curandero* outside of Cielo Solo to get what he needed to cast the spell."

Nick knew what she meant; the villagers believed that some part of the victim had to be used to achieve a successful curse—a broken fingernail, a lock of hair or an object of that person's, like a medal, or even some of his clothes. Stifling his frustration, he suggested quietly, "Maybe there's another explanation for his death."

"It could be the *curandero* in Pitahaya," Liliana agreed, missing his point entirely. "Nowadays Pablo spends much time there, and he has enough money to pay for whatever he wants."

"You said that before," Nick reminded her, fighting a sneaking suspicion of where Mama Luz's money might have ended up. As far as he was concerned, those hard-earned dollar bills would be better used as winter kindling than payment to Cielo Solo's "witch." Or to Pablo, in obsequious pleading to call off his *curan dero*'s curses. "But you didn't tell me how he comes to be so rich."

Liliana flushed, but fear, not guilt, now stained her dark, broad features. "I don't know for certain, Nico, but I know he does not get his money by doing the hard work of a good man. He sells everything he can get his hands on to an American who meets him in Pitahaya. Drugs, birds of many colors, guns, *nopales*—"

"*Nopales*?" Nick repeated, suddenly picturing a burro cart loaded with tiny plants. "He's involved with smuggling cactus plants across the border?"

Liliana nodded. "He says he is the leader of the men who do this. He says they will do whatever he tells them to do. They would—" she blanched as she forced out the words "—they would take a woman, he says, as soon as a shipment of guns or a saguaro."

He got it then; Pablo hadn't changed a bit, except perhaps to get nastier as the years went by. Tonight Nick had heard a rumor that Pablo had killed a man in prison, though nobody had ever proved it; Nick had no doubt that he'd kidnap a woman without a twinge of guilt. "He still wants you, Lili? He's still threatening to get you back any way he can?"

She fought back tears of naked fear. "It is not *me* he wants, Nico. He wants only to prove that he can have anything or anybody that he chooses. He thinks you took me from him, so he hated you and he tried to take me back. He hated Meleseo for the same reason. He does not understand that I loved my husband in a way I could never have loved Pablo."

Humiliation claimed her eyes as she grappled with her memories, but Nick wasn't about to let her off the hook; he couldn't afford to be so magnanimous. If he did nothing else in Cielo Solo, he had to cut through this old scar tissue with Liliana. He had to know, just once and for all, what had really happened that last terrible night when he'd abandoned her.

"Lili," he said softly, "I have to know. I came back here to see Mama Luz...and to find out from you what really happened. Please tell me the truth."

She stiffened slightly. "I told you the truth the night you left. I answered all your questions."

"And you gave me answers that didn't make sense. That's why I couldn't believe you."

Suddenly her eyes grew wide. "I was trying to protect you, Nico! You were talking crazy! I was afraid you'd go for him, and he would find a way to kill you and say it was your fault!"

Quietly he reached out for her hand to calm her. "Lili," he assured her, "I'm not feeling crazy now, and I'm not going to do anything stupid. I just want to know. I *need* to know. I need to know everything before I go back home."

Slowly she nodded, then took a step or two away from him. She faced the mighty saguaro, as though it were judge and jury, as she began to tell her tale. "I did not want him, Nico, not ever," she pleaded softly. "Oh, maybe when I was very young, for a few weeks in the beginning. He was dashing and made me feel beautiful, and my mother did not like him so I felt daring and brave. I grew reckless and I tempted him in order to test my power as a woman, but when I decided the game had gone on long enough he would not let me quit. Maybe it is not quite fair to say he forced himself on me, Nico, but the truth is that he gave me no chance to say no. I was sick with shame when he made it clear what he wanted, but he threatened to tell my mother what I had already done—a few lies, a few kisses in the dark that seemed so sinful then—and I was so scared, and so ashamed, that I didn't know quite how to stop him.''

She looked pathetically young and vulnerable in the moonlight, and Nick was moved with the same kind of pity he'd have felt for a frightened child.

"It wasn't until you came to Cielo Solo that I found the courage to tell him he could never come to me again. I loved you so much, Nico, and I was sure you would protect me.''

Suddenly her voice broke, and her eyes filled with tears as she burst out, "I know it makes no difference now, Nico, but I wish you could believe me! I loved you because you were so sweet and honest and true. All I wanted was a life with you—here, there, any-where!—and when I found out I was pregnant I wanted to die!'' Sadly she slumped down on the crumpled sa-guaro skeleton and wept. "I was so afraid you wouldn't forgive me. You wanted me to be so innocent and pure.'' She met his eyes, tears streaming down her face. "But I *was* still innocent on the inside, Nico. When I married Meleseo, he said I knew nothing about men.''

Nick sat down beside her on the bones of the decay-ing cactus, wishing he had a handkerchief to wipe her face. He wanted to soothe her, to stop the tears, but he was afraid to touch her; afraid that Kelley would mis-understand if she ever saw his fingertips grace another woman's tearful face. It wasn't a logical fear, because they couldn't have been more alone in the empty des-ert. But he would know and that would be enough to mire him in guilt, and he was buried in enough of that already.

Liliana shivered in the warm night air. "Even now I am afraid when I think of how it would feel to have him touch me. He knows I am afraid. He wants me to be afraid! When he comes to the village, he follows me and stares. He stands by my little house; he smiles at all my children." Her eyes met Nick's with trembling fear. "This is the first time I have been this far from the village in weeks, Nico. The women will not go this far at night because of the jaguar, and no other man will dare to walk with me." She swallowed hard and stifled yet another sob. "I am so afraid, Nico! I am living in a cage. And there is no one who can set me free."

CHAPTER FOURTEEN

KELLEY SPENT A SLEEPLESS NIGHT that had nothing to
do with the tired old mattress on the freshly swept dirt
floor. In her dreams she kept seeing Nick's face, warm
and loving, as he reached out for her over and over
again. Each time, when he was just about to kiss her,
he'd suddenly turn his head and call out, "Liliana!"
Mercifully, the fifth or sixth time that she'd awakened, a silvery sunbeam had been slipping in through
Carmelita's adobe hole window.

The day wasn't much improvement on the night.
She'd seen Nick several times, from a distance, and
once he'd even waved and trotted toward her. But one
of the older women had instantly headed him off, and
he had tossed her a look of helpless exasperation as
he'd been towed away.

Kelley's hostess had kept her pretty busy as well,
suggesting herbal cures of interest and sharing everything she knew about the Opata villages, *curanderos*
and plants in the area. In fact, Carmelita was so helpful that Kelley was beginning to wonder if she intended to keep her guest too busy to make contact with
her nephew, a suspicion that intensified when the older
woman made arrangements for Kelley to spend most of
the siesta hour with Cielo Solo's *curandera*.

"*La zarca* knows everything about healing," Carmelita had insisted as she'd tugged Kelley to the out-

ermost house on the east side of the village. "She will tell you everything you want to know." And then, almost in the same breath, she asked, "Did you bring money to pay her?"

"Money?" Kelley asked. "I have to pay her just to talk to me? I don't need any cures. I just want information."

Carmelita flushed, and Kelley was sorry she'd been so blunt.

"Please understand, Kelley, that no one in Nico's family would ever accept money from his friend. Anything we have is yours." She sounded so sincere that Kelley felt guilty for her previous suspicions. "But *La zarca* is not a Morales; she is—how do you say—the dark side of Cielo Solo. We do not even call her a friend."

Kelley respected Carmelita's honesty, but her words were hardly reassuring. "If she's not a friend of yours, what exactly is she?"

Carmelita shrugged uncomfortably. "Some say she is a witch, but only when she cannot hear. She is the one who cures us, and sometimes the one who makes us sick. She lives by herself and never joins us when we celebrate; that's why she's the only one in the village that you have not met. We do not talk to her if we can help it, but we cannot take the risk of *not* talking, if we find ourselves near her house."

"What do you mean she sometimes makes you sick? Do you mean sometimes she makes mistakes with her—" Kelley struggled for a simple Spanish word for diagnosis "—her cures?"

"Mistakes?" Carmelita smiled ruefully. "For us they are mistakes. For her they are . . . the higher price. She does not seek evil, but she does not turn away from it if she will be paid more for doing evil than she would for doing good.''

Kelley shivered, suddenly realizing the reason Nick viewed *curanderismo* with such venom. "*Señora*," she suggested bravely, "there is a fine new doctor in Pitahaya who sewed up Nico's thumb when he injured it on the way here. He told us he would come to any village if someone sent for him.''

Carmelita stared at her. "That is nice, Kelley, but why would we send for him when we have *La zarca*?''

Tongue-tied, Kelley answered, "Well, for one thing, he only takes money to heal people. For another thing, he knows . . . more about healing than . . . many *curanderos* I have met.''

Despite Kelley's cautious tact, Carmelita flashed her a smile that was almost condescending. "No one knows more about healing than *La zarca* does. We are lucky to have her.''

Kelley was mystified by Nick's aunt's logic. "How can you be lucky to have someone so nasty?''

The other woman looked surprised. "The barrel cactus has thorns that can tear a man's hand if he does not know where to place his knife, but the flesh inside can keep him from dying of thirst, Kelley.''

While Kelley was still struggling to decipher this strange metaphor, Carmelita led her to a ramshackle dwelling on the outskirts of town that boasted an *olla* full of dried corn next to the outdoor stove and a dead bat hanging by a leather thong from the palm-leaf roof.

She ushered Kelley into the darkened hole, which lacked the fresh-swept feel of Carmelita's own modest home. In one corner perched a scrawny old woman on her knees, waving her arms over a small boy lying on a palm-leaf mat. Four candles, staked out in a surrounding square, illuminated his bloated stomach and the row of dried plants that lay scattered on the dirt near the wall. The old woman shook a gourd over his head and chanted a quasi-prayer, then turned to acknowledge her new arrivals.

Her eyes were pale blue, with the nearly clear gaze of the blind, but she stared at Kelley as though she had the power to desiccate her soul. Without a word she held out one hawk-like claw for money, but said not a word as she waited to be paid.

"My money is back at Carmelita's house," Kelley confessed awkwardly, wondering how much this old crone's information might be worth to the Institute of Southwestern Studies. "I'll go get it after we talk."

"Yes, you will," *La zarca* proclaimed in a clear hard tone that would have quelled all but the very brave. "You will get it...or you will be very sorry that you did not."

IT WAS JUST AFTER siesta time on his second day in Cielo Solo that Nick found himself unable to avoid putting off any longer his all-important talk with Mama Luz.

He was still dozing on the mattress in the main room when he heard her join him. That is, he heard her totter in and sink down on a chair that had once been made with planks and glue but had since been shored together with cut saguaro ribs and dried palms. Her steps were slow and heavy, but the tuneless hum that touched his ears was full of joy.

When Nick opened his eyes, she was watching him. Her face split into an exuberant grin as she met his sleepy gaze.

"Look at you, Nico," she chided. "Such big muscles, and hair on your chest. You were so very skinny as a child."

He laughed. "It's been a long time since I was a child, Mama Luz."

She shook her head. "Not to me. Never before have I seen you as a man."

He could not meet her eyes as he whispered, "I'm so sorry, Mama Luz. I know I don't deserve your forgiveness for—"

"Hush." She cut him off, her voice throbbing with feeling. "There is nothing to forgive. I always knew you loved me; I always knew you would come home, even when everybody else had given up and called me crazy. And now you are home to stay," she concluded joyfully.

Instantly Nick's eyes flashed up to meet his grandmother's, but before he could clarify his position, she said, "I know, I know, you have a life there now. But it is only part of your youth. Now that you are certain where your place is, you will decide to stay with us." Her eyes bore into his. "This is the only place a Morales man belongs."

"Mama Luz—" he protested in vain.

"Besides, Liliana needs you. Not the way she did before . . . she is a woman now. But she is afraid, Nico, and she needs a man to help her."

This was one fact he couldn't deny. "I know she's in trouble, Mama Luz. And I'll do what I can to help. But there is another woman who—"

"Who is a good friend. A passing fancy. If it were any more than that, you would have said, 'Mama Luz, this is my woman; this is my bride.' But you did not say that when you introduced us to your Kelley. She is a nice girl, for a *gringa*, but she would not be happy in your village for a lifetime. She does not belong at your side.''

Nick wasn't quite sure how to answer that. He couldn't deny that Kelley didn't belong in Cielo Solo, but then again neither did he. And he couldn't very well explain his reticence to proclaim Kelley as his woman without confessing the hold Liliana had had on him for so many years. Feeling awkward and clumsy once more, he forced himself to say, ''Kelley is...very special to me, Mama Luz. We just haven't known each other...very long.''

''Long enough for her to follow you from Los Angeles to Sonora!'' she replied with a hint of disdain.

Nick shook his head, feeling trapped and helpless. He'd already explained Kelley's project in some detail, and Mama Luz had already promised to ask around to see if somebody might be able to help her. But for an elderly woman of her traditional values, it was difficult to understand why *any* decent woman would travel overnight alone with a man who wasn't a close relation.

''It's different over there, Mama Luz,'' he tried to explain, tossing his head in the direction of the States. ''A woman does not have to know a man's family for years to travel with him. We have mutual friends.''

She met his eyes directly. ''I do not know your friends. I have not even seen a picture of your house though you tell me it is very clean.''

Nick couldn't meet her eyes. A decent two-bedroom starter home in East L.A. was a veritable mansion in this part of Sonora. How could he justify such luxury—indoor plumbing, hot water, central heating and air—to a woman who was proud of a meticulous adobe hut that wouldn't even pass building safety codes for a garage back home?

"It's a safe house, Mama Luz," he assured her. "The neighbors are friendly and make no noise after dark."

"Do they let their pigs and chickens in the house?" she persisted.

Struggling to keep a straight face, Nick told her, "No, they don't even have a pig. Where I live, it is the custom to buy our eggs and meat at the store."

She gawked at his words. "Are you sure that the eggs stay fresh?"

He nodded, feeling more guilty every second. "They have...special boxes of ice to keep everything cold until we buy it."

Mama Luz nodded in some relief, settling back in her chair until Nick forced himself to open a topic of conversation that had been troubling him since the moment he'd arrived. "I sent you enough money to buy a new house, Mama Luz. I tried to make sure you had enough to buy anything you needed."

For the first time her eyes darkened with a hint of censure. "I did not need your money, Nico. I only needed you."

He swallowed hard and slid over on the mattress until he could touch her hand. In his position, sitting practically on the ground, he felt like a little boy, a supplicant.

"I couldn't come, Mama Luz. I just couldn't come back here. I couldn't face Liliana. I couldn't face Pablo. I couldn't face...you."

He'd said it now, forced out the terrible words. "I'm so ashamed, Mama Luz. I'm so terribly sorry that I left you alone for so long."

His grandmother reached out gently to pat his face in a gesture of infinite forgiveness. "I have never been ashamed of you, *mi hijo*, so never be ashamed of yourself. I understood what you had to do, and I understood why you sent me the money. I have kept it, kept it all, and it helped me bear your absence. I knew it would not stop coming until you had forgotten me."

Something inside him seemed to break. "You never spent it? None of it?" He didn't know which hurt most—the memory of how desperately he'd needed that cash in the early days of his business, or how terribly destitute his grandmother's life had been because she refused to make use of the money he'd sent her. "But I sent you enough to—"

"To ease your guilt, *mi hijo*, and to tell me you still loved me. It was money well spent. Do not grieve for it now."

"It's not the money I grieve for, Mama Luz. It's all the lost time."

She reached down to hug him, her dry lips a whisper of autumn leaves against her grandson's cheek. "Do not grieve for that either, Nico. The time we have left together will be even more precious because of the time we have lost."

KELLEY WAS MUSING on the contrast between the taste of a microwave-heated frozen burrito and the marvelous taste of Carmelita's homemade *taquitos* the next morning when Nick knocked on the door frame on his way into his aunt's house. After the most cursory nod in the older woman's direction, he declared in terse English, "I need to speak to you, Kelley."

It was the first time he'd addressed her so directly in nearly two days, and his vehemence took her by surprise. Actually, so did his interest. Left to fend for herself almost since her arrival in the village, Kelley had made good use of her time...not to mention Carmelita's hospitality. Not only had she arranged for Kelley to spend that unnerving afternoon with *La zarca* the day before, but she'd also scheduled an interview with a genuine Opata healing woman only one day's walk from Cielo Solo.

Out of sheer courtesy, Kelley had intended to drop by Mama Luz's to tell Nick that she and José were leaving in the morning; by this time, she doubted that he had much interest in her plans. Certainly he'd lost all interest in her feelings, or he would have found a way to speak to her alone before now. In her second miserable night in Nick's hometown, Kelley had come to grips with the reality she'd tried to dodge before: she had lost Nick to his people. Well, maybe not to his people, exactly, but to his memories of them and his longing to make everything right.

If Nick had given her any more encouragement, she might have lied to herself a little longer, clinging to a futile hope that somehow, when he came to his senses, he'd return to her bed and her heart once more. As it was, her second-place status was almost laughably clear, and she hadn't the slightest inclination to submit herself to any more false hopes and devastating discoveries. She'd lost him, that was all there was to it—assuming she'd ever had him at all.

It's better this way, she told herself fiercely. *I'll do what I came here to do and go home on my own. It will be a relief to know I'll never have to see Nick's face again.*

A sharp pain gripped her as she battled the last lie, but she kept her expression blank as she faced the man who'd machetied her heart.

"Sure, Nick, I've got a few minutes," she answered as nonchalantly as she could. "Have a seat till I'm done."

"Now, Kell." His tone implied he'd brook no opposition.

"Returning to our macho roots, are we, Nico?" she asked, unable to conceal the resentment that had been building up for two terrible days. "There's a saying in Spanish as well as English, I believe, that you can catch more flies with honey than—"

"Kelley!" This time she heard urgency rather than command in his deep, hushed tone. Nick's worried brown eyes seemed to beg her to overlook any unsettled issues between them, seemed to plead with her not to make a scene in front of his aunt.

Belatedly, Kelley realized that Carmelita was watching them both intently. "Nico and I have some things to discuss about my research, *señora*," she quickly said in Spanish. "Would it be okay if we go take a walk while we talk?"

"Of course. You are safe enough with Nico," Carmelita assured her.

The older woman's words surprised Kelley. She'd been asking permission to leave as a form of courtesy to her hostess, but clearly some imminent danger caused Nick's aunt to misinterpret her request. She made a mental note to get more information later.

"I'll look out for her, *Tía*," Nick promised, taking Kelley's arm a bit too brusquely as he led her out the door.

"Do you mind telling me what that was all about?" she asked as soon as they were out of earshot. Nick had marched her past a gaggle of children and three women talking near the prickly-pear fence, then led her rapidly over the knoll that ended near the great saguaro. "What is there to be afraid of, and why were you so rude?"

"Rude?" he asked. "*I'm* not the one who was rude."

Ignoring his snide reference to her behavior, she said, "It's rude to speak English in front of anybody in the village. It deliberately shuts them out—"

"Right now I want to shut them out. All of them. They've managed to keep me from having a single moment alone with you since we got here, and I'm beginning to suspect a bit of collusion."

"Collusion?" Kelley echoed.

"Collusion. As in, Nico's home, Nico will marry Liliana, Nico will stay forever…and Kelley will go back to the States alone."

His tone was so sharp, so disbelieving, that Kelley took heart that possibly that scenario was too far-fetched for Nick to consider. "You see a flaw, perhaps, in that vision of the future?" she asked as they hiked over the low hill out of view of the village.

Nick didn't answer her question at once; he glanced back over his shoulder to make sure that they were alone. Then he jammed both his hands into his pockets and said bluntly, "Liliana just told me that you've arranged for a trip to Tepari on your own."

"That's correct."

"What the hell is the matter with you?" he demanded. "We just got here. I can't go running off to the high country this soon! Mama Luz—"

"I don't expect you to go running off *anywhere* with me, Nick, and I don't think *Mama Luz* has anything to do with it! In the first place, I came here to do ethnobotanical research, not to watch you and Liliana in the first throes of the mating dance of spring. In the second place, since my Sonoran guide is obviously too involved with his courtship rituals to concern himself with his promises to me—personal or professional— I've used my native resourcefulness to fend for myself."

"Kelley, give me a break!" he interjected. "I haven't had one minute to myself."

"Fortunately, your aunt and uncle have been exceedingly helpful in making the arrangements I need to carry out my study," Kelley continued, trampling his protest. "I don't know whether their motivation has been sheer generosity or a desire to get me out of their hair or to leave a clear field for Liliana, but in any event, Carmelita used the women's village-to-village grapevine to send the word over hill and dale that a friend of hers needed an Opata *curandera*, so somebody named Yazmín Arizpe is ready and waiting to see me in Tepari. And your uncle, bless his heart, is willing to take me there tomorrow. So unless you have some strenuous objections to—"

"You're damn right I have objections! I object to you taking matters into your own hands in my territory and making me look like a fool. I object to you taking chances just to spite Liliana. And I—"

"Taking chances? Nick, I told you that your uncle is taking me. How can you have a problem with that? Don't you think José can protect me as well as you can?"

Nick sighed heavily, then glanced away. It was obvious that she'd punctured his defense. For a moment he said nothing, just stared at the omnipresent saguaro while he tugged awkwardly at the chain around his neck. "Yes, he can protect you," he admitted reluctantly, his eyes dark with frustration. "I guess I just wanted to take you there myself."

"What you want," Kelley pointed out tersely, "is to have your cake and eat it, too. And that's one option you just don't have, Nick. You made it perfectly clear before we ever came down here that you would either stay with her or go home with me, and it's excruciatingly clear that you've already made your choice. I've accepted that, but that doesn't mean I have to sit here day after day and watch you cavorting about with Liliana!"

"Cavorting?" He looked as though she'd slapped him in the face. "You've seen Liliana, Kell! Talked to her! She's a sweetheart, but she can't hold a candle to you! How can you possibly be jealous of her?"

"Oh, gee, Nick, I don't know," she scoffed. "Maybe it has something to do with the fact that even while you made love to me, you were still crying in your heart for her!"

"That's not true!" he snapped. "There was nobody but you in my heart that night, Kelley. Nobody but you!"

"Wonderful, Nick. I held your interest for a couple of fun-filled hours. But you left me in the morning...left me for Liliana even though she wasn't even there! How do you expect me to feel?"

"I never left you for her!" he pleaded, sliding both warm hands over her shoulders. "I had a problem I had to solve. I told you that again and again. It's got nothing to do with how I feel about you or even how I feel about *her*, really. It's how I feel about myself, Kelley. What's it going to take to make you understand that?''

His brown eyes were desperate, bathing her with the tenderness that always bound her to him. She could never stay angry when he looked at her that way.

More gently she said, ''I do understand your dilemma, Nick. Really I do. And in my saner moments, I feel for you.'' She considered telling him how terribly moved she'd been by his reunion with Mama Luz, then decided that it might give him too much advantage. ''But that doesn't change the fact that some other woman is more important to you than I am. Some other woman keeps getting in our way. When you think about your future, it's Liliana's heartbreak that troubles you, not mine.''

He dropped his hands and sighed deeply. ''I don't think that's true. But even if it were, it would only be because you've got so many more choices than she does, Kell. So many more resources. Even if you don't end up with me, you'll be all right. Hell, you probably make more money than I do, and if you went broke tomorrow, some friend or family member would bail you out until you got back on your feet again. But Liliana could put everything she owns in a knapsack, Kelley...if she even owned one! And even though all these people love her dearly, they're all poor as church mice themselves...and even if they were wealthy, they couldn't protect her against Pablo Villalobos.''

Ignoring the heart of his soliloquy—she had no answer to his need to guarantee a fine future for this woman—she seized on his final comment. ''Why does she need protection from Pablo? You're the one he threatened to kill, and I don't see you shaking in your boots. Besides, it happened nineteen years ago!''

''No,'' he countered sadly. ''I'm afraid the latest episode of this soap opera happened just last week. He's been hounding Liliana and threatening her children.''

A flicker of fear darted through Kelley. Was Liliana—or worse yet, Nick—really in some kind of danger? ''I don't think I understand, Nico,'' she was forced to admit. ''I thought Pablo was in prison.''

''So did I, *corazón*, or I never would have brought you down here.'' His tone was harsh with regret. ''But for some reason Mama Luz never let me know they'd released him. My uncle told me the day we arrived.''

Kelley stared at him, trying not to choke on her fear. ''How could she forget to tell you something so important? Was she afraid it would keep you from coming back?''

Nick closed his eyes for a long moment of frustration. ''I don't know, Kelley. More than likely she thought it was bad luck to mention him in a letter...or maybe she didn't want Lili upset by having to write the words to me.''

He shook his head and took a step closer, reaching for Kelley's hand as though he still had the right to touch her as he chose. Gently he tugged on her fingers, trying to recapture the tenderness that had once sung between them so vibrantly in the night.

Pull away from him, Kelley, she commanded herself. *Be proud, be strong; he made his choice and it wasn't you.*

But she couldn't seem to loosen his loving grip, and worse yet, she realized quickly, she didn't even want to.

Until he declared with sudden fervor, "If she were my woman, I would have taken care of him long ago."

A moment's helpless rage swept through Kelley as he pulled away—rage against Pablo's malignant nature, rage against the power Liliana still had over the man that Kelley loved. "You said he would have killed you, Nick," she felt the need to point out.

"That was when I was a kid. Green as grass. My God, Kelley, I'm a man now. I've been to war. I—"

"Okay, so you're strong. So you're tough. But you're no killer, Nick! You'd never think of settling a problem by violence in L.A. Even in Mexico you don't want to risk carrying a gun! Just because you're spending a couple of weeks in Cielo Solo doesn't mean you have to regress."

"You just don't get it, do you, Kelley?" he demanded, eyes full of anger now. "You're right—I'm just too civilized to stoop to his level. And I'm too civilized to forget what I feel for you so I can snuggle up to Liliana and make everything right. But I'm also too civilized to just turn my back on her and waltz off with you as though I owed her nothing! I'm stuck between a rock and a hard place—every way I jump I'm going to lose. I know these last few days have been hard for you, Kell, and I know you'll feel a lot better when we're headed north and you know that all this trouble with Liliana is behind you. But at least *you* know that there's a light at the end of the tunnel. You know that you've got a beautiful house, a fine career, a decent man who'd do just about anything for you."

"I do?" she questioned. "You must be reading a different script. All I've got besides a house and a job is the memory of a two-timing man who used me for a night."

Kelley regretted the words the instant they flew out of her mouth. Despite her anguish, she knew that their night under the desert stars had been just as special for Nick as it had been for her, and everything that had happened since then to drive them apart had far more to do with the qualities she loved in him than it had to do with any willful betrayal.

For one terrible moment Nick's face darkened with grief. If he'd yelled at her, Kelley could have shrouded her hurt with anger, but his sadness and frustration were more than she could bear.

"I'm so sorry, Nico," she whispered, reaching out to touch the bearded stubble on his face. "I didn't mean that. Even in my darkest moments, that's not what I think of you." He didn't pull away, but he made no move to hold her, either. "Maybe I'm not being fair to you, Nick," she admitted, "but you're so bound up in your own problems right now that I don't think you really have any idea how very much you've hurt me."

At first he just stared at Kelley, grappling with her words. Then, quite tentatively, his warm and gentle hands slipped around her shoulders, his eyes asking for permission to complete the embrace. When she offered no resistance, Nick slowly pulled her toward him, resting his face against her crinkly red hair.

I know I shouldn't do this, a voice within her cautioned. *I know I should keep this man at bay.*

But another voice, a voice of love stronger than the most rational side of her scientific nature, overruled the warning, even overruled the hurt.

Instinctively Kelley pressed against him as he murmured in her ear, "I never meant to hurt you, *corazón*. I warned you over and over again."

"I know. It's my fault," she whispered. "But I wanted you so much, Nico. . . ." She buried her face in his chambray shirt and tried not to cry. But when Nick cradled her head with one warm hand and ever so gently kissed her temple, the tears spilled over anyway.

"Tell me you still want me, Kelley," he pleaded. "Please tell me you can ride out this storm. Just a few more days while I straighten everything out with Liliana and make sure she's safe from Pablo. Just a few more days and we can be together."

Kelley tried to speak, but no words came out.

"It's *you* I want, Kelley, not Liliana," he urged. "Promise me you won't forget that while you're in Tepari."

Kelley lifted her head just enough to kiss his throat in a tender gesture of submission. "I'll remember it, Nico," she promised tearfully, pressing her cheek against his chest, "but I'm not at all sure that I can believe it." She gulped back a sob before she confessed brokenly, "There's no way I can tell you how much I wish I could."

CHAPTER FIFTEEN

THE TRIP TO TEPARI only took eleven hours, but Kelley felt as though she'd crawled halfway around the world by the time she reached the Opata village. The foothills near Cielo Solo, generously covered with creosote and cacti, were positively bare compared to the hackberry, leather stem and cat's claw acacia that cloaked the dense mountains; without some prior knowledge of the deer trail maintained and expanded by the steady foot travel of generations of wolves and javelinas, even a talented guide like José would not have been able to deliver her safely.

After her brief stint in Nick's hometown, Kelley didn't really think that any Mexican village could surprise her, but Tepari was even more primitive than she'd expected. The village itself was nestled in a hollow at the upper end of a riverine valley cloaked with floodwater fields of maize. Two or three dozen huts of wattle-and-daub construction formed the "residential neighborhood," and a crumbling adobe in the center of town appeared to be a church where some sort of activity was going on. Everybody inside the church—and everybody within earshot of the commotion—rushed to greet the newcomers. Or at least to stand and gawk.

Only two or three of the men were as tall as Kelley, and all the women were considerably shorter. They wore baggy skirts and striped *rebozos*, as did the Cielo Solo women, but their facial features were heavier, especially their pendulous earlobes. In her dusty designer jeans, wilted oxford shirt and straw sunhat, Kelley felt like a brazen tourist on an Indian reservation; she was glad that she hadn't been able to find her camera before she'd left Carmelita's. Even Maleta, adorned with Kelley's plant press, looked a bit overdressed in comparison to the Tepari pigs and chickens, which freely ambled in and out of the crumbling mud-brick mission.

Nonetheless, in Kelley's mind there was a majesty to the tiny village because Mama Chayo had been born in one just like it. Being here was the closest she would ever come to being with Mama Chayo again. *This,* she reminded herself joyfully, *is the reason I came to Mexico. Not for Nick Morales; not to win his love or break my heart. If I can unlock the secrets of the Opata, I'll never regret that I made this trip.*

The silent speech didn't do a thing to ease Kelley's ache for Nick's smiling face and fervent kisses, but it did enhance her terrific sense of accomplishment that she had bravely traversed so far to achieve Mama Chayo's dream. How she'd loved that dear old woman! How she wished that Mama Chayo, not a stranger named Yazmín Arizpe, would soon appear to welcome her to Tepari.

"Come with me." A little boy in rags beckoned. His cherubic face radiated good wishes, and unlike the city urchins of Hermosillo, he didn't hold out his hand for cash. "The *curandera* is waiting for you, *señorita*. She sent me to show you to her house."

Without waiting for confirmation, José motioned for Kelley to follow the boy. He only greeted one or two of the curious onlookers, but most of them followed the newcomers to their destination.

A moment later, a robust woman dressed in a dark shapeless dress and black shawl came bustling toward them from a blanketed doorway. Toothless mouth smiling, she took both of Kelley's hands and pressed them heartily between her own as soon as José had introduced his companion.

"I am Yazmín Arizpe," she declared in a raspy, friendly voice that instantly set Kelley at ease. She looked as different from *La zarca* as night from day. "You are the friend of the *sobrino* of my *comadre's* sister's cousin's friend in Cielo Solo?" Almost before Kelley could nod in reply, the woman rushed on, "They say you speak our language very well."

Kelley smiled at the compliment. "I do speak Spanish, *señora*, but I don't speak the language of the Opata," she confessed.

The old woman laughed. "Neither do I! No one does anymore." She gestured around her, as if to include the curious crowd. "But we still remember the old ways. They are not lost. You will soon see. In *quince días* we will celebrate the *semana santa* as our grandfathers did. You will still be here for the *desfile*, no?"

"A parade for Holy Week?" Kelley translated uncertainly. "But Easter's not an Opata celebration. That's—"

"You will see," Yazmín said, abruptly changing the subject. "Now we will talk of other things."

Before Kelley could explore those other things, José was seized by a fit of coughing, a pattern that had been disturbingly common on the trail today. With the memory of his little girl's death from bronchitis still in her mind, Kelley had urged him to go see Dr. Ramirez.

He'd tried to mollify her concern with the news that *La zarca* was treating him with some poultice made with *nabos*.

"*Nabos*?" Yazmín repeated when Kelley reiterated her concern. "Come with me, *señor*, and I can give you something better than turnips for a cough."

"Later, perhaps," he demurred. Clearly embarrassed by all the fuss, his doleful frown reminded Kelley painfully of Nick's expression when she'd tried to doctor him with Opata herbs. "First I must take care of the burro."

As soon as he took off to tend to Maleta, the *curandera* ushered Kelley inside her hut and gestured for the herd of gawkers to leave. "You must forgive them," she said, clucking indulgently. "It is not often that we have guests in the village from over the border. Sometimes years and years go by without one. But you are the second one this month."

"I am?" Kelley asked in some surprise, fearful that some other botanist would steal her project out from under her nose. "Who else could—"

"A big man with a terrible voice who called himself Rinsland. We sold him all the *nopales* we could find."

"All the cactus plants?" Kelley asked, fighting a wave of terror and despair. Rinsland here! She'd noticed a dearth of cacti in the area but had assumed that it had just been cleared away to add more land to the village.

Yazmín shrugged. "All that we do not need. We eat the fruit of the saguaro, and the leaves of the prickly pear, but all the others?" She laughed, then grew more serious in the face of Kelley's dark expression. "Some of our babies will not go cold this winter," she soberly revealed. "We are very lucky that he came."

Kelley couldn't very well reply to that, so she stifled her anguish over the desecrated landscape and said simply, "It's very good of you to see me, *señora*. I understand you know all there is to know about Opata medicine."

Again she smiled, but this time sadly. "There is not as much to know as there once was. But I was taught by my grandfather, and he learned from his mother, and she from her mother before her. What I know is right."

Kelley nodded, longing to start taking notes already but knowing that she didn't dare act like a scientist too soon. Just stepping inside the adobe hut was exciting. She was fascinated by the dirt floor, the large woven mat and the bed made out of cane poles strapped together. A hand-carved cross was jabbed into a chunk of dried mud between the bricks, and a collection of crooked branches strapped together with palm leaves provided the *curandera* with a table to store and mix her herbs.

"I'm very eager to learn everything you can tell me," Kelley confessed as she lowered herself into the rickety willow-reed chair Yazmín indicated, while Yazmín herself sat on the floor mat. "I have always had great respect for the Opata way of healing. When I was little, I always drank *flor de manzanilla* tea whenever I had a stomachache."

Yazmín crossed her arms and studied Kelley carefully, her eyes a mixture of caution and delight. "How is it that you know of these things?" she asked with genuine surprise. "How did you come to hear of our cures so far away from Sonora?"

Suffused by the quiet memory of Mama Chayo, Kelley said, "There was an Opata woman who came to be my grandmother. She loved me very much, and she wanted me to learn about her father's way of healing. She taught me all she could before she died, and I promised her that I would . . . put everything on paper so that the knowledge would not die with her.''

Kelley didn't confess her love for Mama Chayo, but it must have lingered in her voice, because from that moment, Yazmín dropped all signs of reticence.

''Then we shall achieve your grandmother's dream,'' she said gently, her toothless mouth framing a smile. ''Then you will be happy, no?''

Kelley smiled back, and a ghost of tension slipped away. Thanks to Nick, she might not go back home with her heart intact, but at least her debt to Mama Chayo would be paid.

FROM THE MINUTE Kelley left for Tepari, Nick knew he'd made a mistake. It wasn't that he missed her so terribly—although he did—and he wasn't too worried about her journey because he knew that his uncle was the best guide in the world. What troubled Nick was that he'd let Kelley go without convincing her that he cared for her deeply—and that his love for Liliana was a thing of the past.

It was galling that he could blame nobody but himself for his frustration. How could he persuade a sharp cookie like Kelley to believe something that wasn't yet true? Oh, it was true that he wanted her, true that she stirred him in a way that no other woman ever had. But he couldn't convince her that he was ready to turn his back on Liliana until he managed to convince himself. And even if he could bring himself to believe that there was no debt left to be paid to the other woman, he could not turn a deaf ear to the terror in her voice every time she mentioned Pablo Villalobos.

Kelley had been gone nearly two weeks when Nick came home one night to find a visitor waiting for him in Mama Luz's house. His grandmother was out for the evening, attending a rosary for an elderly neighbor who had died. Nick, who'd barely known the man, had made a token appearance to satisfy his family but was looking forward to a bit of privacy while he sorted out his next plan of action. He wasn't used to living cheek by jowl with so many people who felt snubbed and cheated if he failed to inform them every time he drew a breath. He also wasn't accustomed to finding a strange man in his living room, gripping the handle of a knife.

"Por fín, Morales," a thin whining voice greeted him as soon as he slipped through the door. "At last you have come back to face me. Like a dog with its tail between its legs you come, it is true, but at last I can finish what I once began."

It was already dark in the village, but Nick needed no light to recognize his challenger. The last time they'd met it had also been dark, and Pablo Villalobos had taunted him with his insults and the veiled threat of his knife.

"You should have killed me when you had the chance, Pablo," he growled, too angry to be frightened. "I was a kid then. Helpless. Gullible. It might be a little harder to finish me off now."

"True," the weasely voice agreed. "And not nearly as much fun as the plan I have in mind."

Nick forced himself to parry. "Your life must be pretty boring if you need me to entertain you."

Pablo responded with a wicked laugh. "But, Morales, you do not know how entertaining you can be! Even the way you mangle your mother tongue could be sold for healing laughter. It is hard to believe you ever passed yourself off as a true *mexicano*," he sneered.

Nick stifled the rise of bile in his throat. *Forget your pride and think of Liliana,* he reminded himself. *Find a way to use his threats to free her. Remember that she will still be here with him after you go home.*

"What's your point, Villalobos?" he asked nonchalantly. "I mean, is there some particular reason for this visit? Something I can do for you?"

Again the maniacal cackle filled the tiny house. "You can bleed for me, Morales! You can cry for mercy and beg for me to spare you...and your woman."

His last three words made Nick sick with fear. Surely Pablo meant Liliana when he said "your woman," but was it possible that he knew about Kelley... where she was right now and what she meant to him? He nearly gagged at the thought. Kelley would be alone in Tepari until Nick went to collect her in another week or two.

Before he could summon up a safe reply, the other man darted across the dirt floor and pressed a long, sharp knife against the side of Nick's throat; the blade was cold and dented the skin without quite drawing blood. "You can beg, Morales, but it will do you no good. I have waited a long, long time to make you pay for what you did to me. Now I will wait only a little longer, and I can guarantee that you will pay the debt in full."

Nick could feel Pablo's hot breath on his cheek. Holding his ground, he said stoutly, "I'm ready any time you are, Villalobos."

The cackle came again. "But that is the beauty of it, don't you see? You will not know when I am ready, and neither will your woman. I give you only one warning, Morales," he finished with venom in his tone. And then, with a flash of silver, he hacked off a piece of Nick's hair. "This is what I came for, Morales," he growled. "And I already have what I need from the woman."

"THREE WEEKS, SHE SAID. That's six more days at least." Mama Luz muttered the words as she patted the tortillas into shape, stacking one on top of the other in preparation for the first morning meal. It wasn't yet daylight, but Nico had already been dressed and standing in the doorway—eyes on the darkened desert—when she'd starting cooking at five. "Do you think you will last that long, *mi hijo*?"

Nico looked startled by the soft intrusion on his melancholy reverie. "I'm sorry, Mama Luz. What did you say?"

She smiled indulgently, then crossed the room to pat him on the cheek. The flour made him look childish, but he didn't seem to notice. He had noticed very little since the redheaded *gringa* had gone off to Tepari, and even though his uncle had told him over and over again everything there was to tell about the journey, he still had asked for more.

"This stranger who bought the cactus plants—he'd left the area? Cleared out for good?" Nico had prodded his uncle. "And nobody thought he'd come back?"

José had coughed, then answered, "Why would he come back? There are no more plants to take."

To Mama Luz, the business of the missing cacti had seemed unimportant, but Nico had harped upon it most of that first evening. She had finally concluded that he was simply jealous of the possibility that Kelley might find another American man attractive in his absence. But now, almost two weeks later, Nico was still brooding about the woman; he hadn't even wanted to stay at last night's rosary.

Of course, Liliana hadn't gone to pray for the dead either, claiming that she had a stomachache, and Mama Luz had hoped that the two might have wanted a moment to sneak off together. But as she gazed at Nico's tense back—so rigid in his loneliness for the American woman who had claimed his heart—she realized that her dream was not to be. Whatever was troubling him this morning had more to do with Kelley than it had to do with Liliana.

"You think it was wrong of your uncle to leave Kelley in Tepari by herself?" Mama Luz asked gently. "She assured him that she would be very happy with Yazmín."

"Oh, I'm sure she is," Nico snapped. "She doesn't have enough sense to be afraid."

Mama Luz turned on him with a touch of anger. "Why are you so afraid for Kelley? It is Liliana you should fear for. It is *she* that Pablo wants."

"No, it's not!" Nico suddenly roared as he turned to face her. "It's me he wants to injure, and he'll use anything or anybody to make me suffer! Liliana's only in danger until he knows that Kelley is—"

Mama Luz blanched. Surely her old ears had deceived her; Nico had never raised his voice to her before! But now, as shame overcame him, there was fear in his eyes, fear for his woman in Tepari, fear that overruled even his respect for his grandmother.

"What have you not told me, *mi hijo*?" Mama Luz demanded sternly. "What do you know about Pablo that I do not know?"

Quickly he shook his head. "It doesn't matter. It has nothing to do with you."

She flattened her palms on her hips and glared at him. "If it has to do with you, Nico, then it has to do with me. You were not afraid for Kelley when she left for Tepari; you were not even this scared when José came home. But now you are frightened, terribly frightened, because you know something that you do not want me to know!"

Nico sighed dramatically as he stared at the lime-washed kitchen wall. He jammed both hands in his pockets, then faced her miserably. She knew he didn't want to burden her with his fears, but neither would he lie to his grandmother.

"Pablo came to see me last night," Nico finally confessed. "He cut off a lock of my hair."

Serpentine panic looped around her heart as Mama Luz realized the intent of his words. "A curse!" she wailed. "He's going to pay a *curandera* for a curse!" At once she reached for the lard cans of cash Nico had sent her over the years, all but spilling them on the bundled-log table as she pulled out the money and thrust it at him. "You must go to *La zarca* at once! He cannot have paid her this much. You must protect yourself before the curse—"

"Mama Luz," Nico interrupted her bluntly. "Forget the *curandera*. Forget the stupid curse!"

She stared at him in consternation. How could her Nico speak so terribly to her!

"I know you believe in this . . . this way of healing," he told her, struggling to regain his calm. "But I'm a lot more afraid of Pablo than I am of any curse. If he's that determined, he'll find some other way to make me suffer when he finds out that the curse doesn't work. Right now it's Liliana he's trying to frighten because he thinks I came back for her. But once he figures out that Kelley is the woman I—"

He broke off again, frustrated and afraid, but Mama Luz read the truth of his words. It was hopeless for her to dream of Nico coming back to live in Cielo Solo, hopeless to think that he would ever take Liliana for his wife. This new woman—nice, but oh, so very foreign—would be his future now. A future that left Liliana and all those he'd once loved in Cielo Solo very far behind.

"If Kelley is the one for you," she declared stoutly, "then you should take her home with you now. Before Pablo can hurt either one of you."

Slowly, sadly, Nico met her eyes. "I just got here, Mama Luz. Do you really want me to leave so soon?"

Tears clouded her eyes as she reached for both his hands. "I do not want you to go. I want you to stay here forever. But I would rather know you are alive and happy far away than see you dead in Sonora." She brushed back her tears and picked up the lard cans again. "He will kill you, Nico, if you do not run away...or stop him. I had hoped he had forgotten, but I see now that he has not. And a man like Pablo Villalobos will never forgive."

Nico met her eyes squarely. "I don't care if he thinks I'm a coward, Mama Luz; I'd take Kelley home tomorrow if I thought that would be the end of it. But he was hassling Liliana even before I got here. And what's to keep him from bothering you or anyone else after I'm gone?''

"Liliana is already ill! She had stomach pain last night!" Mama Luz cried out, paralyzed with fear as she put two and two together. "Let me pay *La zarca* for you and for her... and for Kelley, too, if she is also in danger. I do not need the money for anything else. I will pay for her protection for all of us, and then we will be safe even after you are gone. Please, Nico, please."

He shook his head in one single, angry gesture, which killed her last hope for her plan. "Mama Luz," he growled, "I swear to you, if you ever spend one single centavo of my money on witchcraft I will never forgive you. Feed it to the vultures for all I care, but promise me you'll never give it to *La zarca*!"

Frustration and anguish crippled her thoughts. How could he be so stubborn! Safety lay in the palm of his hand, but he would toss it away in the desert sand before he would go back on the vow he'd made when he'd lost his mother!

"I love you, *mi hijo*!" she wept. "Please let me save your life."

"If you love me, honor my wishes, Mama Luz! Promise me you won't pay that vile old crone!"

A sob burst from her dry, thin lips, but she knew she could not oppose him. Humbled and feeling hopeless, Mama Luz nodded her head. "I would never do anything to hurt you, Nico," she promised. "All I've ever wanted was for you to be happy."

He reached out for her then and pulled her gently into his arms, dropping a kiss on the top of her white-braided head. "I'm sorry I yelled at you," he whispered, shame laced with tenderness in his tone. "But I won't help the people who took my mother's money and helped her die."

Mama Luz did not refute him; she knew there was no way to convince her grandson that it had been God's will, not the *curandera*'s, that his mother should move on to heaven.

"I'm going to leave for Tepari at daybreak," Nico suddenly announced, his determination to protect his woman unswerving. "But I want José to stay here in case there's any trouble. Kelley's probably okay, but I won't sleep a wink until I see her with my own eyes."

He'd been gone so long that Mama Luz didn't know if he'd remember how to hike through Sonoran thorn scrub; he hardly remembered how to speak the language of his birth. But she knew she couldn't stop him, so she tried to gird him with her love and strength. Blinking back her tears, she struggled to smile, then patted his cheek once more.

For an instant the tension slipped from Nico's face. He dropped a kiss on her cheek, then said, "While I'm gone, will you tell José to keep a close eye on Liliana?"

"Of course I will. And I will pray for her safety."

"It's Kelley who needs your prayers, Mama Luz," Nico answered grimly. "She's the one he'll kill if he can."

CHAPTER SIXTEEN

FOR THE REST of her life, Kelley knew she would remember the Opata Holy Week ceremony. It was unlike anything she'd ever imagined, a blending of a two-thousand-year-old Catholic celebration with a traditional Indian ceremony—perhaps just as old—that heralded the history of the Opata before the first European ever set foot on New World soil.

It had all started very early in the morning on the Thursday before Easter. By the time Kelley was up and dressed, the women had been busy in the old adobe church for hours, cleaning the mud walls and decorating the altar with lupine, prickly pear blossoms and bright orange poppies. By late afternoon the men who took the role of Pharisees had draped the altar with a black curtain and donned rather striking mustachioed masks. Now, at sundown, the first parade was about to begin.

"This man is called the Centurion, the Roman soldier who will capture *Jesucristo*," Yazmín explained to Kelley as they stood beside the old mansion. Near the doorway, an Opata man in a brilliant military costume was mounting the best horse in town. He wore black and red satin-edged trousers, a white wool jacket and a knee-length green skirt for good measure. A cluster of green feathers sprouted from his cardboard helmet, which was adorned with an assortment of mirrors, silver buttons and bits of red cloth.

Once the Centurion mounted his horse, he waved his paper-tassled scepter in the air while he rode hell-bent up and down the tiny street with two small boys hanging on to his silver-studded stirrups. The horse had cocoon rattles strung around his hooves, which jangled like strings of bells and intensified the festive air that permeated the proceedings.

"Now they will capture *El Señor*," Yazmín continued, pointing to a three-foot-tall statue of Christ. "They will drag him to the church and tie him to the rack of cane at the altar."

They did exactly that, hauling the blindfolded statue through the dusty streets of Tepari before an organized mob of wailing women and bantering men who seemed as determined to keep the whole event as lighthearted as the female *cantoras* were to make it serious.

Kelley watched, fascinated, for the next hour while the drums pounded and the women sang and the men leapt and cavorted in exaggerated compliance with their ancient ritual. Yazmín had told her that it was very rare that a foreigner was allowed the privilege of observing this event. Still, now that the celebration had finally begun, Kelley was finding herself acutely aware of how far away from home she'd be when Bonnie started serving Easter dinner. How special it would have been to celebrate this Opata Easter with Jimmy's family! And how special it would have been to share it with Nick!

Oh, give it up, Kelley, she chided herself, realizing that it was hopeless to blot out her deepest desires. *You want to share everything with Nick. And if you go home with fourteen burros full of sample plants and notes, it won't mean diddly if you go home without him by your side.*

Fourteen burros might be a bit of an exaggeration, but Kelley was very pleased with the material she'd gathered and stored in the tiny hut Yazmín had arranged for her to stay in. No bigger than her kitchen back home, it had a flat roof made of loose straw, which probably had to be replaced after every summer storm, and piles of rocks set with mud framed the uneven walls. Kelley had been using an old piece of ironwood as a desk and had cleared a space along one rock wall as a shelf for her notes and herbarian samples.

And what notes and samples she already had! She'd gathered data beyond her wildest dreams! Many of the plants used by the Opata were standard in this part of the world—aloe for burns and mint leaves for pain—but there were medical applications of countless other herbs and plants known only to the Opata. Kelley had even had an opportunity to sample a cure firsthand when she'd been stung by a poisonous scorpion one night. Yazmín had fixed up a poultice of houseleek to draw out the venom and ease the burn.

Yazmín had also given her a native cactus-spine hairbrush to replace the one she'd lost somewhere on the trail to Tepari, and she'd tried to anticipate Kelley's every need. Everyone else had also been very kind to her, but the Opatas' friendliness had done little to ease the ache in Kelley's heart. Once she'd looked so blue that Yazmín had offered her a shoulder to cry on, and she'd surprised herself by pouring out her heartbreak to the sympathetic woman, just as she'd shared all her teenage traumas with Mama Chayo.

There was no doubt that Kelley missed Nick sorely— missed his smile, his laughter and the feel of his warm, magic hands on her skin—but the worst part of their separation was that she'd left him with everything so uncertain. José was scheduled to return for her in another week or so, and Nick had given her the impression that he'd find a way to wrap up all the loose ends with Liliana before she got back.

Now she desperately wanted to put things right; she desperately wanted to hear him say that he'd finally made permanent peace with Liliana. She wanted him so much she—

"I want him so much I'm imagining things," she said out loud, suddenly struck by the realization that one of the men heading toward her through the crowd did not have a mask or those long and fleshy Opata earlobes, either. He had smooth, square features that looked just right with the Dodgers' T-shirt and baggy white cotton pants that showed off his muscular thighs, and he had a smile that made Kelley shiver and glow and stammer as she struggled desperately to think of something, *anything*, to say as he caught her eye from across the dancing procession.

But suddenly Kelley realized that she didn't need to say anything, and neither did he. She hadn't the slightest idea what Nick was doing in Tepari or how he'd made the trip, but when he bolted through the dancers and seized her in his arms, she knew it didn't matter. She adored him with every ounce of her being, and the time had come to let him know.

NICK CRUSHED KELLEY to him with a searing kiss, starving for assurance of her physical well-being and her need for him.

"Oh *corazón*, how I've missed you!" he confessed with a groan, kissing freckle after freckle on her glow-

ing face. "Tell me you're all right. Tell me you're glad
to see me. Tell me there's somewhere in this village
where we can be alone!"

He was rewarded with a jubilant kiss from Kelley's
warm and hungry mouth, then the giddily whispered
confession, "Yes, yes and yes!" before she firmly
pushed him away. Breathing heavily, she reminded
him, "We're visitors here, Nick, and they're in the
middle of a religious ceremony. We should try to
maintain some...decorum."

"Decorum?" he repeated with a grin. "Does that
mean I shouldn't start unbuttoning your blouse yet?"

She shot him a warning glance, but it held no sting.
He laughed out loud, thrilled to be with her, as he
pulled her back into his arms in a slightly more platonic fashion.

Eyes glowing, Kelley asked him, "Would it be silly
to ask what you're doing here?"

"If you can't guess that then you're not smart
enough to be a Ph.D.," he teased her, feeling incredibly light and joyful. "Or don't botany classes cover the
ludicrous things a male Homo sapien will do to find a
mate?"

She laughed. "Surely you didn't have to hike
through that unholy thorn scrub just to find a woman,
Nico."

"To find *a* woman? No, ma'am." Now he sobered;
it was important that Kelley understand. He hadn't
gone through the hell of the past two weeks for nothing. "But to find *the* woman, the only woman, a tough
journey was a prerequisite."

Nick had undergone an exhausting trek through
hellish terrain, not to mention the burden of his ever-
increasing worry that he might not get to Kelley in time.

Now that he actually held her in his arms, his suspicions about Pablo seemed utterly ludicrous, and he didn't want to spoil her joy by revealing that it was fear as much as desire that had forced him to make the journey. What difference did it make anyway? Both emotions were spawned from his growing love for Kelley.

Her eyes grew big with hope and confusion as she took in his words, but before she could answer, the crush of the procession forced Nick to pull her back against the nearest adobe. Only then did he become aware of the elderly woman who had appeared beside Kelley, and was now smiling at him as though she knew exactly who he was.

"You are just in time," the old one greeted him with a teasing glint in her eye. "I am needed at the church and I was going to ask some handsome young man to take care of our guest."

Kelley beamed as she quickly stepped out of Nick's arms. "I guess I don't need to tell you that this is my Nico, Yazmín," she confessed with an embarrassed chuckle.

There was something sweet and bravely tender about those possessive words: *my Nico*. A month ago they would have frightened Nick, but now they seemed just right. He did belong to Kelley, whether she believed it or not, and the fact that he still hadn't found a way to resolve Liliana's problems with Pablo didn't change that irrevocable fact.

"It is an honor to meet you," Nick told the old woman when Kelley finished the introductions. In spite of his instinctive prejudice against *curanderos*, he couldn't help but be polite. "Thank you for being so kind to Kelley."

Yazmín stretched out her hands in an expansive gesture. "*De nada*," she assured him, her warm smile confirming his suspicion that Kelley had earned more than a little of the old one's respect. "We have learned much from each other. But I am glad you have come to make her happy. And I hope you will enjoy the fiesta."

"I thought this was a religious ceremony," Kelley countered.

With her chin, Yazmín gestured to the south. "For the Yaquis who live by the sea, yes. It is very serious. But for us—" she grinned mischievously "—it is a time to pretend we are all very young."

Yazmín explained a few more details of the proceedings to Kelley and Nick before she excused herself and melted into the crowd. When Nick took hold of Kelley's hand again, the drums were still pounding—like the backbeat of desire in his heart. He kneaded her fingers with increasing tension as he watched the Lenten mourners, and he moved close behind her so he could slip one hand around her waist.

"I don't think I can take too much more of this, *corazón*," he whispered in English. Even though nobody could hear him, what he had to say seemed too private to share with the hoards of celebrants. "Wouldn't this be a good time for us to slip away?"

"And miss this once in a lifetime event?" she teased him, resting the back of her head against his chest. "Don't you think this is fascinating, Nick?"

"Fascinating," he breathed, dropping a kiss on the top of her head. "But crowded, Kelley, and confusing. Maybe if you could take me somewhere quiet to explain it all to me..."

"Explain it to you?" she asked, tugging his free hand around her waist until both his arms were draped around her. "Shouldn't it be the other way around? You're the one who was raised in this part of the world."

"I wasn't raised an Opata," he pointed out, gently stroking her fingers with his own. "And anyway, I've forgotten everything I ever learned before we met."

"Everything?"

"Everything," he vowed solemnly, struggling with his memories of the last time he'd held her just like this. They'd been alone in the desert under a canopy of stars. *Come on, Kelley,* he silently urged as the celebrants edged away from them in the wake of the parade. *Have mercy on this poor man who's aching for your touch.*

He pulled her closer, dropping an enticing kiss on the rim of her ear. And then, forgetting the thinning crowd that still milled around them, his tone grew husky as he vowed, "If you can't find a way to take me behind closed doors in another five minutes, Kelley McKinney, I think I'm going to go stark raving berserk."

Her eyes grew bright as she dazzled him with a Mona Lisa smile, struggling to hide her pleasure. "Well, we can't let that happen, can we, Mr. Morales?" she asked, her sauciness tempered by the tenderness of her hands as she eagerly gripped his fingers with her own. "Where would I find another guide to get me safely home?"

"You couldn't, lady, so you better be nice to me," he cajoled her.

"I'll be sure to give you a big tip in the morning for services rendered," Kelley teased, tugging him toward a moonlit corner of the town. "Did I happen to mention that I booked a private room for two while I was in Tepari?"

Nick grinned, suddenly certain that all of his troubles would soon be resolved. "No, I don't think you mentioned that. But it shows excellent foresight on your part, Dr. McKinney, and if you'll consent to share your lodgings with me this evening—" he caught her eye as they shared a laugh "—I promise to pick up the tab."

Neither one of them spoke as Kelley led Nick through the haphazard streets to her humble but oh-so-private temporary dwelling. She suspected that protocol would best be served if she asked Yazmín to find an "official" place for Nick to spend the night, but at the moment she needed him too much to worry about such details. After all, nobody was likely to pay much attention to either one of them until the celebration was over, and it gave every sign of lasting well into the night.

Nick made no comment as Kelley lifted the crude blanket that served as a door, but his fingers were warm as they laced through hers, and his thumb etched intoxicating invitations on her delicate inner wrist. She tried to speak—to welcome him to her temporary home, to confess how terribly much she had missed him—but the combination of Nick's tangy male scent and the aroma of fresh-cut herbs swamped her senses like an aphrodisiac, and the simplest of words were beyond her.

Fortunately, Nick didn't seem to be in the mood for conversation, either. He cupped Kelley's face with both hands, then tipped her head back until his lips were just a breath away from hers. Slowly he teased her with a lingering kiss on one corner of her mouth, then a second kiss on the other side. His thumbs traced erotic patterns across her sensitive throat until she felt breathless with desire.

With deceptive laziness, the heels of his hands insinuated themselves on the swelling upper curves of her breasts. "Oh, Kelley," he groaned against her forehead, his face warm and flushed with desire as his hands moved lower yet. "Don't ever go away this long again!"

Kelley didn't answer; she just cradled his head as she covered him with kisses, revelling in the feel of his urgent hands on her breasts. For a long, tantalizing moment he traced circles around her swelling nipples with his palms, then his fingertips closed around each yearning peak.

When Kelley couldn't stifle a cry of ecstasy, Nick instantly covered her mouth with his own, thrusting his tongue deep within her sweetness as a foreshadowing of things to come. As he deftly unbuttoned her blouse and freed her breasts, she wrapped her arms around his back, pressing herself yet closer as his hands slowly worked their way down the front of her body, skating along the ridge of her hipbones until he firmly grasped her thighs.

Kelley moaned as she quivered against his kneading fingers, trying to remember why she'd left him in Cielo Solo with things so uncertain…and how she'd lived for two whole weeks without his touch. But rational thought was already impossible. Outside the drums were still pounding, compelling her to do their bidding; and Nick, his tongue tracing lazy circles around the tips of her aching breasts, eclipsed any lingering ghost of doubt about their future.

Desire fired Kelley as she lifted her face to kiss him fiercely—once, twice, then again and again beyond counting. They fell together to the cane-pole bed, arms and legs intertwined as their bodies sought to meld in the darkness of the night.

"I've got to have you, Kelley," he choked out in a hoarse, hungry whisper, crushing her against him as though he'd waited a lifetime to hold her in his arms. "I've never wanted anything so much in my entire life!"

With ecstasy she gave Nick what he wanted, and he returned the gift again and again until the desert sparkled with dawn's first light.

CHAPTER SEVENTEEN

NICK AND KELLEY left at sunrise three days later, after the Easter festivities had come to a close. It was a beautiful day in the desert mountains…clear and crisp with only a memory of dew on the ocotillo thorns by the time they took their leave of everyone in Tepari.

Poor little Maleta was all but staggering under the load of plant specimens and artifacts that Kelley had collected. Nick cheerfully observed that he'd probably have to buy a trailer—or at least a second burro—just to get all of Kelley's belongings back to the States.

Despite his good humor as they took off, Nick seemed to be quite determined to press on in a hurry. From Kelley's point of view, the trip to Cielo Solo was too far to travel comfortably in a single day; propriety had forced José to do it, but she would have expected Nick to deliberately linger so that they could have a solitary night on the trail. It irked her that he was so adamant about reaching his village by nightfall.

"You know, Kell," he commented as they plowed through the dense thorn scrub in the blistering heat of the afternoon, "these past few days I've been learning just how American I really am. There are things about L.A. that I miss so much…things I take for granted and never even think of when I'm at home."

"Such as?"

"Well, Chinese food for one. I'm sick of *frijoles*! And how easy it is to get from one place to another, or call a woman for a date—'' he grinned at her affectionately ''—or find out the daily baseball stats. Do you realize that when we left home, the Dodgers were only a game and a half behind the Braves, and for all I know they could be in first place or in the cellar by now?''

Kelley, who could have cared less about baseball, answered solemnly, "I don't miss any of those things very much, Nick. But I did miss my family at Easter. And I have to admit that I rather missed you after a day or two in Tepari.''

He smiled and reached out to ruffle her hair, then took her hand for just a moment. The terrain was simply too difficult to traverse holding hands, so he squeezed her fingers with his own, then let her go. "I missed you, too, Kell. Honestly, I started to speak English to the cacti. I'm ready to sell my soul for a dip in a swimming pool or even five minutes in an air-conditioned lobby. And if I have to have one more conversation with anybody about weaving mats or gathering *nopales* for dinner, I think I'll lose my mind.''

Kelley studied him coolly as she realized what he was really telling her. When he'd first arrived in Tepari, Nick's eagerness to see her had been terribly flattering but almost too hard to comprehend. She'd had the feeling all along that it wasn't just the prospect of her company that had prodded him to rush to the Opata village. "In other words, Nick, you were desperate to see another American.''

"Desperate might be a little strong, but eager, yes," he admitted readily. "No doubt about it.''

"It's nice that I was...so nearby. Otherwise you might have been forced to track down Rinsland for company. Or some other smuggler."

Nick must have missed the somber tone of her voice, because he cheerfully agreed. "Yep, he was next on my list. Lucky I stumbled on you first or I might have ended up in hell instead of heaven."

Kelley glared at him. "I'm glad you found my Opata adobe such convenient lodging, Nick. I suppose you would have shared it with any other American woman who was occupying it at the time."

This time her tone was so sharp that Nick stopped in the middle of the trail, his eyes narrowing. "Kelley, I can't imagine why I'd have to explain to you that I was kidding, but by the look on your face, I'd guess we're getting our wires crossed again."

"I'm just trying to be honest with myself, Nick. When we were in L.A. and you had dozens of women to choose from, you found your desire for me quite easy to restrain. When we were in Cielo Solo and you had Liliana at your fingertips, you didn't want me, either. It's only when I'm the only choice for miles around that I seem to whet your appetite." Her tone mirrored her cold expression. "Does that pretty well sum everything up?"

"It does not sum everything up!" he protested. "I wanted you in Los Angeles; I wanted you in Tucson. By the time we got to Hermosillo I had nearly lost my mind with wanting you! I'd vowed to hold on till we reached Cielo Solo, but I just couldn't do it—especially since you made it very clear that you wanted me just as much as I wanted you."

Kelley had to look away; she could not refute him.

"Now as to Tepari, you were hardly *convenient*. I dragged myself through this tangle of eagle's claw and Texas Ranger thorns just to be with you a few days sooner, Kell, and if you're going to condemn me for that, then I shouldn't have come at all." He exhaled sharply. "The simple truth is that I have made my decision; I want us to be together. From where I stand, you're the one who's holding back now—asking questions, pointing fingers, raising objections even where there aren't any to be found."

Kelley could see his point and she knew that their relationship was simply too new and fragile to sustain a broadside hit. Yet what had he said in that long, passion-filled night, or the secret nights that had followed, to assure her of the depth of his feelings? Oh, he hungered for her, as a man hungers for a woman, but did he love her the way a husband might grow to love a wife?

"Kelley," Nick finally reproached her as he tugged on the medal at his neck, "I know that my feelings about Cielo Solo have greatly clouded the beginning of our romance. And I'm genuinely sorry about that. But it couldn't be helped, and it certainly can't be changed now. I thought when I came to you in Tepari that I'd made it clear that we're embarking on something very special and very... long term. It's probably too soon to say for sure if it's permanent, Kelley, but I honestly thought we were moving in that direction. Frankly, I'm surprised to hear that you think otherwise."

Kelley met his eyes solemnly, then took a step in his direction. She didn't know why she was always so uncertain. Yet she couldn't seem to stifle the sense that Nick was always holding something back, always struggling with some dark feeling that he wasn't yet ready to share with her. "I just keep getting mixed messages, Nick," she admitted softly. "And I've still got questions that I'm afraid to ask."

His eyebrows arched. "Such as?"

She reached out to touch the medal at his neck. "What this means to you, for instance. Liliana has one just like it, and you never take it off."

He met her gaze squarely. "I never take it off because it's a family heirloom. My great-grandmother gave it to Mama Luz when she made First Communion as a child. She passed it on to my mother, who passed it on to me. I even wore it with my dog tags overseas."

Relieved but embarrassed, Kelley had to look away. But he continued, "I suspect that Liliana has one like it because the Virgin of Guadalupe is the patron saint of Mexico. Her family probably buys their medals at the same puny spot in Pitahaya where my great-grandmother must have shopped."

"I'm sorry, Nico," she whispered. "If it weren't for Allan, I'm sure I'd be more patient. It's just that I've been here so many times before—"

"Not with me you haven't," he said brusquely. "And frankly, Kelley, I'm as tired of hearing about Allan as you are about Liliana. Why do you insist on tarring me with his brush? This is a different case entirely. What I feel for Liliana isn't passion, it's guilt. It's obligation. It's the need to atone for a great injustice I once did to a trusting friend."

"But it's over, Nick. There's nothing you can do about it now."

"About the past? No, there's not. But maybe there's still something I can do to stop Pablo."

"Stop him from what?" Kelley asked, realizing that he'd never really clarified this point before. "What do you think he'll do? I mean, he's not vile enough to stoop to rape or kidnap or murder, is he?"

Nick's lengthy silence was unnerving. "I'm just not sure," he admitted darkly. "I'm afraid he's capable of anything. What concerns me most at the moment is that he's paid *La zarca* to put a curse on Liliana, and she's absolutely terrified."

"Nick, that's ridiculous!" The scientist in Kelley fiercely rebelled. "I've met the woman, and I don't doubt that she enjoys manipulating people by tapping their fears. But she's harmless; all she does is light candles and incense. She doesn't know enough about herbal medicine to use it for good or ill. I'm sorry Liliana's so frightened but—"

"But I should just laugh it off because it's nothing more than primitive superstition? I wonder how you'd feel if you were the one shaking in your boots, Kell, and I just laughed at you? What if you were the one Pablo was stalking? If he's got half a brain anyway he's realized by now that you are the woman I'd die for!"

Kelley was silent as his words sunk in. At last his urgency began to make sense. No wonder he'd been so relieved to see her in Tepari—no wonder he didn't want the two of them to camp out alone tonight! While his concern for her was deeply touching, Kelley knew that for a man like Nick, a sense of obligation could be just as strong an emotion as love. Hadn't he promised Paul that he'd take care of her? More importantly, hadn't he promised Kelley?

Catching the panic in her eyes, Nick quickly rushed on. "Kelley, I don't have any reason to think he's after you. For all I know, his talk about Liliana is just hot air, too. But if he's serious about casting a spell on her, you need to understand that there's more involved here than fear...though fear can be enough to make somebody feel pretty sick, and Liliana was already feeling poorly when I left the village."

Of course, Kelley scoffed. *And maybe that's why he's in such a hurry to get back to Cielo Solo.*

She knew it wasn't fair; he hadn't pushed her to leave Tepari. Still, the old insecurities were building up inside her, and the joy she'd celebrated for the past three days was starting to subside.

"My point is that a man like Pablo doesn't bother with a curse unless he's deadly serious," Nick explained, wiping the sweat from the back of his neck. "He's got more than a little bit of faith in the evil power of our local *curandera.* But the long and short of it is, if the curse doesn't work on its own, then he'll help it along any way he can. And since he's got easy access to the village, the number of choices available to him are unlimited."

Kelley said nothing, and after a moment, Nick continued. "Worse yet, it's important to *La zarca's* credibility that Liliana show some ill effects from the curse. Which means that if she doesn't start to exhibit symptoms soon, that crazy old woman is likely to start salting her soup with rattler venom...or whatever it is she does to prove her power. When you get back to Cielo Solo, I want you to double-check everything you eat."

"Why?" Kelley asked, surprised and alarmed at his vehemence. "I can see why Liliana ought to be careful, but I thought you said that I had nothing to worry about."

"I hope you don't, *corazón,*" he said quickly. "I just want you to play it safe until we cross the border."

Kelley took comfort from his words . . . and stifled a wave of fear as she realized that the only reason Pablo would want to hurt her would be to punish Nick. "What about you, Nico? Has he . . . has he . . ."

"Put a curse on me?" He tried to laugh it off but failed. "Of course he has. What did you expect? With any luck at all, I'll be dead within a week . . . even if *La zarca* doesn't have any more help from Pablo."

BY THE TIME they made camp at sundown, Kelley was feeling tired and withdrawn. It didn't help any that they'd taken a wrong turn through some look-alike shrubs and lost several hours in the stifling heat getting their bearings; they were still half a day from Cielo Solo. After their earlier discussion, Kelley's anticipation of a private romantic evening was more than quelled by her concern for their safety, not to mention her new uncertainty regarding their future.

As they ate cold tortillas in the gathering darkness, neither one was inclined to talk. Even Maleta seemed too tuckered out to graze. It was another exquisite starspangled night that lifted at least a little of the heaviness in Kelley's heart. Nearby she could smell the nocturnal blossoms of the beaver-tail cactus poking through a maze of surrounding gray thorn. Off to the right she heard the evening call of a tiny elf owl from his secret saguaro cave, and nature's own clown, the roadrunner, jogged through their tiny clearing in search of a more easily traveled path.

Kelley was trying to decide whether she should suggest that they zip their sleeping bags together when Nick rose purposefully from his spot on a good-sized boulder and strolled over to her side.

"Is this seat taken, ma'am?" he asked, plopping down beside her on the dead trunk of an apache pine she'd appropriated as a bench.

"No, sir. There's plenty of room for one more."

Nick smiled and slipped his arm around her waist. "I'll miss this," he confessed. "I do love those city lights, but I'll miss the desert sunset."

"Will you miss these eerie night sounds?" Kelley asked, as the rumbling roar of a big cat rent the air.

Nick laughed. "I doubt it. But I must confess that I've been hoping for a glance of a wolf ever since I saw that pair at the museum outside Tucson."

"You can keep your hopes to yourself," Kelley told him. "I wish them well, but I can live without the sight of a pack of wolves bearing down on me in the middle of nowhere. I understand that they've been growing increasingly bold down here lately."

Nick nodded. "Well, you can't blame them much, Kell. Humans keep moving into their terrain and killing off their game. They're hungry." The cat snarled again, closer this time, and Kelley shivered in Nick's embrace. "I guess that jaguar is, too."

"Jaguar?" she asked, stifling the jab of alarm in her heart. "How can you tell? I thought this was puma country."

"It usually is," he agreed. "But pumas snarl like fighting tomcats; jaguars roar like lions. Have you ever heard a calico kitty sound like that?" he asked as the rapacious rumble echoed over the night again.

"Can't say as I have," Kelley answered uneasily, desperately wishing that the awesome noise would stop.

"Well, I have. Once or twice when I was young, jaguars started tracking game near Cielo Solo. They're more common farther south, but they roam for hundreds of miles when they're feeling restless. Or hungry.''

"I wish he'd roam back where he came from," Kelley declared. "If he gets any closer, I'm going to start wishing you'd decided to bring that gun after all.''

"Don't worry, *corazón*," Nick promised as he pulled her closer, planting a kiss on her cheek. "I'll protect you from the creatures of the night.''

"You will, huh?" Kelley teased, brushing against him provocatively. "And who will protect me from you?" She turned up her face in invitation, and was rewarded with a gentle kiss, the first since they'd exchanged their hard words earlier.

"You're very special to me," Nick whispered, his voice tender in the moonlight. She nuzzled his neck and pulled him closer, dropping quiet kisses along the length of his firm jaw. He closed his eyes as Kelley's mouth found his; he breathed her name as their tongues slowly joined in an age-old waltz.

For several moments the land was silent, and Kelley's need for Nick eclipsed all her other senses as his fingertips explored the delicate path along her collar bone to her throat. "I'm not much with words, Kell," he confessed between kisses, "but I really don't think I've ever felt quite the same way about anybody else that I feel about you.''

Kelley didn't know how to answer that, so she just stroked his beard-stubbled face with one warm hand, then pressed her lips more urgently to his. His answering kiss was vibrant, eager, full of tenderness and growing passion. She knew at once that the time for words was past, and that any doubts would have to be put off until tomorrow.

Nick's arms tightened around her, and his tongue began a gentle seduction of the sensitive curl of her ear. Kelley swayed toward him, floating on the new crest of bonding between them, suddenly certain that the future would take care of itself.

And then the jaguar roared. It didn't roar on the distant mountain, or from some neighboring scrub oak. It roared from a point that was far too close for comfort, in an endless, terrifying litany of rage that kept growing louder and louder as each second passed—as though it were moving their way and moving very fast.

"Nico!" Kelley gasped, pulling away as she jumped to her feet. "What are we going to do? Is he—"

Her words were cut off by another sound, a hysterical, squealing-pig sound, followed by the thunder of tiny javelina hooves clattering through the tangle of thorns. There seemed to be dozens of wild pigs trampling through the underbrush, all of them bellowing with bald terror.

Too late Kelley realized that she and Nick had been following a natural trail that countless animals had carved through the dense thorn scrub...and had camped in a clearing that was smack in the center of the path.

"Stay calm," Nick ordered, reaching decisively for a dead piece of mesquite that was almost heavy enough to pass for a club. "Get as far off the trail as you possibly can and stay absolutely still." His voice was low but urgent, and Kelley did her best to follow his commands.

But there wasn't much empty space beyond the clearing, and the pigs and the jaguar were coming so fast that Kelley knew she couldn't get very far out of the way. And they couldn't really try to turn the javelinas back on their trail—there were too many of them and not much room, and they'd just end up milling around hysterically in the clearing when the cat arrived. It seemed to Kelley that the only hope she and Nick had was that the pigs and the jaguar would roar by so fast that the jaguar wouldn't have time to notice the humans or bother with them.

It was a forlorn hope. Nick had barely picked up the mesquite branch when the first screaming pig plunged into the clearing, going so fast that it might have led the others, and its pursuer, straight through before it noticed Nick or Kelley. But the instant the javelina made its entrance, tired old Maleta jumped to his feet and started to bray.

In the moonlight Kelley could see the spotted yellow cat coming through the night, its heavy, awesome length stretched out as it flew liquidly through the air, pausing only for split-second touchdowns and take-offs. It followed the shrieking javelinas right into the clearing and then, without warning, wheeled off the path to hurl itself at the hysterically honking burro.

Nick didn't wait for the big cat to spy him; he surged forth at once. He got one good hit on the back of the jaguar's skull before it turned on him. Otherwise, Kelley was certain, he wouldn't have stood a prayer.

The cat was a bit wobbly as it leaped on top of Nick, knocking him to the ground. He slammed the mesquite branch in its face, over and over again, doubling up his knees to jab his feet into the big cat's belly. The tactic was effective in throwing the jaguar off his chest, but the animal seized its revenge by sinking its jaws into Nick's right leg, tearing flesh from the cotton-covered calf.

When Kelley heard Nick cry out, she was terrified that he was going to lose the battle if he didn't have some help. Sick with fear, she knew she'd have to fight; Nick was in trouble, and there was nowhere to run.

She couldn't find a branch like Nick's but she grabbed a handful of small rocks from the ground beneath her feet and hurled them at the jaguar, the bursts of pellets peppering its long-fanged face like bullets.

It shook his head and snarled, dropping Nick's leg from its mouth. While the jaguar was disoriented from the hail of pebbles, Nick slammed the mesquite into its skull again, twice, and the big cat rumbled horribly into the night. It was pain this time, not hunger, that drove the beast. It shook itself, bewildered, as Kelley's hail of pebbles and brush continued, and Nick got one more good thwack on its hind end before it bolted away.

A moment later, Nick slumped to the ground unconscious.

NICK THOUGHT HE must have passed out; in any event, there seemed to be a few minutes he'd lost track of, because one minute the pigs were squealing, the burro was braying and the jaguar was ready to tear out his throat...and the next it was stone-cold quiet in the thicket.

"Nico? Nico, can you hear me?" Kelley was crying softly. She seemed to be far away. He opened his eyes and found her, dimly, somewhere near his leg, which she'd wrapped with a tourniquet that had once been her blouse. She was pouring some of their precious water supply over his mangled leg, heedless of the blood that had spilled from his wound onto her jeans.

"I'm...I'm okay, Kelley," he lied, struggling to keep from fainting again. The pain was worse than anything he'd ever imagined, even worse than his memory of that stray bullet he'd picked up in Nam. "Just give me a moment to...catch my breath."

He heard Kelley sigh deeply. "Nick, you've been out for almost an hour. Thank God you're awake! Can you move everything? I know it hurts but—"

"I've had worse," he lied again, determined to lessen her fear. "I'll be fine with a good night's sleep."

"You need more than sleep, Nick!" Urgency colored her strained tone. "You need a doctor."

"Of course I need a doctor!" he snapped, the pain finally overcoming his determined nonchalance. "But we're still a long way from Pitahaya."

"We're not that far from Tepari. It would be easy for me to find the way back there. Yazmín could come and—"

Nick stared at her as though she'd lost her mind. "You've got to be kidding, Kelley. I'm not about to put myself in the hands of a witch doctor!"

"Yazmín is not a witch doctor! She took care of my scorpion sting beautifully; no modern medicine could have worked any better. And it's not like you've got cancer or diabetes, Nick. You've got an external injury. She told me all about the Opata cures for bleeding and infection. You use the pulp of the *nopales* for a base with sumac bark or thyme. I've got the notes here somewhere; I could do it in a pinch. But Yazmín—"

"Forget it, Kell!" he barked. "She's not here and I wouldn't let her touch me, anyway. We're more than halfway to Cielo Solo, and I'd rather die there if it's meant to be, thank you kindly. Besides, I don't want you to go anywhere by yourself! Between Pablo and the desert—''

''Nick, this isn't the time to worry about Pablo. You need help and I'm going to provide it.'' Suddenly his fragile, crinkly haired Irish beauty was leaning over him, her expression tense as she laid one cold hand on his sweating face. ''Listen to me, Nico. If I were injured, you'd take care of me, wouldn't you? You'd consider the options and make the best decision you could, and brook no opposition from somebody who was hurt too badly to think very clearly. Am I right?''

Nick new she was leading up to something, but the pain kept fogging up his thinking. ''Of course I'd take care of you, Kelley,'' was all he could say.

''Yes, you would. But I'm not hurt—you are. So I'm going to make the decisions for a while. And I've just decided what we're going to do.''

''Kelley, please—''

''I've washed out the wound and stopped the bleeding for the moment, Nick, and we've still got a few of those pain pills that Dr. Ramirez gave you for your thumb. I'm going to go through my notes while you sleep and figure out what Yazmín would do to stave off infection and reduce the swelling. I ought to have samples of most of the plants we need—and if we don't, they shouldn't be too hard to find in the morning.'' Her voice was stern but loving, the way Mama Luz had chided him when he was very young. ''Then we're going to store my plant press and all our equipment somewhere safe and put you on Maleta and get to Cielo Solo just as fast as we can go. I'll come back for our stuff later while somebody goes for Dr. Ramirez on the double. People have been injured and stranded a lot longer than forty-eight hours and come out okay, Nick. If we can hold you together till then, I really think you'll be all right.''

Nick closed his eyes and groaned. He'd rather die than submit to *curanderismo*, but Kelley was a scientist, Kelley knew what she was doing and Kelley was in charge. Besides all that, Kelley loved him, although she hadn't said so yet. He knew she'd sooner die than let him come to any harm.

"I'll ride the burro to Cielo Solo," he finally relented, unable to deny that his pain was even greater than his pride. "But I'll be damned if I'll let a *curandero* doctor me with rattles and beads, even by proxy. When you run out of pills, I'll just tough it out till Dr. Ramirez can look at me.''

"Suffer all you want, Nick, but I can't leave this tourniquet on forever. You've got to have something to stop the bleeding and draw out the infection. Even house-cat scratches have an uncanny ability to get infected, and I don't even want to think about what a jaguar's claws might do.''

Nick shook his head. "He didn't claw my leg, Kelley. He bit me. Tried to make a dinner entrée out of my leg, come to think of it.'' He sat upright and tried to catch a glimpse of the wound. "He didn't really take too much of my flesh with him now, did he?''

For the first time Nick found the strength to study Kelley's face... and read there the certain knowledge that his leg—perhaps his life—lay in her hands. Despite the calm, angry words that she'd hurled at him in the darkness, it was suddenly clear to him that Kelley was terrified. Not of Pablo, not of the jaguar, not of the night; just terrified for him. Tears glistened along her soft lashes as she tugged a flashlight from her pack and began to search for her notes.

"Kelley," he said more gently, "I know I'm being obnoxious, but I hurt like hell and I feel like a fool."

"Nico, don't you understand?" she suddenly burst out. "There's no room here for your pride or even your personal antipathy for folk medicine. Don't you think I'd rush you to a hospital if I could?"

She reached out to touch his face, and her fingers were icy cold, trembling. "Nick, I know that you don't want me to treat you with sumac bark and *nopales*, and I wish I could honor your request. But I've—" she broke down for just a second, and her tears wounded him even more than the gaping hole left by the big cat's teeth "—I've seen your leg, and I have to tell you straight. If the only medicine we've got is cactus salve, then we've *got* to use it right away." She swallowed another sob. "If you want to leave Mexico with two good legs, Nico, we just don't have any other choice."

CHAPTER EIGHTEEN

"MAMA LUZ! *¡Aquí vienen! Su nieto está herido!*"

Your grandson is injured! The words pierced her heart like a fierce ocotillo thorn. How many times had she awakened with such fears when he'd been living so very far away! But now that he was home, now that she had thought him safe, he'd come to harm because of Pablo. Her worst fears had been confirmed: the curse was working. Liliana was terribly ill, and now Nico was also going to die.

"*¡Nico! Qué te pasó?*" Carmelita cried out, rushing ahead of the others to greet her nephew.

He perched clumsily aboard the burro, his good leg occasionally scraping the ground. The other leg was tightly wrapped in some kind of material that had once been white but was now dark with blood.

The story spilled out quickly. Nico did not want to speak of his bravery, but Kelley quickly told the growing audience how he had saved her life by fighting off the jaguar. He, in turn, gave her credit for saving his leg by using the Opata cures she'd learned in Tepari. The *zumaque* had done wonders for his pain, he insisted, and thanks to the *nopal* poultice, there was no pus in the wound.

Still, the sight of it tore his grandmother's heart, and she feared that it was only a matter of time before infection set in. It would take more than herbal cures and good luck to counteract the spell that had been cast on her grandson. "You must go to see *La zarca* at once!" she counseled urgently, knowing that somehow she must convince him to pay the woman now. It had taken all of her strength to keep her promise to him while he'd been gone. "You must give her whatever she asks for, Nico," she begged him. "Surely you can see now that the spell she's cast on you is very strong! You may not have much time!"

Fatigued and hurting, Nico studied her solemnly, then reached out to touch her face. "Mama Luz," he reminded her gently, "you know I'd rather die than pay that snake a single penny. I need a real doctor; the nearest one is at the government clinic in Pitahaya. Now I'd rather not bounce from here to there on the back of this burro, so I'll be more than happy to use that money to pay somebody to go tell Dr. Ramirez that I need to see him at once."

A cry of protest slithered through the crowd, and terror shot through Mama Luz as she realized his intentions. "Nico, nobody can go to Pitahaya for you! Nobody can take the chance that the curse will turn on him as well! Your only chance is *La zarca*. If you send for the doctor she will be so angry she will never reverse the curse no matter what you pay her!"

Nico was starting to look less patient. "I'm worried about saving my leg, Mama Luz, not hurting that witch doctor's feelings. I thought that I could count on you to help me out when I was in trouble. Was I wrong?"

Before Mama Luz could respond to the terrible words, Kelley took a step forward and reached out her hands. "Mama Luz," she said gently, "Nico means no disrespect. You know that he loves you very much. But he is not a man of the desert anymore, and desert medicine will not do for him what it might do for you. He needs the kind of medicine he's used to, or his leg will never heal." Her eyes met Mama Luz's, woman to woman, as she urged, "Please send someone to Pitahaya right away. If Dr. Ramirez has a Jeep or a very fine horse, he might get here by tomorrow."

In anguish Mama Luz cried out, "Kelley, can you not see that it does not matter what the other doctor will do for him? Maybe he is a good doctor; maybe he is a good man! But unless the curse is lifted, my Nico will die! Poor Liliana is almost beyond help already!"

Nico's eyes flared when Mama Luz mentioned Liliana; tenderness for the girl he'd once loved filled his weary face. "What's wrong with Liliana?" he demanded. "Has that old bag poisoned her food?"

This time it was Carmelita who intervened. "She has terrible pains in her stomach! She has not moved since the day after you left! What more proof do you need?"

Panic skittered across Nico's face. "Take me to her," he commanded. "Somebody help me walk there or I'll hop all the way on one foot!"

His eyes beseeched his aunt, and then his uncle, for some ghost of understanding, but José slowly shook his head as if he thought Nick were crazy, and led Carmelita away. The rest of the group drew back, as though it might be dangerous to get too close to this madman.

In the end it was only Kelley—pale with fatigue and worry—who stepped forward to help him hobble toward Liliana's house on his saguaro-rib cane.

NICK KNEW SOMETHING was terribly wrong the minute he slipped into Liliana's shack. He had assumed,

from all the witch talk, that her problem was psycho-
somatic, intensified, perhaps, by some unsavory sub-
stance slipped into her soup or tea. But her face was
chalky white, and a grimace of pain took hold of her
even as she tried to greet him. There was no trace of joy
in her once sunny face.

"Lili," he croaked in dismay, hopping to her side.
"What has that witch done to you?"

Liliana's mother, who had hardly spoken to Nick in
the two weeks since he'd arrived, crossed the dirt floor
with a fresh supply of *yerba buena* leaves, scowling at
the gawking crowd gathered outside.

"The curse is working on her stomach," she revealed in hushed tones. "She says the pain is on her
right side, very low."

"What has she eaten since I left?" he asked, ignoring Liliana's mother's disapproving glare while he
probed the midsection of her stomach with a doctor's
care. He could smell the mint leaves and other herbs
that had been rubbed on her skin in futile hopes of
vanquishing the pain. "Anything that somebody could
have put something in?"

Liliana shook her head weakly. "I don't think I have
eaten since you left, Nico." She barely mouthed the
words. "The curse came on, hard, as soon as you were
gone."

He felt helpless, angry, as he turned back to Mama
Luz and the others who now spilled through the doorway. "She's been like this for five days and none of you
have gone for a doctor?" he upbraided them. "What
kind of vultures are you! How can you just sit around
and wait for her to die?"

A terrible hush swept over the crowd followed by a
whisper of anger. "Who are you to tell us how to live?"

Liliana's mother demanded harshly. "If you had acted like a man, Pablo would be dead now!" Suddenly she turned to Mama Luz, who cowered silently in the doorway. "Ask Mama Luz why Liliana is dying! She has the money to pay *La zarca* all the money you have sent her over the years! But would she spend one centavo to help her? Would she lift a finger to help my girl?"

Mama Luz could not meet the hostile woman's eyes, and Nick knew she could offer no word in her own defense without revealing that Nick had forbidden her to use her hoard of cash to pay a *curandero*. His grandmother had followed his commands, and now, because of him, the very people who filled her world with love had turned against her.

"My grandmother was wise to hold on to her money," he declared stoutly. "Now she has the money to pay a real doctor who can still save Liliana if someone can bring him here in time! Send somebody—anybody—to Pitahaya and I'll pay him any price! Just get a doctor for Liliana before it's too late!"

His virulent exhortation was greeted with silence. A dozen pairs of eyes glared at him with naked fury. The only friend Nick was sure of was the redheaded woman who pressed against him in watchful silence.

Finally Mama Luz struggled for words to pacify her friends. "He may know something that we do not," she pleaded in his defense, even though Nick new that she had no more faith in Dr. Ramirez than did the others. "He means well; you can see that! He has just been gone so long . . . he has forgotten many things."

"He has forgotten the land of his birth!" hollered one man.

"He has forgotten how to be a man!" called another.

"I haven't forgotten how to stand by a friend!" Nick roared back, heedless of the impact he was making on the hostile crowd. "I haven't forgotten how to tell that a woman has pain in her stomach that wasn't caused by a witch doctor!" He turned to his grandmother, his very last resort. If he couldn't reach her, he could never reach the others. "Mama Luz, have you forgotten how my mother died?"

Nick was consumed with helpless rage. He'd come back to Cielo Solo to make things right with Liliana, and instead he was going to watch her die! He would have crawled to Pitahaya on his hands and knees if he'd thought it would do any good, but he knew he'd never get there in time in his current condition. Whatever was wrong with her—food poisoning, gallstones or even appendicitis—was far too serious to disappear with a good night's rest and a cup of herbal tea. She desperately needed something he just couldn't give her, and nobody—not one person in this squalid village, no matter how much they loved her—was going to be brave enough to go to Pitahaya for help.

And then, quite suddenly, he felt a gentle hand on his shoulder. Surrounded by the villagers who loved Kelley's rival, it was Kelley herself who stoutly proclaimed, "If I start right now, Nico, and follow the moon, I should be there by morning. If he's got a four-wheel drive or even a great horse, he just might get here in time."

TWENTY-FOUR HOURS LATER, the villagers were still fussing over Dr. Ramirez and his pretty nurse, asking questions and demanding to see Liliana, when Kelley slipped out of Cielo Solo and over the hillock toward the great saguaro.

Her fatigue was absolute and all-encompassing. She'd won the battle but lost the war, and she was ready to lay down her arms. After emergency surgery for appendicitis, Liliana was alive, and Kelley was grateful; she couldn't have lived with herself if she hadn't done everything she could to save a human life. But from the look on Nick's face when Dr. Ramirez had first arrived—as though God had just decided to renew the world's lease by another million years—she knew that the peasant woman had won the final round. Even if Nick didn't try to marry Liliana and take her back to the States with him—it was too late, entirely too late, for Kelley to ever again be foolish enough to believe that what he felt for her might ever grow into a once-in-a-lifetime love.

It was a peaceful night on the desert—quiet and clear. The silence was soothing, and the tombstone-shaped cacti seemed to welcome Kelley. Heartsick, she rambled aimlessly through the creosote for half an hour before the distant sound of machinery reached her ears. At first the low drone did not alarm her; after all, she lived in a world where honking horns and the squeal of rubber were commonplace at all hours of the day and night. But here in the desert, where every sound was part of nature's private orchestra, the groan of a straining engine had no place.

Coupled with the squeaky crunch of a slow-moving truck was the sound of men's voices, low and furtive. As the darkened truck—armed with a menacing hydraulic cradle—approached the great saguaro, Kelley knew at once that something was terribly wrong.

It was hard to make out the faces of the four men in the darkness, but there was no mistaking the one voice that cursed in English and executed such clumsy Spanish commands to his companions. Kelley had heard that gravelly voice once before, on the day Nick had seen a burro cart full of cacti outside of Dr. Ramirez's office. It had to be Rinsland, and if Rinsland had brought other men and machinery to the great saguaro, then—

"No!" Kelley screamed, her panic obliterating common sense. She was too tired, too angry and too depressed to care what happened to herself; all she knew was that *this* saguaro, this mighty symbol of Nick's dreams for his lifesaving homecoming, could not be torn from desert ground. "It belongs here! It's sacred! You let it be!" she shouted, running breathlessly toward the fifty-foot-tall cactus. "It took two hundred years to grow there!"

For a moment, her spontaneous rescue tactics worked; the men, stunned by the appearance of a red-headed cactus angel, froze in the darkness and stared in speechless dismay. Belatedly Kelley remembered that she was speaking English, and probably only Rinsland could understand her.

"This cactus is the symbol of Cielo Solo!" she beseeched the men in Spanish. "The landmark. The way the people find the village when they've been away."

She was about to wax poetic when the Anglo in their midst stepped toward her, menace darkening his tone. "Nobody needs to find this village, sister," he snarled. "Ain't nobody worth remembering ever comes this way."

Only then did Kelley realize what an incredible blunder she'd just made. She, a lone, unarmed woman, was confronting four strange men in the middle of no-where and expecting them to demonstrate *honor* to a cactus…let alone honor to *her*! Now that she was close enough to study them, she realized that Rinsland's companions had nothing in common with Nick's uncles and cousins. Rinsland himself bore no resem-blance to any man she'd ever known in the States. They were all hard men, with cold, lifeless eyes, and the one who was laughing now wore an expression of glee that made her throat feel dry as dust.

"So it is Morales's redheaded princess," he whined in Spanish, "delivered right into my hands. What good fortune! Kelley, do they not call you?"

When he reached forward to grab her hand, she pulled back instantly, but his grip was bulldog cruel. And his laugh—that smug, incredibly self-satisfied cackle—was downright brutal.

"Who are you?" she demanded, suddenly terrified by the maniacal gleam in his eye. "How do you know my name?"

He chortled again, and the eerie sound made Kelley shiver. She struggled desperately to pull away from him. But all that achieved was a cuff to her neck, and double the pressure, now applied with both hands.

Morales's redheaded princess, he'd called her. That meant he knew Nick. *Oh, dear God!* she suddenly thought, realizing at last who Rinsland's terrible co-hort had to be. Pablo Villalobos, Nick's old tormen-tor. Cactus, drugs, guns…and maybe murder as well! He'd cast a spell on Nick and Liliana to seek his re-venge, and now he had Kelley in his hands!

She shuddered as she recalled Nick's hastily re-tracted words in the desert. *If he's got half a brain anyway, he's realized by now that* you *are the woman I'd die for....*

She didn't doubt that Nick would die for her; he'd proven that with the jaguar. And even if his love for Liliana did come first, Kelley knew that if Nick had the slightest idea she was in trouble, he'd find a way to rescue her. But judging by the weakened state he'd been in the last time she'd seen him, Kelley didn't think she'd even cross his mind for a day or two. And nobody else in the village was likely to think of her at all.

"I know everything about Morales, every way to make him bleed," Pablo boasted proudly, dragging the squirming Kelley toward the truck as the other men laughed. "I have waited nineteen years for this moment, *señorita*," he assured her. "Taking your life will be even more gratifying than making Morales watch his other woman die."

As NICK STEPPED OUT of Liliana's tiny house at midnight, he took a deep breath of relief. At last he knew that he was totally free to give his love to Kelley; at last he was free from his guilt and shame.

By the time news had reached him that three horses were galloping toward Cielo Solo, he'd all but given up hope that Kelley had reached Pitahaya, let alone that Liliana would live another hour. The miracle of Kelley's safe return had overwhelmed him, but he hadn't gotten a chance to convey his joy to Kelley before *La zarca* had descended on the gathering, uttering dire threats and warnings about how everyone would sicken and die at the hands of the government doctor.

Dr. Ramirez had simply ignored her. With Rosa's help, he'd operated on Liliana, then stitched up Nick's leg and checked his thumb. He'd also pointed out, man to man, that Nick was in need of psychiatric care, not medicine, if he ever intended to let a woman of Kelley's courage slip out of his grasp.

Nick had agreed wholeheartedly with the doctor before he'd hobbled off to his uncle's house to find her. It occurred to him that underneath that solid trooper spirit she had so bravely shown to the village, Kelley might be uneasy with the steadfast loyalty he'd shown to Liliana. Nick honestly believed that he would have defended anybody in the village from witchcraft, ignorance and death, but he had to admit that, in a way, he was relieved that it was Liliana whom he'd managed to save. For the first time in years, he felt light and free from nineteen years of guilt. He'd repaid Liliana for all his past crimes with this one single gesture: payment for his old betrayal with the fresh gift of her life. Nick knew that Liliana wouldn't see it that way, and maybe Kelley wouldn't either, because neither one of them ever considered him guilty of his crimes. But he was free now, utterly free, to love any woman he pleased. And the woman he loved was Kelley.

"She is not here," Carmelita told Nick when he reached the house. "I have not seen her since the doctor arrived. I thought she was with you."

Uneasily Nick toyed with the medal at his throat. "No, I only saw her for a minute. Then I had to tell the doctor everything I could." Unable to help himself, he reproached her, "He said if he'd been called even one day later, Liliana would have died."

His aunt couldn't meet his eyes. "They say she is sitting up already, Nico. Talking to them. Still weak and sore in her stomach, but not . . . not at all like she was before."

"That's right," he said coldly. "It wasn't a curse; it was a ruptured appendix. It could have happened to anybody, anywhere. Easy to fix with a real live doctor. Impossible to cure with witchcraft."

This time Carmelita met his eyes defiantly as she pointed to his bandaged leg. "Was it witchcraft that killed your pain and stopped your bleeding?"

He couldn't hold her gaze very long, not with the memory of Kelley's makeshift herbal cures, which had worked wonders for him. "No, *Tía*," he finally had to admit. "It was herbal medicine, which isn't exactly the same thing as witchcraft. Maybe Kelley is right— maybe it's good for teething and morning sickness and even my bur sage allergy. But when somebody's really sick, no *curandero*, even a very good one, is a substitute for modern medicine. Please believe me."

She nodded slowly, as though Dr. Ramirez's miracle cure had indeed made an impression on her. "I do believe you, Nico. But I did not before. I only thought you wanted to . . . well, to show us that your new ways were better. We have always taken care of our sick ones this way."

"And a lot of them have died, *Tía*. Died when they didn't have to. Promise me that you won't let that happen again. Even if the men are too stubborn—"

"I will do more than promise you," she conceded, her tone an urgent plea for Nick to feel her love for him again. "I will make your uncle see your doctor before he leaves for Pitahaya. José's cough has hung on far too long, and *La zarca* has not been able to *cure* it."

"I'm glad to hear it, *Tía*," Nick said, relieved that he'd inadvertently helped his beloved uncle as well as Liliana. "Now where did you say Kelley was?"

Carmelita lifted her hands. "I did not say, Nico. You might check your grandmother's house. After that—" she smiled "—you know her better than I do."

He returned the smile, but his uneasiness heightened, especially when he discovered that Mama Luz hadn't seen Kelley, either. In fact, nobody in the village had seen her for several hours.

Is it possible that she's gone back for her plant press and notes by herself? Nick asked himself, doubting that she'd be that foolish. Granted, she'd proven herself to be a true desert rat in that solitary hike to Pitahaya, and she certainly was capable of making the journey back to the jaguar's territory alone. But she had to be utterly exhausted after all she'd been through, and besides, no matter how confused or upset she might be feeling, she would never just go off without leaving a message for him. Surely she knew that he'd be frantic if he couldn't figure out where she'd gone.

And by now, he was getting frantic. Every instinct in his body told Nick that something was terribly wrong. By the time he started over the knoll toward the great saguaro, limping heavily on his saguaro-rib cane, he didn't really expect to find Kelley out there talking to a blooming Queen of the Night. But there was a chance she'd come out to think in solitude, a chance she—

Nick froze as he suddenly realized that he was not alone on the north side of the hillock. There were noises, people noises, coming from nearby...about halfway between Nick and the great saguaro.

In an instant he recognized the jarring sound that had no place in the peaceful desert night. It was the hideous sound of laughter. Pablo Villalobos's laughter...coupled with Kelley's terrified scream.

FOR MINUTES—or maybe hours—nothing but stillness gripped the desert after Pablo tied up Kelley and tossed her into the truck. And then, without warning, every silent cactus seemed to spring to life.

At first she thought it was only her own desperation that caused her to believe that there were suddenly far more than four furtive voices whispering in Spanish as her captors dug feverishly into the ground. But suddenly the night was shattered by wild hoops and hollers reminiscent of Apaches on a sunrise raid. A moment later a host of human forms appeared from the direction of the village, swarming like ants over the landscape, the smugglers and the truck.

From Kelley's vantage point, it was hard to tell what was happening; she could only see glimpses of faces as they rushed by, hear yelps of surprise, submission and defeat. She didn't know how Nick had realized she was in trouble, but she knew instantly that only he was responsible for her rescue. And somewhere in this crush of bodies and chaos, he had to be looking for her now.

She tried to scream so he could find her, but the dirty handkerchief stuffed in her mouth kept Kelley from uttering a single clear sound. Off to her right she heard a quick scuffle, then Nick's angry shout.

"I know you've got her, damn you! Now you tell me where she is! If you've touched one red hair on my woman's head, Villalobos, I swear to God I'll kill you right where you stand!"

The next voice was meek, frightened and subdued. It was clear to Kelley that all the fire had gone out of Liliana's lifetime tormentor. "Your woman's in the truck," Pablo whined. "She's still alive."

A moment later the cab door burst open, and Nick's beloved face swam before Kelley's tearful eyes.

She'd never seen him look so angry, joyful and re-lieved, all at the same time. In an instant he had pulled off her gag and struggled to free her hands and feet.

"Kelley, did he hurt you?" he beseeched her. "Do you need the doctor, *corazón*? Do you—"

"I only need you," she whispered brokenly, unable to stifle her pent-up sobs of relief. "Oh, Nico, I never thought you'd find me in time! I never even thought you'd notice I was gone!"

"Not notice you were gone?" he echoed, cradling her tear-streaked face against his chest. "Kelley, I nearly went crazy looking for you! I was so afraid that—" He broke off abruptly, his eyes full of an-guish as he faced her on the tattered seat of the dirty truck. For a minute Kelley could do nothing but stare at this man she loved and marvel at the sudden burst of joy within her. Not only was she going to live to see the light of day, but maybe, just maybe, she was going to see the miraculous rebirth of Nick's love for her, too.

And then Nick pulled her into his arms, his grip so urgent that it was almost painful. But Kelley didn't care; it was a sweet, delicious pain, a declaration of his adoration, and she hugged him back with equal might.

"My God, Kelley, I love you so much," Nick con-fessed for the first time as he buried his face in her hair. They were awesome words, beautiful words, words Kelley would have sold her soul to hear a week ago . . . and words she desperately needed to hear right now. But she'd been there before, too many times, and she knew that prudence hinted that Nick's promises might take on a different shade of meaning when his fear receded.

"I know what you're thinking," he chided Kelley as she trembled in his arms, "but you're wrong." He pulled back then, eyes soft and tender in the moonlight, as he reached up to unhook the chain that held his family medal . . . and transferred it from his neck to hers. The spontaneous offering moved Kelley unbearably; she knew that Nick held nothing he owned more dear. His beautiful brown eyes were rich with feeling as he met her tearful gaze, then kissed her gently on the mouth. "I won't change my mind in the morning, *corazón*, and I won't change my mind when we get back home," he promised. "I've never been so sure of anything in my life."

She only wished she could believe him.

CHAPTER NINETEEN

A WEEK AFTER the kidnapping, Nico and Kelley loaded
up Maleta just before the first whisper of dawn swept
across the saguaro-studded foothills of Sonora. Mama
Luz, hovering among the crowd of gathered relatives,
struggled not to cry as she watched her grandson prepare once more to leave his homeland. But this time,
she was certain, he *would* return to Cielo Solo. It was
Pablo Villalobos who'd been banished forever.

Between Liliana's illness, Nico's injury and Kelley's
kidnapping, it seemed to Mama Luz that her poor little village had had more excitement in the past week
than it usually had in several years. The men still
boasted about the way they'd trapped Pablo and his
gang and bravely herded the smugglers into Pitahaya;
Liliana still told everybody who would listen how
Nico's persistence and Kelley's courage had combined
to save her life. And Nico himself kept telling his
grandmother that he'd finally found the woman who
was meant to be his bride.

But Kelley hadn't said much of anything since the
night Nico had rescued her from Pablo. Her silence
worried Mama Luz.

But now, as Kelley slipped away from Nico to bid
Mama Luz goodbye, she looked very grave—almost
tearful—as she fingered the ancient Virgin of Guadalupe medal that Nick had lovingly bestowed upon her.

Before the young woman could fumble for words of farewell, Mama Luz reached out to hug her with all the tenderness that Kelley's own Mama Chayo had surely once lavished upon her. *"¡Ay, mi hija!"* she proclaimed with all her heart. *"No te llores.* You have earned the right to call yourself Morales."

The fair-skinned girl clung to her tightly, fighting tears that seemed to take her by surprise. "I know that I wasn't your first choice, Mama Luz," she admitted in a hushed, apologetic tone, "but I love him terribly, and I promise you that I'll do my very best to make him happy."

"Hush now," Mama Luz insisted, stroking the wrinkly red hair in her gnarled old hands. "If you are his first choice, Kelley, then you are my first choice. You are part of Nico's family now."

Kelley hugged her mightily, gulping back a sob, then broke away to take her leave of Carmelita and José. Mama Luz would have turned to Nico then, but she found him gingerly embracing Liliana, who had hobbled to his side to say goodbye.

"I owe you my life, Nico," the young woman said simply. "I will never be able to repay you."

"It is my own debt I have paid, Liliana," he assured her, planting a brotherly kiss on her cheek. "You owe me nothing but the promise that you will write to me—in your own words from now on—and let me know if Mama Luz ever needs me."

Liliana's sunny smile widened. "This I will promise you."

Mama Luz swallowed her own impatience while Liliana turned to Kelley, lowering her voice as if she were about to impart a great secret. "You will look out for him, yes?" she beseeched Kelley. "I know that Nico is a rich man now, but he still will not eat right if he does not have a woman to cook for him.''

"I will do my best for him, Lili," Kelley promised graciously. "Nico is . . . very important to me."

"And you, Kelley, are very, very important to Nico!" she cheerfully countered. "I am so glad you will be with him now! For so many years I worried about my dear friend, alone in that dangerous foreign land with nobody who loved him! But now my thoughts of Nico will only be happy ones."

Kelley studied the other woman for a moment, her expression perplexed but satisfied. Finally she took Liliana's hand and squeezed it warmly. "I hope the time comes when you won't be alone any longer either, Liliana."

Liliana shook her head. "I am not alone, Kelley. I am surrounded by my children and my friends, and my Meleseo—" she laid one hand over her heart "—my Meleseo still walks beside me. Now that you and Nico have saved me from Pablo, I have nothing to fear."

As she contemplated Liliana's joyful relief, Mama Luz suddenly realized that *she* no longer had anything to fear, either. Even though her grandson had not come home to stay, her greatest dreams for Nico really had come true. He had a woman who loved him and a life that gave him ease . . . a life he'd carved for himself out of hard work, integrity and sheer determination. She would miss him terribly, but she was oh, so proud of her boy, full to bursting with love for him!

Slowly Nico worked his way around the circle of well-wishers, listening to their prayers and contradictory advice, offering good wishes and tender farewells of his own. Finally there was nobody else to say goodbye to; he'd left the hardest for last.

When he came to stand before her, Nico did not speak. His brimming eyes told her all that he might have said if he could have found his voice—how very much he loved her, how hard it was to go—and when his strong young arms closed around her, she clung to him with all her ancient might.

"Nico, *mi hijo*," she whispered against his cheek, "is there any hope that I will ever see your beloved face again?"

He gave her a squeeze, his poignant grip confessing even more than his trembling words. "Mama Luz," he promised in a grave, hushed tone, "I swear to you that I'll be back each time the Queen of the Night comes into bloom."

She pulled away from him, old eyes cloudy with joyful disbelief. "Nico, have you been away so long that you do not recall that the Queen blooms every spring?" she tried to chide him.

He shook his head, then leaned over to kiss her leathery cheek with infinite care. "No, Mama Luz, *no se me olvidó*," he told her. "From now on, God willing, I'll come back to Sonora once a year."

Before Mama Luz could respond, her grandson—this strong and honorable American man who still bore traces of the little Mexican boy she had always loved so deeply—turned away before his emotions could betray him. She did not want to hold him against his will, but it was very hard for her to let him go! Her gnarled fingers clenched the sleeves of his shirt as she tried to release and yet hold him. Trembling, she whispered, *"Qué te vayas con Dios, mi hijo."*

Nico touched her face again, his eyes tightly closed with feeling. "Is there anything I can do for you before I leave, Mama Luz?'' he pleaded. "More water from the spring, more money for—''

The braided old head shook emphatically. "You have come to see me; you have promised to return,'' she reminded him stoutly. "And so, my grandson, you have given me everything I have ever needed.'' Mama Luz reached up to kiss his cheek just one last time, then choked out her farewell benediction. "Go with God, Nico. Go now with God.''

IT WAS ALMOST supper time when Nick and Kelley arrived in Los Angeles three days later, but when Kelley offered to defrost something in the microwave or order pizza, Nick declined.

"No, thanks, Kell,'' he was quick to tell her. "I've got a yen for Paul Lee's egg *foo yung* and I need to check up on a few things before I can relax.''

They'd driven straight through from Pitahaya to Tucson in one terribly long day, then gotten up before dawn to reach Los Angeles without spending another night on the road. Kelley had agreed to the tight schedule Nick had suggested, certain that they'd both feel a lot better when they got home. Nonetheless, his eagerness to conclude their journey had troubled her right from the start. He'd been just as solicitous as ever during their travels, but she couldn't shake the feeling that kindness, not lifetime love, might have been his dominant motivation.

Last night was the first time they'd shared a bed since Nick's encounter with the jaguar, but those few hours of sleep had hardly smacked of moonlight and roses. Once they'd showered and climbed in between the sheets, Nick had slipped his arm around Kelley's shoulders and pulled her close enough to snuggle. But neither one of them had had the energy to indulge in more than a good-night kiss.

At the time, Kelley had been heartened by the unspoken intimacy of the sleepy cuddling; but now, as Nick's eagerness to take his leave grew more visible by the moment, she began to wonder just what he'd been thinking of last night while she'd been dozing off to sleep. And what he was thinking now that he realized that his official obligation as Kelley's "guide" had ended?

"I guess I should thank you for the trip, Nick," she declared rather stiffly, trying to smother her sudden insecurity as he hurried toward the door. "My project was certainly a success. At least, I have plenty of data to get my preliminary report launched no matter what Paul's successor thinks; the successful application of Opata cures to your injuries will certainly spice up my findings. And I—" she struggled for the proper words "—I really did enjoy getting to know your family."

Nick's eyebrows raised dubiously as he stopped in midstride, jangling his keys in one hand. "I appreciate your gratitude, Kelley, but I have the uneasy feeling that you're about to offer me a handshake instead of a kiss."

"Apparently you've had enough of my kisses for the time being, Nick," Kelley snapped without thinking. "I don't believe I've ever had a date quite so eager to say good-night and be on his way."

Nick's eyes narrowed as he studied her face. "I've been away from my shop for a month, Kell," he pointed out, ignoring the sharp tone of her voice. "I need to check up on some things before Jeff takes off. I'm only going to be gone for a few hours, not a few days."

A slow, steady pounding started in Kelley's heart as she contemplated the true meaning of his words. "A few...hours, Nico?" she repeated, hope and joy commencing battle with her doubt. "You mean you're coming back tonight?"

"Of course I'm coming back tonight!" he ground out in some exasperation. "We haven't really talked about our future."

"Do we have a future, Nick?" Kelley asked. "Are you sure?"

This time there was no denying the dark shadow that crossed Nick's face. His biceps tensed as he deliberately tapped the medal at her throat. "What's it going to take to convince you that I'm crazy about you?"

Tears claimed her eyes as she tried to answer. "Oh, Nick, please forgive me! I don't mean to doubt you. It's just that so much has happened lately that I feel like I'm still in Never Never Land, and any minute I'll wake up and find out that everything that's happened between us is just a dream!"

Nick did not reply at first, but he laid one strong hand on her trembling cheek as if he sought to warm her. It was such a tender gesture, so loving and yet so sad, that it tugged unbearably at Kelley's scrambled emotions. She knew that Nick only wanted to soothe her, but fear and fatigue suddenly overwhelmed her, and she began to cry.

Ignoring the tears, Nick edged yet closer and cradled her head with both hands. He touched her lips with his own in the gentlest form of bonding, then kissed her again with the promise of passion yet to be fulfilled.

"I love you, Kelley McKinney, and I'm going to love you for the rest of my life," he insisted, his voice hoarse and low as he tenderly pressed her face against his chest. "I just wish I could find a way to make you believe that."

"So do I, Nick," Kelley whispered. "So do I."

NICK HADN'T LIED to Kelley when he'd said he had a few errands to run, but at the moment the shop was the least of his concerns. He'd spent the last month tying up all the loose ends of his life, and he still had one tiny thread left to knot.

"You were right, Juanita," he declared by way of greeting when he reached his old friend's classroom half an hour after he left Kelley's house. "You were right and I'm deeply indebted to you."

Juanita Martinez sat at her desk and stared at him, then stood up to lay one cool hand on his forehead. "Are you all right, Nico?" she asked, only partly in jest. "It's not the first time I've ever heard you admit you were wrong, but—"

"I was wrong and you were right. Right to push me back toward Mexico...and right to leave me, too."

"Nico..." There was no humor in her voice now. Juanita looked stunned and more than a little concerned.

"I just wanted you to know that you're doing the right thing to marry John," Nick declared. "It wasn't Liliana that kept us from getting closer, though. You were wrong about that, Juanita. I think the world of you—you know that—but there was...well, somebody else who was meant to be my sunrise and my sunset."

This time she did smile at the unexpected sight of seeing Nick Morales all but tongue-tied over his newfound love; but it was a tender smile of relief and joy for the happiness of her old friend, so he was not embarrassed.

"I'm so glad for you, Nico!" she exclaimed. "I only wish I could have persuaded you to go down there sooner."

"So do I," he admitted, "but I try to learn from my mistakes. This time I'm not going to let any grass grow under my feet when I've got a problem waiting to be resolved." The dramatic solution to Kelley's problem that Nick had in mind was embarrassing and somewhat ludicrous, but he was willing to do almost anything to quench her fears once and for all. Toward that end he asked, "Can you give me Kelley's brother's phone number?"

Juanita looked perplexed. "Sure, Nick. But may I ask why you need it?"

Nick had hoped she wouldn't ask, but nonetheless he confessed, "I've got this crazy idea that won't work without somebody special from Kelley's family. Besides—" his grin was positively sheepish "—I might need somebody to bail me out tonight when I'm arrested for disturbing the peace."

KELLEY HAD DOZED OFF on the couch waiting for Nick, but it was not a knock at the door that woke her up at midnight. It was the high, clear sound of a tenor voice slipping in and out of her dreams until she bolted upright with the sudden realization that she wasn't imagining the haunting melody. Somewhere nearby— somewhere *very* nearby—there was a man singing a Spanish song. Maybe two men. Or even three!

Kelley rubbed her eyes and struggled for consciousness as she realized that since her stereo wasn't on, one

of her normally circumspect neighbors must have gone
crazy or be throwing an incredibly wild party.

And then, with sudden insight, Kelley realized that
she knew the love song that lilted so romantically
through her living-room window. It was *Las Mañanitas*, that incredibly sentimental number she'd heard the
night she and Nick had stumbled on the mariachis ser-
enading the young girl in Hermosillo. What had Nick
said about the song? *If I wanted to tell a special lady
that she walks right next to my heart, this is the only
song I'd sing.* But then he'd gone on to say that he
couldn't sing for beans and hiring mariachis was ludi-
crously expensive, anyway.

A moment later Kelley realized that nobody in her
staid Anglo neighborhood would ever play mariachi
music on the stereo in the middle of the night, even if
they had gone stark raving berserk! And no recording,
no matter how eloquent, could ever replace the majesty of a live guitar, let alone the hearty strum of the
quitarrón.

Without taking a moment to so much as brush her
hair, Kelley ran to the window and pulled back the
drapes, certain now that she'd find the street graced
with three Mexican musicians in wide-brimmed som-
breros and black *charro* suits with silver *conchas* glittering down each side.

She was right. In front of her yard stood three mustachioed gentlemen who couldn't have looked more
delighted to be giving a musical performance in the
middle of the night in a quiet residential section of
West L.A. But the mariachis weren't alone. There were
neighbors spilling out onto the street, now, too...

sleepy neighbors in bathrobes and tugged on crumpled jeans who looked by turns irritated, entranced, bewildered and dismayed.

But Kelley was no longer confused about anything; sunbeams had painted all of her doubts with joy. From the inside out, she finally knew that Nick Morales loved her—loved her in every way a man could love a woman. *A fellow would have to be stark raving loony over a gal to shell out that kind of money and risk getting arrested just to let the whole world know he was a besotted chump,* he'd said in Hermosillo. And Kelley was absolutely certain that he was counting on her to remember every word.

Through her haze of joy, she vaguely remembered that the girl's family was responsible for part of this glorious ritual. Wasn't somebody supposed to be ready with dessert? Wasn't somebody supposed to ask these fellows in?

But her refrigerator was empty; she'd been out of town for a month. She was about to do something rash—like ordering a pizza—when she spied another group of familiar faces outside her window. Sandwiched in among the neighbors was Jimmy carrying a thermos and the baby; picnic-basket-laden Bonnie was wiping her eyes as she herded the other three kids toward the porch.

Although the streetlight did little to illumine the romantic setting, Kelley finally spotted the one face she longed to see. As he stepped from the shadows to join the musicians, Nick's smile was awkward and embarrassed, but his eyes were full of joy. He'd shed his jeans and now stood resplendent in a full-dress tux that dramatized the regal set of his shoulders. His shoes were black and shiny; he even had ruffles on his crisp white shirt.

It was not the way Kelley had ever imagined Nick Morales in her dreams, but she couldn't deny that he looked positively gorgeous. But there was one thing about his appearance that didn't make any sense to her. He was holding an earthenware clay pot that was home to one limp blackish-green plant. Its solitary white flower leaned toward her precariously as she tried to determine its genus and species.

It wasn't until Kelley threw open the front door, clapping along with her neighbors as the sentimental number ended, that she got a good look at the nocturnal blossom. Even then it was hard to believe that her eyes did not deceive her.

It was a Queen of the Night cactus in full bloom.

"Oh, Nico," she whispered into the darkness of the empty house, unable to believe the symbolism of this precious gift . . . or his luck in finding one in bloom tonight. "If you had any idea what this means to me...." *But he does know. Of course he knows! And that's why he's here,* she suddenly realized, too overwhelmed to speak. The tears of joy spilled over as the first mariachi reached the front door, complimenting Kelley on her home, her Sonoran cactus garden and her radiant beauty.

She nodded and wept and welcomed the whole troop inside—Jimmy laughing, Bonnie crying, the kids giggling while the mariachis continued to play—until at last Nick stepped up on the porch, eyes glowing as he recognized her joy.

"You know, *corazón*, if you let me in tonight," he pointed out with infuriating calm, "the neighbors will think you're ready and willing to marry me tomorrow.''

All Kelley could do was nod her head.

"And I'm likely to get the same impression, so you might want to give this some more thought before I close the door."

The tears flowed freely now as Kelley reached out to grab his arm and tug him into the hall. Still he didn't touch her, except with his love-warmed smile. He waited until she shut the door, then presented her with the clay pot.

"I read somewhere when you come to call on a lady, you ought to bring her flowers. I know this is sort of an ugly old thing, but I thought you might like a memento of Sonora...though I made sure this was raised in a reputable nursery and not scalped from the land."

Kelley seized the pot with both hands and pressed it against her ribs, as though it were a baby. Still she sobbed, until Nick reached out, ever so gently, and took the cactus from her hands and set it on the floor. Then he pulled her into his arms and clung to her while she wept against his chest.

Kelley couldn't speak, so she just slipped her fingers through Nick's thick hair and pulled his head down to rest against her tearful face. Without another word he pressed his cheek to hers and rocked her softly, letting his heart do the talking for him.

The mariachi music continued, unheeded, in the living room, but Kelley never really heard it. All she knew for certain was that each new melody was a celebration of Nick's love for her, and every beat heralded his lifetime passion.

"I love you so much, Nico," she whispered, joyfully. "I never thought I could love anybody as much as I love you."

She could feel Nick's fingers trembling as he soothed her back; his lips warm and tender as he dropped soft kisses on her sensitive scalp. He held her with a passionate kind of tenderness she'd never felt in him before, and Kelley knew that his next words would not frame a joke or a lie or even a platitude designed to please her. Whatever he said to her now would be the truth of his deepest emotions, a truth she could count on for the rest of her life.

"Kelley, you are my queen," Nick whispered, his rough male tones quivering with the depth of his unveiled emotions. He lifted her chin to kiss her lips, just once, with a fullness of love that cast sunshine on every nook and cranny of her soul. His love swallowed up all the empty places that had ever troubled her heart; peace soothed the memory of every rough patch of ground she'd ever trod.

"You'll be my queen for a lifetime, *corazón*," Nick confessed with a throbbing intensity her heart could no longer doubt. "You're my only...Queen of the Night."

And this time, she believed him.

Harlequin Superromance

COMING NEXT MONTH

#286 OF TIME AND TENDERNESS • Kelly Walsh
Even if David Mansfield weren't surrounded by
mystery, architect Sabrina Hutchins would still find
him irresistibly intriguing. But David is not welcome
at the Louisiana mansion Sabrina is in charge of
renovating, and she's determined to find out why.

#287 STOLEN MOMENTS • Janice Kaiser
When Lacey Parlett meets Garrett Royston, she falls
passionately in love with the kindhearted professor.
But how can they have a future together when she's
wanted by the FBI for kidnapping her own daughter?

#288 HIS AND HERS • Pamela Bauer
Sassy Montana rancher and rodeo champ Jenna
Morgan is easy in the saddle and a whiz with the
lasso. But when Harrison Drake, New York
financier, rolls into town, Jenna starts feeling
distinctly skittish.

#289 MORE THAN EVER • Eleni Carr
Sara Crane is juggling her studies, a career and
motherhood. Psychologist Andrew Lorimer is quick
to see that she is taking care of everything but her
own needs. And, ever so subtly, he sets out to change
Sara's priorities....

Six exciting series for you every month... from Harlequin

Harlequin Romance®
The series that started it all

Tender, captivating and heartwarming...
love stories that sweep you off to faraway places
and delight you with the magic of love.

◆

Harlequin Presents·
Powerful contemporary love stories...as individual as the women who read them

The No. 1 romance series...
exciting love stories for you, the woman of today...
a rare blend of passion and dramatic realism.

◆

Harlequin Superromance®
It's more than romance...
it's Harlequin Superromance

A sophisticated, contemporary romance-fiction
series, providing you with a longer,
more involving read...a richer mix of complex plots,
realism and adventure.

Harlequin
American Romance™
Harlequin celebrates the American woman...

...by offering you romance stories written about American women, by American women for American women. This series offers you contemporary romances uniquely North American in flavor and appeal.

◆

Harlequin Temptation™
Passionate stories for today's woman

An exciting series of sensual, mature stories of love...dilemmas, choices, resolutions... all contemporary issues dealt with in a true-to-life fashion by some of your favorite authors.

◆

Harlequin Intrigue™
Because romance can be quite an adventure

Harlequin Intrigue, an innovative series that blends the romance you expect... with the unexpected. Each story has an added element of intrigue that provides a new twist to the Harlequin tradition of romance excellence.

Harlequin Books·

PROD-A-2